FIGHTING FOR LUCY (SPECIAL FORCES: OPERATION ALPHA)

PREY SECURITY: ATHENA TEAM
BOOK TWO

JANE BLYTHE

Cover designed by Q Designs

Dear Readers,

Welcome to the Special Forces: Operation Alpha Fan-Fiction world!

If you are new to this amazing world, in a nutshell the author wrote a story using one or more of my characters in it. Sometimes that character has a major role in the story, and other times they are only mentioned briefly. This is perfectly legal and allowable because they are going through Aces Press to publish the story.

This book is entirely the work of the author who wrote it. While I might have assisted with brainstorming and other ideas about which of my characters to use, I didn't have any part in the process or writing or editing the story.

I'm proud and excited that so many authors loved my characters enough that they wanted to write them into their own story. Thank you for supporting them, and me!

READ ON!
    Xoxo
    Susan Stoker

ACKNOWLEDGMENTS

I'd like to thank everyone who played a part in bringing this story to life. Particularly my mom who is always there to share her thoughts and opinions with me. My wonderful cover designer Amy who did an amazing job with this stunning cover. My fabulous editor Lisa for all the hard work she puts into polishing my work. My awesome team, Sophie, Robyn, and Clayr, without your help I'd never be able to run my street team. And my fantastic street team members who help share my books with every share, comment, and like!

And of course a big thank you to all of you, my readers! Without you I wouldn't be living my dreams of sharing the stories in my head with the world!

CHAPTER ONE

January 21st
   10:43 A.M.

"What's happening?" Lucy Elrod demanded.

The plane was making a horrible sound, and an alarm was blaring, screaming at them that something was wrong.

"We're going down," the pilot said. Considering what he'd just told her and the kind of wailing sound coming from the engine, he should not have said those words with such a steady calm.

The man didn't even look the teeniest little bit panicked while terror was clawing at her insides with a viciousness she hadn't felt in a long time.

It wasn't so much their likely impending death that had her hands growing clammy and her pulse kicking into high gear, after all, you didn't live your entire life with an illness that controlled everything you did and still get terrified of death.

Nope.

What had her heart hammering in her chest was the fear that had been on the face of her friend and fellow Prey Security colleague while they'd been video-calling just seconds ago. Scarlett Madden had just lived through a horrific ordeal. Kidnapped twice, accused of being a traitor, and of making plans to sell a drug that all four Athena Team members had created together to a notorious weapons trafficker.

With her name cleared and a fledgling relationship with SEAL Tate Laurier, Scarlett should be on cloud nine. Yet as soon as she'd glimpsed something in the plane she'd freaked out and demanded to see the pilot.

"Lucy, whatever happens, don't trust him," Scarlett's voice screamed through the phone she'd dropped and was now lying on the floor at her feet. "That's Zander, my brother. He's supposed to be dead. If he's there then you're not safe."

Shock had her turning to gape at the pilot.

At Zander Madden.

A man who was supposedly killed in action a little over eighteen months ago.

How could a dead Delta Force Operator be flying a plane for Prey?

Not possible.

While she hadn't met Zander many times in the years she'd been friends and teammates with his twin sister, what little she knew of him was that he was incredibly smart, driven, and determined. He also loved his sister despite the distance that had grown between them after he enlisted in the Army.

But that Zander would never allow Scarlett to think he was dead when he clearly wasn't.

So, if he'd been prepared to deceive his twin in the worst possible way, what else was he willing to do?

Was it a stretch to wonder if he was somehow the mole who had framed his sister to take the fall for him? How would Zander even know about the Reactivator? They'd started working on it six months before his supposed death, so there was a chance Scarlett had talked to him about it.

But why would he want to sell his twin sister's drug to a weapons trafficker?

And why had he taken this job when he knew it would put him in contact with Prey and someone who knew his sister?

There was no time to quiz the man on what exactly it was he was doing here and what he hoped to achieve because the plane engine was still whining, and Zander—who had introduced himself to her as Zeke when she met him at the airfield—was the only thing standing between her and certain death.

Did she trust him?

Nope.

Not as far as she could throw him.

Which was not far at all. While physical fitness was important to her, a way to compensate for her epilepsy, and she spent a minimum of an hour working out in the gym every single day, there was no way her slight five foot three, one hundred and ten pound frame could so much as budge Zander's.

He had to be at least six foot three and close to two hundred pounds of pure muscle. His eyes were blue, but she knew he had to be wearing contacts because Zander Madden's eyes were brown just like his twin's. With a deep tan and his hair a little darker than she remembered, it was no wonder she hadn't recognized him.

"Why are you here?" she demanded as her hands curled around her seatbelt. Not that the belt across her stomach was going to do her much good when they crashed. From the way Zander was fighting with the plane and the ground

3

quickly rushing up to meet them, she knew that it was the inevitable outcome.

"To fly the plane," Zander muttered, making her roll her eyes. So he was a smart alec as well as a liar.

"Real funny, wise guy," she shot back. "You know who I am. You're not here by accident. Does Eagle know who you really are? Are you here because of what happened to your sister? Are you the one who set Scarlett up?"

Throwing her a quick glare, Zander asked, "You really want to have that conversation now? Because I'm thinking I'm the only thing standing between us and certain death."

Yep, he was a smart alec all right.

The thing was that with Scarlett's revelation, Lucy had no idea if she could trust a single thing about this man. For all she knew, he was faking an issue with the plane in order to gain her trust. After all, everything had been going smoothly right up until she'd gotten the call from Ella Whitlock, another member of Athena Team, and spoken with Scarlett.

Then all of a sudden, the plane started blaring an alarm.

So forgive her for being suspicious of the ghost man.

"Are we really going to crash?" she asked.

Shooting her an incredulous look, he shook his head at her like he wasn't convinced she wasn't crazy. "Not if I can help it."

"I mean, is there really an issue with the plane or are you faking it?"

"Are you for real? What does it look like?" Zander waved his arms to indicate the flashing warning light on the control panel and the alarm that still blared.

"Gee, forgive me for being suspicious of you, ghost man," she muttered, wishing she knew more about flying planes. While she was a total adrenalin junky, chasing highs wherever she could find them, there was a lot her epilepsy prohibited her from doing. Flying planes was one of them, heck, she wasn't even allowed to drive a car because, unfortunately, for her even with her medication there was a chance she would have a seizure behind the wheel.

Ignoring her, Zander kept doing whatever it was he was doing, which didn't seem to be working if you asked her because the green of the jungle beneath them was quickly getting closer. Which left her with nothing to do but think about the fact that she was mere moments away from likely dying.

Leaving behind her parents, who had always been there for her, standing at her side during her lowest moments, and her four siblings, who drove her crazy but who she loved fiercely, would be hard, but it was leaving her fur baby behind that hurt the worst. While all of her family would grieve her, at least her parents and siblings, nieces and nephews, would all understand what had happened, but her poodle, Cotton, would never understand why she didn't come home.

The thought of her sweet, slightly neurotic, fluffy baby forever waiting for her to walk through the door had tears blurring her vision.

Lucy didn't want to die, she didn't want to leave behind so many people that she loved and cared about. Practical, sensible, no-nonsense, those were all the words people would use to describe her, but in this moment, she didn't feel any of those things. She just wanted to scream and cry that it wasn't fair, that her life shouldn't end like this.

"Brace for impact," Zander announced.

"I thought you were going to stop us from crashing," she snapped, glowering at Zander. Somehow, she couldn't help but feel like this was all somehow his fault. Just because she didn't know how didn't mean it wasn't. Although why he'd risk his own life just to kill her she had no idea.

Looking over at her, there was still not an ounce of panic

or concern in his eyes, despite their situation, and she envied his ability to not care that he was about to die for real. "We're going to crash. There's nothing I can do about it, but I'm going to do everything I can to make sure we survive the landing."

There was zero reason why she should believe him.

Yet she did.

Giving him a shaky nod, Lucy adopted the brace position and started counting seconds, wondering if she was counting down to the end of her life.

She had to be.

Right?

There was no way, even if he was the most skilled pilot on the planet—and Zander had been in Delta Force, he wasn't in the air force so his skills couldn't be the best—that he could really land the plane with mechanical problems in the middle of the jungle.

No way.

Moments later, her worst fears were confirmed when they collided with the trees, and she was tossed about, held in place only by her flimsy seatbelt. It was no match against the force of the crash, and when her head slammed into the side of the plane it was lights out.

* * *

JANUARY 21ST

10:56 A.M.

AGONY SPEARED through Zander Madden's skull.

Trying to open his eyes turned out to be a big mistake.

Sunlight shot through them, and he promptly turned his head and threw up.

6

Great.

A concussion.

That was the last thing he needed right now.

It had been a big risk to take on this flight, but his entire future was riding on this job going smoothly. He'd been hoping that given what had just happened to his sister, he wouldn't have to make contact with her because while he could fool anybody else there was no way his twin wouldn't recognize him the second she laid eyes on him no matter the changes he'd made to his appearance.

Damn his twin for ruining this.

If everything he had worked so hard for fell apart because of Scarlett, he was going to be furious. Not *with* his sister, Scarlett was the only person in the world who loved him— well, she *used* to love him, but there was every chance she now hated him—but with the world in general.

This wasn't how he'd wanted things to turn out, but in life you had no choice but to play the hand you were dealt.

That was all he was doing here, but it still sucked.

However, looking on the bright side, he *had* survived the crash.

Shockingly.

Despite the fact he'd played it cool when they were up in the air—he had no choice, it was the only thing that gave them a chance at living—inside he'd been panicking. He didn't want to die for real.

He hadn't wanted to fake his death either.

But again, it was the whole playing the hand you were dealt thing.

This time, he inched his eyes open more slowly. One eye was harder to open than the other, and when he lifted a hand to brush at it, he found that blood had dribbled down over it, sticking to his eyelashes. An impressive set, the kind that made girls jealous, his sister had always told him.

The set of eyelashes on his gorgeous passenger was also pretty impressive.

Actually, everything about Lucy Elrod was impressive. Zander was a sucker for a beautiful blonde, throw in a set of baby blues, and he was a goner. She was everything he usually looked for in a woman, pretty, intelligent, and down to earth. He'd been attracted to her from the first time he met her, but since you didn't date your sister's friends, he'd never done anything about it. For the last several years he'd merely admired her from afar. Respected the hell out of the fact that she never once allowed her epilepsy to hold her back from doing anything. Sure, there were times when her condition prohibited her from doing something she wanted to, but instead of complaining or moping about it, she just looked for a workaround, an alternative.

In the plane, she'd been afraid when his sister spilled the beans on who he was, but she hadn't backed down, hadn't cowered, she'd still sassed him right up until the end when he'd yelled at her to brace for the inevitable crash.

Had Lucy survived as well?

Honestly, his life would be a whole lot easier if she'd died on impact. Awful as that made him sound, it was the truth.

Prying open his other eye, Zander did a quick inventory of his body. There were aches and pains all over, but there was nothing that screamed at him that it was a life-threatening injury. The head injury was probably going to be his biggest concern. Concussions sucked, he'd had a few in his years in Delta Force, and he knew the nausea, headaches, and dizziness were going to make traipsing through the Mexican jungle that much more unpleasant.

At least the plane had landed right side up, that was a small plus. Unsnapping his seatbelt, Zander shoved to his feet, barely sparing Lucy a glance. It was better for her if she was dead, and if he was going to sell her death then he didn't want to risk slipping up by checking to see if she had survived.

So he bypassed her and headed to the back of the plane to grab his survival pack. Always be prepared. The Boy Scout's motto. An acceptable extracurricular activity as far as his parents and grandparents were concerned, and the only one he'd been allowed to do as a kid. While he certainly hadn't expected to crash, he'd done what he always did and packed everything he would need to survive if the situation arose.

Just as he was hefting the pack onto his back, needing to keep one hand on the warped metal of the plane to keep his balance, he heard it.

About the worst sound he could have heard in this moment.

Not the sound of gunfire, or an explosion, or the sound of approaching footsteps, which out here were likely to belong to one of the cartels.

A moan.

A small one.

A pained one.

And there was only one person it could have belonged to.

Damn it.

Lucy had also survived the crash.

Too bad for her. A quick death would have been preferable to whatever Raul Castillo was going to do once he got his hands on her.

The notorious weapons dealer was not a man who was known to give up on something he wanted. Especially when he had already invested a lot of time and money on it. If Raul had decided that he was going to own the Reactivator, a drug created by Scarlett, Lucy, and the other two members of their team, then he would keep going until he got his hands on it. It was a wonder drug if ever there was one. When finished, it would help to give injured soldiers in the field a better chance at surviving their injuries by helping to dull pain, encourage fast healing, slow bleeding, and provide extra adrenalin to keep them on their feet.

Initially, Raul wanted the drug to sell to the highest bidder, and he'd kidnapped Scarlett in hopes of forcing the formula from her. When his sister had refused to give up the intel she'd been horribly tortured. Even after she'd been rescued, Raul hadn't been willing to give up on his plans, and managed to kidnap her a second time.

Just because Scarlett had been rescued then, too, and she was surrounded by too many people to make a third attempt successful, Raul was still determined to get what he wanted.

Enter Zander.

This game had always been risky, but it had just gotten much riskier.

Now that he knew Lucy was alive, he had no choice but to take her with him.

"Damn it, sassy girl, why couldn't you have just died and made both our lives so much simpler," he murmured aloud.

Turning back to the front of the plane, he did a visual sweep of Lucy. Like himself, there was a gash on her head, and blood streaked her face. One of her arms hung limply at her side, the other was resting on her lap, from the angle of it there was no doubt it was broken. Still, at least it wasn't a compound fracture. Out here infection would have gotten her for sure.

Strike that.

It would be *better* for her if infection killed her before Raul got his hands on her.

Crouching at her side, he battled another wave of dizziness as he ran his hands up and down her body in search of other injuries. There was nothing that stood out to him, although since she wasn't conscious there was always the chance of internal injuries he didn't know about.

Another moan tumbled from her lips, and her eyelashes began to flutter on cheeks that had lost their rosiness in the aftermath of the crash.

"Lucy? Come on, sassy girl, wake yourself up," he encouraged, cupping her cheek and sweeping his fingertips across her cheek with a gentleness that could wind up being dangerous. It didn't matter how attracted he was to Scarlett's friend, how attracted he had *always* been to her, there was no way he could allow it to develop into anything more.

"Mmm ... Z ... Zander ...?" she murmured as her eyes finally opened. They weren't focused and he didn't have to ask any other questions to know that she also had a concussion.

"Yeah. I'm here."

"You ... did it. We're ... alive." Clear incredulity was in her voice, and he smiled despite the awful situation they found themselves in.

"Yeah, told you I could."

"You did good, ghost man."

A flash of pain shafted through his chest, and it had nothing to do with the crash and his injuries.

He *was* a ghost now, and that was how it should have stayed. Scarlett should never have learned that he was still alive. She was never supposed to. There was no going back from the choices he'd made, and while it was fair that he had to live with the consequences it sucked that his twin sister had to as well.

But there was nothing he could do about that.

Nothing he could do about what was going to happen to Lucy either.

CHAPTER TWO

January 21ˢᵗ
    11:04 A.M.

THEY WERE ALIVE.

It was nothing short of a miracle.

Whatever game Zander was playing, he'd gotten them safely down onto the ground in one piece.

Well relatively speaking.

There was a headache raging between Lucy's temples, and her chest sent stabbing pains through her with every breath. One of her arms felt broken for sure, and then there were bumps and bruises littering everything else in between.

But she was alive.

Everything else could be fixed.

Eventually.

If they could find their way out of the jungle.

"Did you get a mayday out before we crashed?" Lucy asked.

The blue eyes that looked back at her were odd. Not the

color, it was perfectly realistic, but because she'd seen the man's photo almost every day as there was a picture of a teenage Zander and Scarlett on her friend's desk in the lab, and she knew he had brown eyes.

It was a stupid thing to worry about at the moment, but she wanted to see the real Zander. There was nothing to do about his darker hair color, and she kind of liked the tanned skin, but she wanted to see his real eyes.

Maybe it would make her feel a little less like this man was the enemy.

Was he?

Honestly, she had no idea.

There was every chance that there was a perfectly logical reason for why Zander had faked his death, and it had nothing to do with the Reactivator, Raul Castillo, and Athena Team.

Or she was clutching at straws because if Zander was working for the enemy, then that was not good news for her.

The two of them were alone out there. There was no backup. She had no idea where exactly they'd crashed, and injured as she was, she had no idea how she was going to get herself out of the jungle and back to civilization.

She needed Zander right now.

An annoyance on top of being scary since she had no idea if she could trust him. Growing up with a condition that impacted her day-to-day life, her parents had been overly cautious when it came to her doing pretty much anything. They coddled her, her siblings, too, even her little brother and sister, and getting them to see her as a strong, competent woman, one who didn't need a keeper had been hard. She'd fought for her independence and didn't want to give it up for anyone.

Realizing Zander hadn't answered her question, she repeated it. "Did you put out a mayday before we crashed?"

"We were on the phone with your friends when it happened, I think everybody knows and will be looking for us."

Not an answer.

And it didn't pass her by that he had called them her friends, with no mention that one of her friends was his twin sister. Was it guilt over faking his death that made him want to put distance between himself and Scarlett, or was it something more?

Like he knew he had played some part in what had happened to Scarlett at the hands of the weapons trafficker?

No matter what, it was hard for Lucy to believe that Zander would have stood back and done nothing to stop his sister from being tortured regardless of what else he had done. She knew a bit about how Scarlett and Zander had grown up. Parents who refused to give up military careers for their kids. Raised by grandparents who were beyond strict. No real time for fun or all the silly things kids did.

The twins were all each other had, and she knew it had torn Scarlett apart when, upon their grandparents' deaths, she and her brother had been separated and put in foster care. Even during those five years before they aged out of the system, the two had tried their best to keep in contact, and it had been another loss for Scarlett when, upon graduating high school, her brother went and enlisted, following in their family's footsteps. If Scarlett found out her brother had known what was happening to her and not done anything to help her, it was going to kill her.

"My phone might have survived the crash," Lucy said, wondering if there was any chance she could get some reception out there even if the phone wasn't totaled. One miracle a day was probably all she could hope for, and they'd already used theirs up in surviving the crash. Still, she used her good hand to unsnap her seatbelt and scanned the floor of the wrecked plane in search of her cell.

"You shouldn't be moving around until we've assessed your injuries," Zander said, putting one of his large hands on her shoulder and using his superior size and strength to keep her in her seat.

"I don't think the paramedics come out this deep in the jungle," she quipped.

"Haha, sassy girl. I'm serious, Lucy. Stay still. You were unconscious for a while, you probably have a concussion."

Since his concern didn't seem sweet, it was more like he was annoyed with her about something, although she had no idea what, she tried to push him away. "Like you didn't pass out, too. I need to find my phone. Unless you have yours and it survived?"

"Don't have one," he replied.

Okay, that had to be an outright lie. Who in this day and age didn't have a cell phone? She would have guessed at least everyone from middle school age and up did. "Well then, we for sure need mine."

Sighing like he was at the end of his rope, Zander gave her the kind of look usually reserved for toddlers pushing their luck. "Let me deal with your arm first, and then we can look for it."

The deal wasn't completely unreasonable, and those few extra minutes weren't going to change anything. They had been on the phone with her team when they crashed, so Prey would be looking for them. And since they also knew where she'd been heading, they at least had a place to start.

"Fine," she agreed, gingerly lifting her broken arm for him to see.

"It's broken," he said, trailing a fingertip around the small lump in her forearm.

"No kidding, ghost man." Zander's flinch at the nickname

was almost imperceptible, but she noticed it and felt bad. She'd meant it as a joke, but it was clear that despite whatever was going on, he did feel bad about hurting his sister by letting her think he was dead. "Sorry."

His eyes met hers, now carefully wiped free of all emotion. "It's fine. It's true. It's what I am now."

She had no idea what that meant, and from the way he pressed his lips together, it was clear Zander had no intention of explaining.

"This is going to hurt, but I need to try to get it back in place. No idea when we'll get you to a hospital."

It wasn't her first broken arm, she'd had three, two as a kid when she'd had a seizure, and one as an adult when she'd gone skydiving and messed up her landing. Still, she'd never had the bone pushed back into place while she was conscious. Since there was nothing she could do about it, she merely nodded.

"I'll do the best I can to get it straight, but I don't have an x-ray machine to check, might still need surgery later."

"At least I'm alive," Lucy reminded him. She had him to thank for it. She still had no idea whether he was trustworthy, but he'd gotten her to the ground alive, so that counted for something.

With his face an expressionless mask, Zander grasped her arm with confidence like he'd done this a million times before. First, his fingertips pressed to her wrist, checking her pulse no doubt to monitor blood flow, then almost before she even realized it, both his thumbs pressed on the lump on her arm, and one searing second of agony later the bump was gone.

Panting through the pain, Lucy somehow managed to cling to consciousness, although the world did go a little gray around the edges.

Zander's fingers squeezed hers lightly before he grabbed

a bandage and began to wrap her arm from wrist to elbow. "You did good, sassy girl. Didn't even scream."

"You didn't give me time." She managed the small joke as she slumped back into her seat. From this angle, she spotted what she'd been looking for before. "Hey, it's my cell phone. Can you grab it for me? If it survived and we can somehow get reception, we can call Prey, and you can give them the coordinates of where we were just before we crashed."

They weren't all that far away from San Diego. If Prey sent out a helo right away, she could be home in her bed tonight, or at least in the hospital if her arm needed surgery.

Once he was finished securing her bandage, Zander did indeed stoop to scoop up her phone.

But instead of handing it to her, or checking himself to see if there was reception, he dropped it back onto the floor of the plane and stomped it under his foot.

* * *

JANUARY 21ST
10:56 A.M.

"WHAT ARE YOU DOING?" Lucy shrieked. "Why would you do that?"

Because I can't let you call anyone.

Because if anyone knows you're alive your life will be as good as over.

Because no one can know we survived until I get you where I need to take you.

None of those were the answer Zander gave aloud. If Lucy learned the truth, it would ruin everything he had worked so hard for.

There was no way he was going to let that happen.

18

Although by the deadly look the blonde was shooting him, it was going to be hell keeping Lucy around and holding onto his secrets.

"Is Scarlett right? Are you a traitor?"

Wincing at the accusation, especially given what his twin had just been accused of and what she'd suffered because of it, Zander carefully wiped away every trace of emotion from his face. And his heart.

Because despite what his sister might think, he wasn't completely heartless.

"We didn't crash because of mechanical failure," he told Lucy, which was at least the truth, or as much of it as he could reveal without ruining everything.

"W-what do you mean?" she asked. Despite her stiff back and challenging gaze, he could see the pain shadowed beneath. How often did this woman hide her pain so people wouldn't think she was weak?

And why did he care?

Just because he'd always felt an attraction toward his sister's friend didn't mean he had ever intended to do anything about it. Even less so now. His choices might have been because he had been backed into a corner, but he still could have said no.

"Someone tampered with my plane, Lucy," he said, holding her gaze so she could read the truth in his eyes. "That means they know we crashed, and they know approximately where we crashed. If your phone survived, it's practically a honing beacon for anyone in the area to track us. Nobody good lives in this part of the world, and I don't think we want visitors right now when neither of us is at one hundred percent."

Indecision warred in her light blue eyes. "I guess not."

"Trust me." She shouldn't, but … part of him hoped that she might. It would be nice to feel like a good guy again instead of the bad one he'd become. "We don't want to be tracked right now, and cell phones are the worst for broadcasting your location, its why I no longer have one."

"You really don't have a cell phone? I thought you were lying about that."

One of the only honest things he'd said to her. "I really don't."

"Because you don't want anyone to know you're still alive."

The accusation hit its mark just as she'd intended it to if the disapproving tone was anything to go by. That wasn't exactly true. Hurting his sister sucked. For most of their lives they had been all each other had, and while they had drifted apart and both built new families, he'd lost his while hers was glaring angrily at him.

As much as it hurt to be reminded of his sins, it at least warmed him to know that Scarlett had a whole family of people around her who had her back. Once upon a time, he'd had that, too, until it had all been ripped away from him and he'd become the man he was today.

Suddenly, much too weary, Zander held out a hand to Lucy. "Come on, we have to get out of here."

Again another truth. Every time he spoke something true rather than the web of lies his life had become, he felt a tiny sliver of his soul and his self-respect return. There was no way he could ever be a man who was worthy of his sister's love, but maybe one day he could earn her forgiveness.

Maybe.

But more than likely not.

"Where are we going?" Lucy asked. Her hesitation in taking his offered hand spoke volumes. She had no idea if he could be trusted, and as much as he'd love to be able to reassure her that he wasn't a threat to her, he couldn't.

Because he was.

"Away from the plane so when whoever made sure we crashed comes looking for the wreckage, they won't find us in it."

"I guess it was the mole at Prey who must have sabotaged the plane." Lucy was still staring at his hand as though a tarantula was sitting in his palm, and it was more than obvious she wasn't positive that he wasn't the mole.

A crime he wasn't guilty of although he was guilty of committing many sins.

"Maybe we should split up," she suggested somewhat hesitantly. "That way if we do get found they don't get both of us."

Her comment felt like a test, one he was sure he was going to fail because there was absolutely no way he was letting this woman out of his sight. "We stick together," he told her.

"But if they—"

"We stay together," he repeated, this time in the cold, hard voice he had perfected. The one that said argue at your own peril.

Lucy's already pale face faded another couple of notches, fear turning it a sickly shade of gray, and a fine tremor rippled through her. As much as he hated scaring her, reminding her of their size differences, and how defying him wouldn't go well for her, Zander straightened to his full height and stared down at her with expressionless eyes. A look he knew could make grown men cower let alone tiny women who were injured and scared.

"Let's go," he ordered, this time not giving her a choice and taking her hand. Since he wasn't a complete monster, his grip was gentle and he eased her to her feet slowly, knowing with the head injury she was going to be dizzy. Ready to catch her if she fell, he kept hold of her once she was upright.

Out of necessity, Lucy's fingers tightened around his,

clinging to him with her eyes scrunched closed as she took in several deep breaths. As much as he wanted there to be something he could say or do to make this situation better for her, there was nothing he could do to change their circumstances. So, to that end, he said nothing. Just held her hand, his thumb brushing absently across the inside of her wrist.

It wasn't until Lucy's eyes opened, widening slightly, and dipped to their joined hands that he realized he was doing it.

What was he thinking?

He had no business comforting this woman.

None at all.

Knowing he should stop, withdraw his hand, and keep things as distant between them as possible didn't seem to help. For some reason, he couldn't seem to stop. There were so many things he wished he could explain, so many questions he wished he could ask, but in the end none of it would change a thing.

Abruptly, he released his hold on Lucy's hand before he did something stupid like pull her flush against him and kiss her until they both forgot everything else, including their own names. It was tempting, the kiss would be phenomenal, Zander already knew that. This woman was so smart, logical, and practical on the outside, but he was positive that if you could get her to lose control, she would be all fiery passion on the inside.

With her wild blonde mane of silky locks and those huge, long-lashed baby blues, the kind of eyes you could drown in, he didn't have to guess to know that Lucy would be amazing in bed. Once she let her inner goddess out there would be no stopping her. She'd be tight, and hot, and wet, and a breathy moan would tumble through those plump lips as her head tipped back in pleasure.

Picturing what Lucy would be like in bed was a

dangerous game, and one he better stop playing before he wound up making an already bad situation that much worse.

Without a word, he climbed through the mangled side of the plane, jumping the three feet down to the jungle floor, then turned to help Lucy down. While she didn't pull away from him, resisting his help, her body was stiff as his hands grasped her hips and he lifted her down.

When he started walking, Lucy followed. Whether he could expect her to stay close or not, for now at least, she seemed too weak and tired to try anything, but he couldn't let his guard down. Lucy was smart and resourceful, and he wouldn't put it past her to try something.

The last thing he wanted to do was hurt the woman, but the facts were, he had to get her to his intended destination. There were no other choices or at least none he could consider. So even though he didn't want to, he would do whatever it took to get her there.

Don't make me hurt you, Lucy.

I've caused enough pain.

Been responsible for enough deaths.

I don't need anything else on my conscience.

CHAPTER THREE

January 22nd
  2:18 A.M.

WAS HE ASLEEP?

Was this her chance?

Lucy lay as still as it was possible to lie when you were on the ground, in the middle of the jungle, inside a small cave that was really more of a rocky outcrop. There were a lot of things in the rainforest that could kill you, and she was doing her best not to think about all of them.

Just because she was usually an adrenalin junky didn't mean she didn't have her fears.

And bugs were at the top of that list.

Plus, there were jaguars, snakes, and scorpions.

Knowing that at any moment any one of them could come out of the dark was enough that there was no chance she was going to fall asleep.

After Zander made her walk for hours through the thick jungle, she finally collapsed when he found this little spot and informed her they would make camp for the night. Exhaustion had her passing out as soon as he'd forced her to drink some water and eat a protein bar.

By the time she'd woken, Zander had been lying beside her, seemingly fast asleep. It hadn't gone unnoticed that he'd taken the side closest to the opening of the little rocky cave, and she wasn't sure if that was because he wanted to be a line of protection between her and danger or because he wanted to make sure she couldn't leave without him knowing.

But leaving was exactly what she had planned.

The more they'd walked, the clearer it had become that Zander knew exactly where he was heading.

They weren't walking randomly, hoping to find signs of a village, road, or something that could lead them back home.

If the plane had been tampered with, and Zander had nothing to do with it—and she couldn't think of a logical reason why he would tamper with a plane he was going to be in—then why did he seem to know right where they were as well as where they were going? His strides had been confident, he'd never once wavered in the direction he was heading. There were no hesitations, and he didn't stop to check their surroundings or use a compass. He just walked.

That would be one thing if she could trust him, but since she couldn't … it was scary.

Scarier still, he was so adamant about keeping her close and the two of them sticking together. It wasn't so much because the idea was stupid, in these sorts of situations, sticking together would be the right move, but the problem was she couldn't trust Zander which meant she was questioning everything he did.

Why was it so important to him that they stay together?

Images of her friend's battered body flittered through her mind.

Was that her fate?

Was Zander leading her to Raul Castillo?

Was she going to be captured and tortured like Scarlett had been?

While it was hard to believe that Zander had played any role in his twin sister's abduction, it was hard to deny the bad timing. Now was when he chose to come back from the dead. There was zero chance he didn't know what risk he was taking by flying that plane. He knew it was a Prey job, who she was, and this was his sister's team.

What game are you playing, Zander Madden? And how dangerous is it to me?

There was no way she could answer that question. Zander himself certainly wasn't going to give anything away. As they walked, she'd asked him question after question, anything to pass the time and distract herself from the throbbing pain spiking up and down her body with each step.

None of those questions had gotten an answer.

The man was a vault, and he'd walked in complete silence almost the entire time, pausing occasionally to warn her of something he'd spotted up ahead or to tell her it was break time.

Well, his voice had been silent, but his eyes were anything but.

Even though she'd wanted to ask him to remove the contacts, she hadn't, but at some point, they must have been bothering him because he'd taken them out and pocketed them. Now that she was able to see more of the real Zander, she'd started noticing the mess of emotions swirling in the deep brown depths.

There was determination there, but so much more, guilt, anger, and helplessness.

It was the helplessness that got to her the most. Lucy didn't have to ask to know it was about a whole lot more than their current predicament.

But what did a man like Zander, a highly trained Delta Force operator, big and strong, powerful and trained, have to feel helpless about?

And why did she feel like the reason he'd faked his death was something you wouldn't immediately guess?

Still, despite her feelings that there was more going on here than Zander was ever going to tell her, Lucy knew she wasn't safe with him. It was the secrets he was keeping that were putting her at risk. If she didn't know what she was up against, she had no way of protecting herself. And since she couldn't trust Zander and his motives, she couldn't rely on him to have her back.

Which meant she was on her own.

The safest option for her was to get away from Zander and find her own way back to civilization. Not an easy task for a young woman alone in this part of the world, but she had a feeling it was still safer than sticking around Zander and his secrets. Plus, she had the added burden of her epilepsy. Since this trip was only supposed to be a couple of hours, she hadn't packed her medication. In the morning, it would be twenty-four hours since she'd had her last dose, so any time after that a seizure could hit. Her epilepsy was unpredictable at the best of times, but without her medicine, a seizure wasn't just a possibility it was an inevitability. This was a when not an if problem.

But it was also a problem for later.

Now she had to sneak away from a man who was trained to wake at the tiniest hint of a sound, especially when he was on an op.

Carefully, Lucy eased herself up into a sitting position, shifting slightly so her back was propped up against the rock wall. Not a single part of her body didn't protest the movement. Worst was her head, her arm, and her ribs. She was positive she'd cracked a couple, and there was no doubt she had a concussion with the nausea and dizziness.

Not that she had time to coddle herself right now.

If she didn't get away, she might not get another chance. Zander might not talk, but he watched her like a hawk, and even when she'd had to go to the bathroom, he'd hovered close enough to grab her if she tried to run.

After waiting a few minutes to see if he was going to stir, and noticing no change in his slow, even breathing, Lucy decided it was time to risk it. If he woke, she could always claim she was just going to the bathroom and then try to run again later.

Time felt like it slowed to barely moving as she pushed to her feet, not an easy thing to do with a broken arm and a battered body.

Once she was standing she froze, again waiting for any sign that Zander was awake.

But he didn't move, and her confidence rose a smidgen.

Since the cave was barely big enough for them both to stretch out in, she had no choice but to step over Zander if she wanted to get out into the jungle and make a run for it.

As she lifted her leg, Lucy could barely breathe, her heart hammered so hard in her chest that she was surprised that alone didn't wake him. Inch by inch, she raised her leg and stretched it out, then lowered it again just as slowly on the other side of Zander.

Next, she lifted her other leg with as much caution, and many seconds later she was standing on his other side, nothing between her and the relative safety of the jungle. Well, if you left out all the animals and the cartels that notoriously owned this part of the world.

Holding her breath, she waited what had to be another five minutes, but Zander didn't stir, and he didn't move. He was injured, too, which was working in her favor, making him tired enough not to hear her.

Not willing to wait another second and risk something else waking the sleeping man, Lucy turned and bolted.

There was no time to waste. At any moment, Zander could wake, and the most terrifying thing of all was she had no idea how he would respond to her escape attempt.

Just because his touch had been gentle at times didn't mean he wouldn't hurt her.

Which told her everything she needed to know about his trustworthiness. If she believed there was a chance that he might physically harm her, then she couldn't trust him. Running was the right thing to do.

Only she'd barely made it a dozen yards before she heard footsteps behind her.

No.

A sob built inside her, but she stamped it down, and shoved every bit of speed and strength she had into putting any distance between them.

If Zander caught her now she'd never get another chance.

Her life could very well be over.

In the end, size won out like it always did. Arms wrapped around her from behind, and she was yanked off her feet.

Despite her desire to put up a strong front and hide any signs of weakness, everything caught up to her at once, and that sob she'd been trying so hard to hold in came bursting out.

* * *

JANUARY 22ND
2:49 A.M.

. . .

DAMN.

She was crying.

Zander felt woefully inadequate to deal with tears.

They'd never been his strong suit with any woman other than his sister, and that was back when they were kids and all he had to do was try to cheer her up and make her laugh. Crying was pretty much forbidden in their house growing up. Unless you'd lost a limb you were expected to suck it up and deal with it without complaint. Even if you'd lost a limb, he was sure there would have been little tolerance for crying.

Sometimes at night, after their grandparents had gone to sleep, he'd sneak into his sister's room, and they'd hide under her covers and whisper to one another about how unfair things were. Occasionally, Scarlett would weep, and he'd do whatever it took to bring a smile back to her face.

They might be twins, but in a lot of ways he'd always been more of a big brother. He'd looked out for her and protected her when and where he could. When they were sent to different foster homes, he'd made sure any other kids there knew not to mess with his sister. Same at school, if any boy showed an interest in his twin, he issued a warning of what would happen if they broke her sweet, big, kind heart.

Their personalities were night and day. Always had been. Scarlett was so sweet, loved everyone, cared for everyone, had big dreams about what her life was going to look like, and he was happy that she'd finally found what she'd been searching for all her life. Her place to belong in the world.

Unlike him, she'd always believed she would find love, happiness, and family.

The kind of family they both used to wish for on their birthdays.

But Zander had always known he was more like their parents and grandparents. He was colder, harder, and able to separate emotions and do what needed to be done.

Only right now, with this beautiful, strong, crying woman clutched against his chest, Zander had no idea how to do what needed to be done. It would be so much easier if he didn't have to interact with Lucy. If he had sedatives and could just knock her out, throw her over his shoulder, and walk out of here, and not just easier because he could walk at a much faster pace on his own.

This was harder than he'd thought it would be.

Lucy had always invoked something in him that he hadn't wanted to examine too closely. She brought out feelings that he had learned from birth to ignore. Somehow, when she was around, he seemed to have a harder time doing that than he should.

"Please, let me go." Lucy wept. She was limp in his hold like everything that had happened had caught up with her all at once and left her too exhausted to do anything other than cry and beg.

Unless it was in the bedroom, and she was pleading for pleasure, he'd be only too happy to deliver, Zander found he didn't like the sound. Usually, a man's pleas were easy to ignore, he was able to block them out and focus on the bigger picture. But he couldn't do that with Lucy. She was different. The only other person who'd ever managed to bring out that same protectiveness in him was his sister.

Only he definitely didn't look at Lucy and think of her as a sister.

Although his life would be so much easier if he did.

"I can't let you go, Lucy," he said softly, dropping his forehead to rest against the back of her head. The ache in his chest was uncomfortable, and he wanted to rub it away, erase it, do what he always did, and focus on the job at hand.

"Why?" The whispered word, spoken through a torrent of tears, only made the ache worse because there was no answer he could offer her.

No satisfactory answer anyway.

"I only have one set of night vision goggles," he said in place of an answer. "How about I carry you for a while. Since we're both awake, we may as well keep walking."

"I don't want you touching me," she said, beginning to struggle against his grip. The only way she was getting free was if he let her and he had no intention of letting her.

"You're weak, in pain, and exhausted." Zander shifted his hold on her so she was cradled in his arms. With her in this position, he had no choice but to look into her eyes. Such a pretty shade of blue, the kind of eyes you could get lost staring into if you'd let yourself. But he couldn't let himself.

That was something he was going to have to keep reminding himself of.

Because there was no way he could throw away everything he'd worked for, everything he was so close to getting. Not for one woman with a tough girl attitude he admired, a sexy body he craved, and a lot of love to offer that he found himself longing to be the recipient of.

Not for anything.

Too much was riding on this.

There was too much to lose if it all fell apart.

Too much to gain if everything went the way he had planned.

"Like you care if I'm hurting," Lucy said, eyeing him defiantly.

The spark of anger in her eyes almost made him smile. If he didn't know it would only make her angry, he'd tell her how much he loved that she wasn't cowering down before him, but standing up for herself. He guessed she had a lot of practice of standing up for herself and proving to those around her that she wasn't weak.

Which reminded him.

"Do you have your medication with you?" he asked.

Annoyance flared in those baby blues that looked at him with such disdain that he wanted to spill his guts, and try to make her understand the position he'd been put in.

"That's none of your business, and how do you even know about my epilepsy?"

"Because I know you, Lucy."

"No, you don't. Not really. We've only met a handful of times."

"Enough," he murmured. Enough for him to have fantasized about her more times than he could count, coming in his hand with an image of her face in his mind, and the echo of the sounds he knew she'd make in his ears.

Enough to know that if he was a different man, and his life wasn't the one he had chosen, he could have pursued her and convinced this fiercely independent woman to give him a chance.

But he wasn't different, and his life was a step away from complete catastrophe.

He could do nothing to ever be good enough for a woman like Lucy Elrod.

Best he remembered that.

"I don't get you." There was exasperation in her tone now. "I know you love Scarlett, yet you let her believe you were dead knowing it would crush her. You show up right as there's a mole at Prey, even though it's a huge risk for a guy who's supposed to be dead to show up at his sister's job. Our plan crashes, you're acting all crazy about us sticking together, and you walk with a purpose. You know what you're doing and where you're going, but you refuse to tell me anything or answer any question I ask. Yet when you touch me, you're so gentle that I can't imagine you ever doing anything to hurt anyone. You're quite the enigma, ghost man."

This time when she called him ghost man it was free of

judgment and the words didn't quite sting as much, reminding him of all his failures.

There was no refuting any of her words. He knew exactly where they were and where he was going. And there was no way he could not be gentle with this precious bundle he held in his arms. Just because he knew there could never be anything between them didn't mean there wasn't a part of him that wondered.

What would it be like to have Lucy as his?

What would it be like to make love to her?

What would it be like to press his lips against hers?

What would it be like to be normal?

And what was the point of wondering about it all? Nothing could change what was. Nothing could take back what had happened or his choices following it.

"I'm not a puzzle for you to uncover, sassy girl," he said softly.

A small smile curled up one side of her mouth. "You should know something, ghost man."

"Yeah? What's that?"

"I love puzzles, and I'm really good at them."

There was a challenge in her voice as well as a promise. Lucy was determined to unravel him, but if she discovered the truth, it would only put her in more danger than she was already in.

CHAPTER FOUR

January 22nd
    5:02 P.M.

WITH EVERY SECOND THAT PASSED, it looked like the inevitable
was drawing closer.

Lucy didn't like it one little bit, this wasn't how she
wanted things to end, and she wasn't even sure she was
capable of following through and doing what had to be done.

You have to, Lucy.

This is your life we're talking about.

*Zander might have been a good guy at one point but he's not
now. You know it.*

You feel it.

That was completely true. As the hours ticked by, she felt
Zander growing more and more distant. Not only did he
refuse to speak to her unless it was to issue an order, but she
could sense him withdrawing. There was nothing in his eyes
anymore, they were just … blank. Like he was more robot
than man.

The pace he was setting was punishing, and more than once she'd collapsed, her battered body simply unable to go on.

When that happened, he no longer touched her with gentleness, cupping her chin as he helped her sip water from a bottle like he had the day before. Lucy hadn't even realized that she'd needed those small human connections to keep her going until he'd ripped them away. Now all she got was the canteen thrust at her while he stood over her with his arms crossed, expression empty, and posture stiff like he was ready for something to happen.

She was, too.

It was the very definition of waiting on tender hooks.

Something was happening, but she was left completely in the dark. She had no idea what to expect and the thought was terrifying.

Risking your safety in some adrenalin pumping activity like sky diving, or bungee jumping, or scuba diving way out in the depths of the ocean was one thing. It was kind of like controlling the danger. You knew what you were doing, you had practiced what to do in the event of an emergency, and you were prepared for all scenarios. It didn't mean the risk was gone, but it definitely mitigated it.

Out here, she had nothing to go on, no way to prepare herself.

That was what made it so scary.

How could she hope to survive when she had no idea what she had to defend herself against?

Zander was giving nothing away, and all she had to go on were theories and suspicions. Just because he had faked his death didn't mean he was working for someone like Raul Castillo. Yet the timing was so suspicious that it was hard to believe his sudden reappearance had nothing to do with the weapons dealer.

All she knew for certain was that Zander was shutting down any sort of connection to her, distancing himself. The only reason she could think of to do that was if he knew what he was going to do with her, and he felt some guilt over it, so he had to stop seeing her as a real person so he could do what he planned.

Not if I can help it, ghost man.

Although to do what *she* had to do, she was going to have to stop seeing the man as one of her three best friends' twin brother.

Because if she couldn't, then she wouldn't be able to take action, and that meant she was handing herself over to Zander and his plans on a silver platter.

Every time she'd called him ghost man, she'd sensed his pain, although he'd tried to hide it. A lot was going on with this man, and while she would love nothing more than to puzzle him out she didn't have the time.

Not if she wanted to live.

So, she had to do this, even if she had no idea how she was going to face Scarlett if she did make it through this ordeal and back home.

It was more than clear that her best chance at survival was getting away from Zander. He was taking her some-where—or to someone—that wasn't safe. That was pretty much a fact as far as she was concerned. So even though there were lots of risks going it alone in the Mexican jungle, it was absolutely the lesser of the two evils in this scenario.

For now, she just had to think one step ahead. If she tried to see the big picture, she was going to get too overwhelmed to act.

While Zander kept a hawk's view on her as they walked and didn't let her out of his sight for so much as a second, there was no way he could stop her eyes from roaming the landscape. Nor could he stop her mind from running through possible scenarios.

Since Zander kept growing more tense, she knew they were getting closer to his destination, so time was running out for her. She had to come up with a way to escape, and since she knew Zander was prepared for her to try something, she had to take him out of the equation.

That meant having to hurt him or possibly even kill him.

The very thought of harming another human being left her feeling sick to her stomach in a way that had nothing to do with the concussion.

But what other choice did she have?

Go with Zander and let him do to her what he had planned?

Not happening.

A huge part of her wanted to believe she was reading the man and the situation all wrong. That those pieces of Zander she sensed that showed his guilt, his pain, his conflicted emotions, were all true. That he had no intention of hurting her or handing her over to people who would hurt her.

If his intentions weren't nefarious, he wouldn't be trying to hide his plans.

It was that piece of information she had to keep reminding herself of. Zander wouldn't be so tight-lipped if he was just trying to get them to some village so they could call Prey, and get back home. There would be no need to.

Be strong, Luce. And smart.

Your life depends on it.

It's great to see the good in people, but not if it costs you your life.

When she saw they were walking close to the edge of a rocky cliff, an idea popped into her head.

Could she pull it off?

You have to.

Steadying her nerves and fortifying her resolve, Lucy stopped walking. "I have to pee," she announced. She didn't really, but she needed to get as close to that edge as possible for her plan to work, and she knew that having to go to the bathroom would allow her a little more distance from her captor than needing a break would.

Zander merely nodded, scanning their surroundings then settling his gaze on her.

Thankfully, for her plan to work, she *wanted* him to be watching her.

Walking a couple of steps closer to the edge of the cliff, Lucy turned her back on Zander like she had the other times she'd had to pee, and awkwardly shoved her pants down enough that she could do her business.

Once she was done, she dragged in a deep breath, ignored the ache in her chest as she did so, and prayed that this would work.

Pulling her pants up one handed was awkward, and her balance was off because of the head injury and exhaustion, so when she swayed like she was about to topple over it wasn't that much of an act.

Like she'd hoped he would, Zander sprung toward her to catch her before she fell.

Just as he was about to reach her, Lucy sidestepped, hoping his forward momentum would be too much to counter in time.

Right as he would have tumbled down, rolling over the cliff edge, a crack split through the air.

Somehow, Zander managed to take her down with him as he fell, angling his body so he took the brunt of the impact as they hit the ground.

Sluggish as it was, it took a moment for her brain to process what had just happened.

A gunshot.

Someone had shot at them.

And Zander was trying to protect her.

Unfortunately, it was too little, too late.

Her plan was working. Together, in a tangle of limbs, they rolled the short distance toward the edge of the cliff. Zander muttered a curse, and then he was shoving her body with a force that sent her tumbling back in the other direction.

The move sent him rolling faster toward the edge.

There was nothing he could do to stop it.

He'd saved her life at the expense of his own.

Lucy cried out in fear and scrambled toward him, praying she could grab onto him in time and stop the inevitable from happening.

But it happened.

In slow motion the bottom half of Zander's body disappeared. Their eyes connected. There was no condemnation in Zander's, no anger, no fear either. Instead, there was almost a sense of peace. Like he was ready to welcome death.

Then his head disappeared, and he was just gone.

* * *

JANUARY 22ND
    5:27 P.M.

PAIN RICOCHETED THROUGH HIS BODY.

Zander groaned as he returned to consciousness.

For a moment, his brain was foggy and unfocused. He couldn't remember where he was, or what had happened, or why it was that he felt like he'd been run over by a truck.

All he knew was the tickle of fear at the back of his mind.

Something was wrong.

Just because he couldn't figure out what didn't mean he didn't know he had to. And fast.

Focusing on the pain, he allowed it to lead him out of the fogginess, let it anchor him. Once he'd gripped his mind onto that pain memories began to trickle back in. The plane crash, the hike through the jungle, the gunshot, the fall.

Lucy had tried to throw him over the side of the cliff.

A grin replaced the grimace, and he blinked his eyes open to find that he'd rolled about halfway down the incline and landed on a mossy outcrop where a single tree grew. It wasn't so much as a cliff as a fairly steep hill that was more rocky than covered in trees like the rest of the landscape. If Lucy thought the fall would kill him, she was mistaken. It was enough for her to get away from him though, since it separated them and bought her a little time.

There was no anger in him at the knowledge she'd been willing to kill him. That she'd actively tried to, or at the very least to incapacitate him.

The opposite.

Pride blossomed inside him. The woman was smart and spunky. It took guts to do what she'd done, and she'd done it so perfectly. He hadn't seen it coming until it was too late to do anything about it, and momentum sent him sailing over.

It had taken every bit of strength he had to shift his trajectory to hit Lucy and take her down when he felt a tingling at the back of his neck one moment before the crack of a gunshot sounded through the jungle.

Had Lucy been hit?

Was she up there now with the shooter?

Or had his shove not been enough to save her from falling?

Fear for her safety was enough to wipe the smile from his face. Maybe the woman was a little too spunky for her own good. If she hadn't tried to get rid of him and go this alone, they wouldn't be separated right now. He had a weapon in his backpack, which thankfully was still on his back, he could have protected them both, but now she was up there alone with someone he wanted desperately to keep her away from.

So much for that plan.

Whatever Lucy might think, he hadn't been walking her toward danger. The opposite in fact. He'd been walking her away from it, taking her to a place where he knew she'd be safe.

Too late for that now.

Now she was alone, unprotected, unarmed, injured, and left to face an enemy that spunk wasn't going to save her from.

The fear that lurched its way through his body, gaining momentum as it went, was something he wasn't accustomed to.

Sure, Zander knew what it was like to be afraid. Knew what it was like to fear for the lives of the people you cared about, those that were important to you, the closest thing you had to family.

But this felt so different.

It had been months since he'd felt anything even close to this, and that week of horror was etched into his mind and his soul. The echoes of his teammates' screams still haunted his sleeping and waking hours. Nightmares plagued him, flashbacks during the day, and the only thing that kept him going was his need for vengeance.

Nothing could mess up his plans because without them he was … nothing.

Nothing but the tragic lone survivor of a hell he was never supposed to walk away from.

Death should have claimed him like it did the seven other men there with him that day. A horrible, unimaginable, agonizing death. Slow and painful, that was the kind of torture those men took pleasure in dishing out.

But he was going to get his revenge, and then there was every chance he was going to die for real. After that, he would have nothing left to live for. His team was all dead, his Delta career trashed, and his sister—the only blood family who had ever meant anything to him—hated his guts.

He was better off dead.

All of them were better off if he was dead.

Not yet, though. Death couldn't claim his soul until he finished his final mission. And part of that mission included getting one strong, sassy, beautiful woman back home where she belonged.

"Hold on, Lucy, I'm coming," he muttered as he placed his palms against the ground and used them to help heave himself into a standing position.

For a second, his body swayed, and he got the sickening feeling that he was going to fall the rest of the way down the side of the mountain. Just because it wasn't really a fall that could kill a man, if he hit one of the trees the wrong way, he could snap his neck, or break a bone, rendering himself useless.

Somehow, he managed to remain upright, and covering his eyes to shield them from the bright sunlight he looked up to the top of the incline. Up there was the last place he'd seen Lucy, their gazes had connected as he was going over the edge. In that split second, he'd felt her fear, regret, and her deep remorse. There were a million things he'd wanted to say, assurances he'd wanted to give, but in the end, there hadn't been time.

All he'd felt, believing his life was about to end, was peace.

Peace he didn't deserve.

Peace he would find only in death.

As nice as it would be to fade into oblivion and finally

escape the torment that would follow him for the remainder of his life, right now he couldn't.

He had to find Lucy.

Knowing she was vulnerable to whoever had shot at them made his gut churn in the most unpleasant way, and there was a constriction in his chest that Zander didn't quite understand. It was one thing not to want to see another innocent die, it was another thing to want to protect a woman who was important to his sister, but it felt like so much more than that.

It felt like *he* needed Lucy to be okay.

The attraction he'd always felt toward her seemed to have grown into something so much more, although he had no idea how it had happened. Maybe it was the first time she sassed him in that plane, maybe it was seeing her anger directed toward him and knowing it was born out of protectiveness for someone she loved. Or maybe it was the way she seemed to sense what he was feeling even though he was an expert at hiding it.

The trail of mangled bodies left behind after he and his team were captured was a testament to that skill. Only with Lucy, the skill seemed to vanish.

Now she needed him, and he wasn't there.

There had been no sound from her. She wasn't still up there and hadn't called out to him or tried to help in any way. Just because her job wasn't one that required her to be out in the field didn't mean she had no idea of what was going on. She knew they'd been shot at, and knew she would have to run if she was going to have any chance at surviving.

"I'm coming, sassy girl."

The words offered him strength severely lacking in his exhausted body, and he gripped the side of the hill, ready to drag himself back up it. A pull in his bicep and the streaks of blood down his arm surprised him, and he realized for the first time that the bullet that had been fired had actually hit him.

Better him than Lucy.

Not wanting to waste time—time Lucy might not have—tending to the wound, Zander ignored it, and instead, somehow managed to find a foothold and began what would be a torturous climb back up the cliff.

Every time he felt like giving up, every time it felt like he couldn't make it, he reminded himself of the woman counting on him and managed to make it another foot.

Foot after foot he climbed.

By the time he dragged himself over the ledge, his arms and legs were trembling, he was breathing hard and coated in sweat.

But there was no time to sit around and recoup lost energy.

At least half a dozen sets of prints told him that people had been here recently, no doubt looking down to see if he'd survived the fall. That meant there were at least half a dozen armed men currently on Lucy's trail.

"Hold on, sassy girl."

Please, hold on.

CHAPTER FIVE

January 22nd
    5:30 P.M.

Check on Zander or run?

Lucy knew the sensible answer to that question was to run.

Now.

As fast as she could.

If she wanted any chance of getting away from the shooter, she couldn't afford to waste a single second.

But ...

It was *her* fault that Zander had fallen.

Because of her trying to get away from him, he'd gone over the side of the cliff and possibly even gotten shot first.

She had to see if he was alive. If he was, then maybe she could run, lead the men away from there, and then circle back and help Zander.

Maybe that was stupid of her to even want to help him

when her entire goal had been to get him out of the way, but he'd tried to save her life.

Twice.

That bullet would have hit her if he hadn't knocked her down, and when they'd both been going to fall, he'd pushed her away, knowing it would speed up his own momentum and take him over.

He had been prepared to sacrifice his life for her.

That had to mean something.

Didn't it?

Creeping on her stomach to the edge of the cliff, Lucy looked down. Dressed all in black as he was, it took her a moment to spot him through the trees, but there he was, lying on a small outcrop.

But was he alive?

"Zander?" she hissed, trying to keep her voice quiet so it didn't carry. Since she wasn't a field operative and didn't have the training everyone else at Prey did, she couldn't make her voice that same wisp of sound all the guys and the Artemis Team girls could. It was way too loud, and she flinched at the sound, sure anyone in the area would have heard it and know that she was alive.

The man she was calling out to didn't flinch though.

Didn't so much as move a single muscle.

From her vantage point, there was no way to tell if he was breathing or not, and she couldn't check his pulse, so she had no choice but to assume the worst.

Zander was dead.

Because of her.

She'd as good as killed him.

Tears blurred her vision as she shakily managed to get to her feet. The pain in her body was forgotten as an ache spread out from her heart. She'd killed a man. A man who, while she knew was untrustworthy, had demons he was fighting. That was something Lucy knew for certain. She felt his pain somehow and spotted the shadows lurking deep in his eyes that he tried so hard to hide. Whatever he'd gotten mixed up in wasn't because he wanted to, it wasn't for greed or selfish purposes, she believed that.

Deep down, she believed Zander Madden was still a good man.

A good man who had made some bad choices, and if he'd just told her what was going on she would have found a way to help him.

Only now it was too late.

He was dead, and there was still a gunman out there somewhere.

Choking on a sob, Lucy turned away from the cliff's edge and started running.

All those hours she'd spent plotting how she was going to get away from Zander and go this alone, now that she was alone, and she'd gotten Zander out of the way, it didn't feel so great after all.

Fear was chasing her every bit as much as whoever had shot at them.

Self-doubt, too.

Had she made a mistake in trying to get away from Zander? What if he hadn't told her what was going on because he couldn't and not because he didn't want to? What if he and his team were working some deep-cover mission and that was why his death had been faked? What if she'd been safe with him all along and thrown away his protection because she believed she couldn't trust him?

There was no point in playing the what-if game. What was done was done. She'd gotten what she wanted, she was on her own now and had to figure out a way to survive and get back home.

It felt like she'd been running for hours when she first heard it.

The sounds of someone running behind her.

Not just someone. *Multiple* someones if she was correct.

A whimper slipped out as she continued to drag in rough breaths. The stitch in her side kept her slightly hunched over, and her ribs protested every ragged breath she was able to draw into her lungs. Her broken arm was pure agony, and keeping it tucked against her stomach did little to protect it from jostling with each step she took.

She wouldn't be able to go on much longer.

The thought was terrifying, and images of Scarlett's injuries superimposed themselves in her mind over the image of Zander's big body lying so still. So much death and pain and suffering, and Lucy knew she could be seconds away from enduring her own hell on earth.

Turned out she was indeed seconds away from capture.

Because less than a minute later, she was knocked to the ground.

Heavy weight pressed her down into the ground, her broken arm crushed between it and both their bodies sending pain shafting through it. A cry fell from her lips, and she thrashed about, trying to throw her attacker off.

If any of the guys from Prey, who had spent hours drilling her in self-defense could see her now, they'd be so disappointed. Her movements had no technique, just plain old panic and fear.

It was one thing to practice in the safety of the gym, it was quite another to have to do those same moves when you were actually fighting for your life.

All at once, the pressure on her body was gone. Meaty hands wrapped around her biceps, pulling her up until she was standing.

Six men stood around her, one leering at her as his grip

on her arm tightened. Despite the terror pounding her chest, Lucy glared at them. Just because she was afraid didn't mean she intended to back down from these men.

They were bullies, plain and simple.

Over the years, she'd had plenty of practice dealing with bullies.

Kids could be cruel, and when you had something that made you different, they latched onto it. Didn't help that her epilepsy hadn't been very well under control back then and she'd had several seizures at school. While she'd never seen herself having a seizure, Lucy knew it could be scary for those watching, and it was no wonder the other kids had treated her as a freak after that.

But she'd never cowered before them.

Not once.

Her parents had drilled into her that she had nothing to be ashamed of, she just had a medical condition, she was no freak. They might have coddled her and worried over her, but they had always told her that just because she had epilepsy, she could still get out and live her life, doing whatever she wanted. They'd just prefer that the things she wanted to do weren't so dangerous.

Drawing on that strength now, honed since childhood, Lucy yanked her arm free and squared her shoulders. Just because she couldn't fight her way out of this didn't mean she had to fall at their feet and shake in fear.

"Leave me alone," she snarled, shooting daggers at them with her eyes and wishing she had a real weapon on her. Wouldn't do much good against half a dozen armed men, but she was not going to go down without a fight.

That wasn't her style.

"You are scientist girl," one of them said, his lecherous gaze roaming her body, making her feel dirty.

By scientist girl, she assumed he meant one of Athena

Team, a safe assumption she was sure. That meant they weren't just cartel members who happened to be out here, they had to have tracked her and Zander from the plane. While she was sure he wouldn't have left much of a trail, she'd been hurt, exhausted, and plotting to get away from him the whole time. She would have pretty much left arrows pointing to the direction she'd walked in.

If these were Raul Castillo's men, they weren't leaving here without her.

"You'll come with us," the same man said, his voice confident.

While she would love nothing more than to refuse, that would be stupid. They were armed, they were bigger than her, and they weren't injured. If they wanted to take her with them, they could and they would.

"Come with you where?" she asked, wanting confirmation so she could make a plan.

"Boss wants to talk to you," one of the other men said.

"Boss?"

"Mr. Castillo," another man replied.

So they were Raul's men, which meant he hadn't given up on getting the formula for the Reactivator. They didn't think he would, but knowing for sure that he hadn't made her skin crawl. Not only was she in danger, but so were her three best friends because Raul could go after any one of them.

It also meant that Zander really was working for the man.

It was the only explanation as to how they knew she was out there and had been able to find them.

Stupid, but as she was dragged off through the jungle, the thing that hurt the most was knowing that she had been right not to trust him. All those things she'd thought she had seen in him were nothing more than her trying to make excuses for a man she was attracted to.

* * *

JANUARY 23ᴿᴰ
   12:31 A.M.

BLACK SPOTS DANCED in front of his eyes.

Bats?

No.

Spiders?

No.

Birds?

No.

Zander crashed to his knees, and with the thud of pain that echoed through his body, the answer to the question filtered through his mind.

The black spots were the beginnings of unconsciousness. He was pushing himself too hard, too far, almost going beyond the limits of what his trained body could endure.

It might not even be forty-eight hours yet since he'd climbed into his plane, but in that time, they'd crashed, he'd argued with himself incessantly about what the right thing to do was, he'd hiked through the thick jungle for hours, gotten no more than snatched pockets of light sleep, fallen off a cliff, and gotten shot.

No wonder he was struggling to remain on his feet.

But he had to.

There was no other option.

Lucy was out there, and she needed him.

It was his fault that she was in danger. Just because he thought he could use this situation at Prey to his advantage didn't mean that he hadn't known there could be repercussions. Not that he thought anyone would sabotage his plane and cause him to crash, but he'd known things could go horribly wrong.

There had been no time to analyze the crash and why someone had tampered with his plane. If it was Raul, then there was every chance his plans had already been discovered, and he, too, was walking into a trap. If it was the mole at Prey, then there was a chance that they were acting alone and had simply planned to kill one of the Athena Team members possibly as a way to scare the others into coughing up the formula for the Reactivator.

Personally, Zander couldn't care less about the drug. That had nothing to do with his goals, and he was proud as hell of his sister and her friends for creating something that could save the lives of men and women serving their country.

Not that it would have done his team any good.

Their injuries had been so brutal there was no chance of them surviving.

Seven good men, friends, his family, all gone now.

There was no way he was losing Lucy, too.

For some reason, he knew losing her would crush him differently than losing the rest of his Delta Team.

If he wanted to save her life, he had to keep going. It didn't matter if his body was running on empty, he had to get back on his feet and keep following the trail.

Somehow, he managed to force himself into a standing position, although he swayed precariously and very nearly ended back up on the ground.

Thankfully, the night vision goggles had been undamaged in the fall, and he'd put them on as soon as it got dark so he didn't have to stop for the night. The trail wasn't overtly obvious, but he had a lot of training and could follow the marks Lucy had left behind. The same marks the men who had shot at them had also followed.

Seven people.

Why did that number continue to haunt him?

Only this time, six of them were the enemy, and one was ...

Important.

That was the only word he would allow himself to consider right now, although it didn't feel nearly big enough to explain the myriad of tangled emotions he felt when it came to the smart, sexy blonde with the bright baby blues.

It was those feelings that had him following the trail again. Even if he was stumbling, he was at least on his feet, at least moving forward and making progress.

Although what he was going to do when he found Lucy he had no idea.

There was only one of him, and since they were close to Raul's turf, he had to assume it was the weapons dealer who had sent his men out to retrieve any survivors from the crash. Raul was a smart man, and more than that, he'd been forced to give up two of his properties in the last month because of kidnapping Scarlett and the rescues. If Zander had to guess, there would be at least two dozen of Raul's men guarding the property, possibly more.

Two dozen minimum against him.

With recon gathered intel, a proper plan, and no injuries, it was possible he could have mounted a solo rescue.

But ...

Like this?

Injured, weak, and teetering on the edge of exhaustion, it wasn't likely he could get Lucy out on his own.

More like impossible.

It wasn't like he had backup, though. His team was gone, he was off on a mission of revenge, alerting Prey would ruin everything he had worked so hard for.

So he guessed it boiled down to one thing.

Was Lucy's life more important than vengeance for his team?

Calling Prey was an option. Just because he'd broken Lucy's phone so she couldn't use it to call for help didn't mean he didn't have a satellite phone of his own tucked away in his pack. Back then, he hadn't wanted anyone to know they'd survived, he'd thought he had everything under control and didn't want interference that could mess up his plans.

But things had changed.

Because of Lucy's injuries, they'd had to walk slower than he would have liked, which meant they hadn't hit his destination. There was no way he could have known Lucy would try to kill him, so he hadn't anticipated the two of them being split up.

Nor had he intended for Lucy to get captured.

Now that she was, he had to do whatever it took to get her out because the thought of her beautiful body marred with the marks of a self-obsessed maniac and her strong soul stained with the psychological trauma that would leave deeper scars made him feel ill. It had been bad enough learning what had happened to his sister, in fact, he'd promptly thrown up when he'd learned about it. But allowing it to happen to Lucy when she was supposed to be under his care was too much.

Another burden his already struggling psyche would struggle to bear.

Seven deaths on his conscience were enough.

No more.

He wasn't losing Lucy as well.

So, he had no choice but to keep walking, forcing his body beyond what it could cope with. A single-minded focus the only thing keeping him vaguely upright.

As he continued searching for evidence of how Lucy and

the others had gone, he kept images of her in his mind as motivation. The way her fingers had curled around his when they'd shaken hands upon meeting that first time several years back. The way her laugh could brighten a room with its sweet melody. The spark in her eyes as she sassed him.

The panic and guilt in her eyes as he went over the cliff.

No.

That memory had to be shoved away.

If he allowed himself to think of Lucy, scared and hurting, the magic was gone. He had to picture her as she should be, all serious logic and practicality. All that wildness she kept bottled up inside allowed her to run free only when she had designated time to let her hair down.

Zander wanted to make her let her hair down and see her all wild and free, head thrown back, laughter tumbling from her lips, and her eyes shining with the freedom of not having to carry around the pressure of always proving you were capable.

He wanted the real Lucy, the one who didn't worry about how others saw her.

Wanted her free.

Completely and utterly free.

And his.

Because no matter how many times he reminded himself that he couldn't date his twin sister's friend he still wanted her. Still craved her with an intensity that was only growing. The last few days together had only made it worse. She was so strong and stood up for herself no matter how scared she was. She was tough and so beautiful, and brave enough to do whatever it took to protect herself.

And she was out there all alone.

Captured.

He'd seen the evidence of the men catching her, dragging her away with them, and was using it to feed his fury.

But it was also feeding his fear.

Just because Lucy could never really be his, he wasn't worthy of a woman like her, his soul was too black, too dirty, it didn't mean that he wouldn't do whatever it took to save her.

Anything.

He had to.

This was his fault, and he wouldn't allow another person to be hurt because of him.

Die because of him.

On and on he walked, his focus narrowed down to only following the trail, there was no energy left in his body to worry about anything else like the predators lurking in the jungle.

Zander walked until he couldn't anymore.

Until his body fell and he was unable to push back up to his feet.

Until the black spots grew until they consumed his vision.

Until unconsciousness stole him away, and his last thought was that, once again, an innocent person was going to pay for his mistakes.

CHAPTER SIX

January 23rd
  10:47 A.M.

You can do this.

You will not back down.

Lucy kept repeating that to herself as she was marched out of the bedroom she'd been stashed in when she was first brought to the house.

Someone had cleaned up her wounds properly, and she'd been given water to drink but nothing to eat and no clean clothes to wear. It wasn't the being dirty in and of itself that bothered her—although she'd love to be clean, she'd gone camping plenty of times and been longer without a shower— it was that it was another way for Raul Castillo to try to exert dominance over her. He thought if he kept her dirty and hungry, it gave him an edge.

He was wrong.

Stubborn might very well have been her middle name.

When you grew up with a condition that could make you

JANE BLYTHE

vulnerable, and you didn't want to let that condition rule your entire life, you learned pretty quickly how to stand up for yourself and fight for what you wanted. If her parents had had their way, she would have been wrapped in bubble wrap and kept in the house her whole life. But what kind of life would that be?

Everything she had she'd worked hard for. Graduating high school at the top of her class, then the same at college with both her degrees. She'd aced the interview for Prey, and every single day she made sure she did the best she could do. When she allowed herself time just to have fun, she sought out the most adrenalin-pumping activities she could to remind herself that she was alive and could do whatever she wanted.

This might be the scariest thing she'd ever done and certainly had more adrenalin flooding her system than anything else she'd tried, but the same principle still applied. She was tough and strong, she did whatever it took to get to where she wanted to be, whether that be sweet-talking her parents at seven into letting her play football, or deep-sea diving in the ocean where it was so dark you couldn't see anything outside of the beam of your flashlight.

Survive.

Conquer.

Never show weakness.

When she was led downstairs into a basement, she kept her back straight and eyes wide open. No cowering. If Raul thought it was going to be easy to break her, he was wrong. He hadn't broken Scarlett, and he wasn't going to get to her either.

Because of what her friend had been through she knew what to expect, and she used the knowledge to mentally fortify herself. Before she'd made a couple of really good friends who she kept in contact with to this day, school had been lonely. The other kids called her a freak, excluded and bullied her, and she had become an expert at finding things to do on her own, usually reading, and pretending that being left out didn't bother her.

Of course, it had, but none of them had ever suspected, and they'd eventually grown tired of taunting her and never getting a response. In third grade when a new little girl had joined her class, they'd hit it off right away. The girl had had cancer and was in remission, but their medical histories had bonded them quickly, and Lucy had finally learned what it was like to fit in and not be treated like you were different.

She'd loved it and never looked back, but the memories of those years when she felt so alone and different lingered, and she could use them now to make her stronger.

In the middle of the basement, there was a large table with cuffs attached to the corners, it didn't take being a genius to figure out that was where she was going to be put.

As predicted, the two men flanking her led her over to it. They didn't ask her to get on, one of them just picked her up and laid her on it, using his superior size to hold her in place while her ankles and wrists were secured.

The awkward angle made her broken arm throb, but it was the least of her worries right now because a man in a crisp, white shirt with black suit pants came strolling in. Recognizing him from his picture, Lucy knew he was Raul Castillo, and with his slicked-back hair and toned body, she could see why women thought he was attractive.

Until you looked into his eyes anyway.

They were dead, and you could sense the malevolence that lived inside him.

"Ms. Elrod," he greeted her formally as though they were business associates having a meeting, and he hadn't brought her here against her will.

"Mr. Castillo," she replied, keeping her tone cool and willing her pulse to slow so it wasn't echoing in her ears.

An eyebrow quirked at her calm tone, and she knew she'd scored a point, even if it was a small one. While she had no intention of taunting the man, she also had no intention of giving him what he wanted. Not just the formula to the drug she and her friends had created, but she wasn't going to cry, scream, or beg, she was simply going to lay here and stare at him.

Not the best of plans, maybe, but what else could she do?

Prey knew the plane had crashed, and she had no doubt they'd be looking for her. Although she rated the chances of them finding her at pretty close to zero. No one was coming for her. Zander was dead, and even if he wasn't, she doubted he'd be of any help to her. So she was on her own. For now, she was going to play this calm, cool, and collected while she bid her time and waited for a moment to escape. Or even better, if she could find one then she was going to take the opportunity to kill Raul Castillo. She and her team deserved to live in peace without the threat of him coming after them again and again hanging over their heads.

"You should know I don't intend to give you the formula," she warned him. "None of us will so you may as well just give up."

Annoyance flared in his dark eyes. "I don't give up, Ms. Elrod."

Shrugging as best as she could with her wrists cuffed, she met his gaze squarely. "Then I don't know what to tell you, but you're wasting your time. I know what you did to Scarlett. How you had her beaten and whipped. About the drug you gave her. I won't insult both our intelligence by saying I'm not afraid, but I know how to control my fear."

"Even in the face of death, Ms. Elrod?" Raul mocked.

"I've been staring death in the face all my life." While it

was unlikely her epilepsy would kill her outright, there was such a thing as sudden unexpected death in epilepsy, SUDEP, that killed more than one person out of every thousand with epilepsy each year. With her seizures not well controlled even with her medication, and the fact that her seizures were tonic-clonic, what used to be called grand mal, she was at higher risk of dying from SUDEP. As a small child, she'd been so afraid of her condition, but as she'd gotten older, learned more about it, and learned that life was never certain and tomorrow was not guaranteed, she'd mastered her fear.

She'd done it then, and she could do it now.

"Ah, yes, the epilepsy." There was clear distaste in his tone, and he looked disgusted by the thought that she had a condition she'd been born with.

Bad move on his part.

All her life there had been people who had looked down on her because of her epilepsy. Maybe they wouldn't outright say anything, but they would treat her like she was less than capable, like she needed someone to do simple things for her, like she was fragile.

That attitude always made her angry.

Most of the time she'd let it slide, just reiterate that there was nothing she couldn't do if she put her mind to it, but right now, she let it fuel her rage.

"Since your friend told you about the drug, I'm sure you're anxious to try it out for yourself, see what all the hype was about. Ms. Madden was lucky, I only gave her one dose then left her alone to think about her choices. I wonder how it would go if I kept injecting you over and over again? How long would you last, Ms. Elrod, before you caved and told me what I want to know?"

Dread pooled in her stomach, but Lucy kept her features schooled.

You can do this.

If you give up on yourself then you've already lost.

"I had promised my men that they could have their fun with your friend while she begged and pleaded for their touch to bring her relief, they were disappointed that we were interrupted last time. Let's see how long you last, shall we? My men are taking bets, whoever wins gets first round with you." Raul gave a soulless chuckle. "But don't worry, Ms. Elrod, they'll all get a turn."

Keeping her mask of control as the needle pricked her skin was hard, and when a flush of raging heat flooded her system a few seconds later, Lucy prayed she hadn't underestimated her own strength.

* * *

JANUARY 23RD
2:18 P.M.

"WE SHOULD JUST KILL him and be done with it, he's too heavy to carry back to the truck."

Those were the words Zander regained consciousness to.

He had no idea how long he'd been out. The last thing he remembered was forcing his body to move even though he knew he was asking more from it than it was capable of giving. Remembered the blackness closing in on him. Then he remembered hazy recollections of panic about Lucy and dragging himself through the jungle, consumed with the need to get to her. Repeating that process over and over again throughout the hours between his fall over the cliff and his capture.

It was the feelings he remembered more than anything else.

Horrible, piercing sensations in his chest as he pictured all the things Raul could be doing to Lucy.

All because of him.

Because he'd failed her.

Failed his team.

Failed the woman who ... made him think all things were possible.

Not something he was used to.

His childhood had taught him that life was already written before you took your first breath. That serving your country and not wasting time on frivolous things like love was all that mattered.

Scarlett had never been afraid to buck against the mold their family tried to stick them in, but he wasn't as brave as his twin.

He'd followed the path set before him like a good little soldier. Thought that if he served, worked hard, and made it into the elite Delta unit he could somehow earn his parents' love.

But he'd been wrong.

Their reactions in the wake of the ordeal that stole the lives of his teammates and broke something inside of him that could never be fixed, proved they were incapable of loving anything other than the military, and he'd given up trying.

Given up on everything.

If it wasn't for Lucy and her needing him, he would be perfectly content to let Raul's men do whatever they wanted to him.

But Lucy was depending on him, so he mustered some last reserves of strength he must have gathered during his last bout of unconsciousness.

In one swift move, he shoved his way out of the hold of

the men carrying him and came up with one of their weapons in his hand.

"You mind telling me why you shot me?" he snarled, aiming his weapon at the closest man but confident he could drop all four of them before any could draw a weapon.

Surprise and a tiny bit of fear widened the gazes of each of the four sets of eyes looking back at him, and he smiled. It didn't matter that he probably looked half dead—felt it too— they knew he was a threat and they were right.

"We didn't shoot at you," one of them said nervously, his gaze darting to one of his friends as though they might be able to come up with a plan to regain control of the situation.

"Then why do I have a bullet wound in my arm?" he growled. Too much lost blood, not enough fluids, and no food or rest meant he was beyond cranky, add in his fear for Lucy and he was ready to rip these men apart with his bare hands.

"Because you got in the way, we were aiming for the girl," another said nervously.

Zander didn't recognize any of them so they weren't high up in Castillo's organization, just grunt men who were used to do tedious jobs like tracking through the jungle in search of him and Lucy.

"You were leading her away from the house," a third said, this time with a hint of accusation in his tone.

Of course, his position with the organization would be precarious after the crash, but there had to be a way to salvage it. Not only did his need for revenge hinge on it, but so did Lucy's life. He had to get back into that house, and not as a prisoner. If Raul doubted him, then it was all over, he could kiss Lucy's life goodbye.

"I have a concussion, idiots," he snapped, waving his free hand at his head and the injury he knew was still visible. "I thought I *was* leading her back to the house."

That explanation drew them up and he could see them all relax.

Good.

He'd gained their trust with the lie, he just had to hope he could keep Raul's as well.

"Misunderstanding," the fourth man said. "When we found the plane and saw you and the woman were heading away from the house, we thought maybe you weren't to be trusted. Orders were to bring you both in dead or alive, but alive if possible."

Making a scoffing noise, he glowered at the men. "Never occurred to you to think maybe we were hurt and didn't know what we were doing? And maybe you're the ones not to be trusted. Someone sabotaged my plane."

Glances were exchanged, and then one of the men hurried to reassure him. "It was not us. Mr. Castillo knows how valuable you are, he would not try to kill you. But his mole at Prey has gone rogue and is no longer following orders."

Anger surged inside him at the mention of the mole. A man—or woman—who had played a huge role in everything his sister had gone through. They better hope he didn't learn their identity because if he got his hands on them, he would make them pay a hundredfold for his twin's suffering.

Strength was slowly returning, but he faked a wobble and let the gun drop as though he were no longer able to hold it up. So far, the men believed he had led Lucy away from Castillo only because he had a concussion and didn't know what he was doing, not because he was trying to keep her safe. That was exactly what he wanted them to keep thinking.

The closest man reached out a steadying hand. "Let's get back to the house. Mr. Castillo's doctor can check you out and you can get some rest."

What he wanted to do was get to the house and then scour it top to bottom in search of Lucy. But that was his emotions talking. Logically speaking, if he wanted to keep her alive and get her out, he needed to regain some of his strength. While he might not be quite as weak as he was pretending to be, he wasn't in top shape, and this was all on him.

Besides, if the first words out of his mouth were demanding Lucy's location then he'd give himself away.

For a few hours he'd have to keep up the charade. Rest, eat, drink, take some painkillers, and get his body on the road to healing then he could figure out a plan to get Lucy out without breaking from his original plan.

And if he couldn't?

Then he already knew what choice he would make.

The one the guys on his team would want him to make.

Save the innocent.

That was why they did what they did. They wanted to rid the world of evil and make it a safer place for those they loved.

While Zander was not in any way claiming he loved Lucy Elrod, he couldn't deny there was an attraction there. More than physical attraction. From the moment he'd first laid eyes on her he'd felt something. Something that he couldn't explore because she was his sister's friend, and he wasn't sure how a woman fit into the life he had chosen.

But that something was still there whether he'd done anything about it or not.

Those hours they'd spent in the jungle together confirmed it.

As did the fact that he was prepared to throw away everything he had worked so hard for, everything he thought he needed to survive.

What did revenge matter if Lucy was dead?

The guys on his team would kick his backside if he prioritized vengeance over the life of a woman they knew he had some sort of feelings for. Feelings he'd never verbalized, not even to himself, but they knew. Knew he was different every time he went to catch up with his sister and saw her friends while he was there. Knew it was because of one of the women on Athena Team, although they might not have known which.

Half the guys on his team had been married, a couple had kids, and their last words and last thoughts had been for the loved ones they were leaving behind. There was no doubt in his mind that any one of them would do whatever it took to protect those loved ones. Because if they didn't, then all the horror they experienced would be for nothing.

Lucy's life trumped everything.

It had to.

If he let her die like she meant nothing, like her life was worthless and easily forfeited, then there was no way he would ever be able to look at himself in the mirror again.

Seven deaths rested on his conscience.

No more.

Especially not hers.

CHAPTER SEVEN

January 24th
  8:04 A.M.

WHO WOULD EVER HAVE GUESSED this could be such horrific torture?

Usually, in the bedroom, all you could think about was orgasms, of the excitement of being worked up until you tumbled over that edge. It was fun and intoxicating and was what made sex so wonderful.

But when there was no falling over the edge, just hour upon hour of standing with your toes dangling over that edge, but that was it, you never got to actually fall, then it was absolute torture.

Lucy wasn't super experienced in the bedroom, she'd always been too busy pursuing other goals to date a whole lot. Casual sex with men she didn't know well wasn't really her thing, so the only time she got sex was when she was in a relationship, and she could quite literally count on one hand the number of relationships that had lasted long enough to get to the sex stage.

It wasn't that she didn't like sex or dating, it was just that sooner or later her epilepsy seemed to become an issue.

Or maybe it was all in her head and *her* issue.

The second they treated her like she was incapable of doing something on her own, coddling her as her family did, then she always ended things.

While it made for a lonely life in some areas, the rest of her life was so full of work, family, friends, and finding adrenalin highs to chase to prove to herself that she was indeed capable. Usually, she didn't dwell on the things missing in her life, she was grateful for everything that she had, and worrying over what she didn't never seemed like a good use of her time.

Right now, though, she was wishing there was a man around who wasn't so utterly repulsive to her that she could beg him to relieve her suffering without feeling like she was disrespecting herself.

So far, she had been good to her promise to herself. There had been no begging or pleading, but she was pragmatic enough to have already come to the conclusion that it couldn't last.

Sooner or later, she would beg.

And plead.

And all but throw herself down on the floor with her legs open and let the closest man bring her body some measure of relief. Her body only because when that day came it would break her mind.

Hearing Scarlett describe what the drug had felt like as it had flooded her system was nothing compared to living it herself. The clawing need low in her belly that felt like a physical being trying to tear its way through her flesh was impossible to explain to someone else. While in theory, it might sound fun to be so turned on that you could have sex for hours without needing a break, in reality, it was pure hell.

Because there was no sex.

There was no relief.

There was just burning in your veins, begging you to set it free.

If her hands weren't bound behind her back, she absolutely would have thrown caution to the wind, put her hands between her legs, and taken care of herself.

True to his word, Raul hadn't allowed her a moment to recover from the drug before one of his men was injecting her with another dose. There had been no reprieve, just hours of writhing and chewing on her bottom lip to keep from begging for someone to bring her a release.

What Raul hadn't mentioned, though, was that he intended to parade her around the house so she was constantly on display for him and his men to enjoy her suffering. She'd been put in a corner of the dining room while the men ate lunch, then outside by the pool while Raul enjoyed some sexy times with some woman Lucy was pretty sure was not here by choice. Again, at dinner time, she'd been ogled and laughed at in the dining room, then several of the men had gotten off in the living room in the evening while they watched porn and played cards.

It was disgusting watching them get off, her body craving the feel of them inside her while her brain was sickened by the whole thing.

At one point, tears had trickled down her cheeks, and a sob had built inside her, but when she'd seen how gleeful her tears made the men she quickly summoned the strength to get them under control.

Worst, though, was being made to spend the night in Raul's room in his bed. He hadn't touched her, well, not sexually, but he'd made her sleep beside him with a fresh dose of

75

the drug in her system, and she knew he'd loved the way her body writhed as need consumed her.

Now she was back in the dining room, men were filing in, filling their plates with food from the buffet, while her empty stomach growled in protest. Another shot had more of the arousal drug in her veins, and with little sleep in days, plus her injuries, she was teetering on the edge of exhaustion.

Which meant she was also teetering on the edge of breaking.

It was close.

Much too close.

Any second now she feared it was going to happen.

Once she took that first step and begged for someone to touch her, then it was only a matter of time until everything else came crumbling down. Less than twenty-four hours on the arousal drug, and she was coming precariously close to giving up the formula for the Reactivator just to get an orgasm.

The knowledge filled her with shame, but the problem was the shame was no match for the raging need that demanded it be quenched.

Tears blurred her vision as the door to the dining room opened, and two more men stepped through. Normally, she wouldn't have paid all that much attention to whoever it was. The men were all the same in her mind and blended into one, but something about this man caught her attention.

There was no way …

But as she looked closer, she saw that it was.

It was … Zander.

Here.

In Raul Castillo's house.

Not drugged and cuffed like she was but walking free.

Walking free *and* clean. His hair was damp, and he was dressed in jeans and a black T-shirt that stretched across his muscular frame. There were no dirty smudges on his face like she knew there were on her own, and she could see a bandage on his bicep, peeking out from under the sleeve of his T-shirt, and butterfly bandages on his forehead closing the wound there from the crash.

As her mouth dropped open in shock, she watched as he laughed with one of Raul's men and piled food high on his plate before taking a seat at the table.

He didn't even spare a glance her way.

Just sat there eating and talking like he didn't have a care in the world.

Rage unlike anything else Lucy had ever felt before built inside her. Boiling hot lava like the arousal burning her from the inside out had turned her into a volcano mere seconds away from erupting.

Zander was working for Raul Castillo.

All those doubts she'd had about whether or not he could be trusted, those flickers in his eyes that she had interpreted as pain, loss, and guilt, the guilt she herself had felt when she thought he was dead because of her, it all added to her rage and fueled it.

Traitor.

He was a traitor.

He'd turned against his country, but worse than that, he'd turned against his own twin sister by working for the man who had kidnapped and tortured her.

How could he?

What could make a man who had made it into the elite Delta Force turn on his country and go to work with a notorious weapons trafficker?

Right now, the whys didn't matter, they weren't going to help her. They wouldn't ease the need drumming through her body, and they wouldn't help her escape. There was no way Prey would find her there and she couldn't expect any help from Zander.

Scarlett had told them how her plan had been to take her own life so she couldn't be forced to give up the formula for their drug. At the time, Lucy had been aghast to know her friend had felt like that was her only option.

Now she got it.

It was her only option, too.

Only she wasn't going to go down alone.

Everyone thought she was too caught up in the haze of need the drug induced to do anything else.

But she wasn't.

If she was going to die, there were two men she wanted to take out with her. Of course, one of them was Raul Castillo, and he would be her priority, but she also wanted to take Zander Madden down with her.

As though sensing her fury, his head suddenly turned in her direction, and their eyes met. A myriad of emotions spun through the blue eyes that looked back at her and she briefly wondered why he'd bothered putting the contacts back in again.

Lucy didn't bother to hide anything she was feeling, letting it all bleed into her gaze. Her arousal, her hatred that her body sang at the thought of Zander's large hands easing her suffering, her anger at him for betraying all of them.

And her promise.

Her promise to take him down with her.

* * *

January 24TH
9:55 A.M.

. . .

SHE WAS GOING to do something crazy.

It had been written all over Lucy's face in the dining room at breakfast.

The worst part was, Zander wasn't sure how to stop her from doing whatever it was she was plotting.

Seeing her in danger was so much worse than anything he'd ever experienced.

This wasn't the first time he'd witnessed an innocent person being tortured. It was always hell not being able to immediately intervene, and he had thanked his near photographic memory more times than he could count for the details he'd been able to relay after an op was successfully completed and victims had been recovered because of it.

There had been no doubt in his mind that being chained to a wall in the relentless heat of the desert, and listening to the screams of his teammates as they were dismembered alive while he was forced to watch was the worst thing he could ever experience.

It had changed him on a fundamental level.

How could it not?

It was his fault.

His refusal to give up the intel the terrorists wanted and to not so much as flinch with each strike given to a man he would gladly suffer and die for, was what had angered them and egged them on.

So much blood shed over those seven hellish days.

So many screams, so many tears, so much anger had taken root inside him.

He'd never expected to survive. Hadn't been counting on the rescue that had come too late for the seven other men on his team and too early for him.

Zander hadn't wanted to live with the guilt of knowing he was responsible for their deaths. Their painful, horrific deaths.

It didn't matter how many times they reassured him that they understood, that he was doing exactly what they wanted him to do, those screams, the stench of blood and decaying flesh, were forever etched into his mind.

Nothing should be able to top that ordeal.

Yet watching Lucy, still in her tattered clothes from the crash, dirt streaking her face, her blonde locks a matted tangle around her head, with her arms tied behind her back and her cheeks flushed with arousal somehow managed to be worse.

Maybe it was because he knew she hadn't signed up for this and had no idea what she was getting herself into.

The way her hips rocked subconsciously, seeking friction that would bring her release, friction that wasn't there and wouldn't be there until she coughed up the intel Raul wanted, was pure torture.

His fault.

He'd gotten her into this.

And he had to figure out a way to get her out.

Because he knew why it was that this was worse than being taken captive with his team and watching their executions. They hadn't hated him. They'd offered him forgiveness, accepted their fates, and understood his decisions.

Lucy did not.

She had no idea what was going on, and mingled with the blood-searing lust in her gaze in the dining room at breakfast was pure, unadulterated hatred.

Aimed directly at him.

And it had met its mark. Spearing like an arrow straight through his heart.

"Let me take a shot at her," he said as he strolled into Raul's personal office.

Although the other man's eyes narrowed in disapproval, there wasn't a lot he could do about it. Zander wasn't one of his men and couldn't be ordered around. As far as Raul was aware—as far as anyone outside a select few who knew the truth were aware—he was a former Delta Force operator who had been warped by war and turned. Blamed his country for the death of his team and wanted revenge on the men who had killed them.

Partially true.

He did want revenge.

Lived for it.

Or at least he had until Lucy came along.

"Why do you think she'll give it up for you when she has yet to beg for pleasure from anyone else?" Raul asked. Despite his annoyance at not being able to be completely in control of Zander, he recognized that they could be mutually beneficial to one another. He got Zander access to the terrorist group responsible for his teammates' deaths so he could destroy them, and Zander would give him the benefit of the connections he had made in his years in Delta.

Win-win.

Only Zander had plans the man knew nothing about.

Plans he had no intention of sharing.

"Because we built a ... how shall we say ... rapport ... while we were in the jungle," he answered vaguely.

"Do you mean there was sexual chemistry between you two?" Raul asked.

"You want the details?" he snapped. It was always a fine line he was balancing. Push Raul too hard, and the man would react in anger, he liked to be in control, and he liked to have his way. But if he didn't push hard enough, then no way would the weapons dealer believe he was warped enough from his ordeal to turn on his country.

The man actually considered his answer and Zander feared that if Raul said he did want details of sex between him and Lucy—even if those details would be fictitious—he would have no choice but to beat the man to a pulp for invading Lucy's privacy like that.

"No, not particularly. But have at it. She's in the third room to the right on the second floor. Remind her that she's due another dose in less than an hour, and my men are chomping at the bit to have a touch of her."

Reining in his anger was not an easy thing to do, but somehow Zander managed it. "I'll get her to talk."

"Promise her a quick death if she tells you. She doesn't have to know that I've already promised her to my men when I have what I need from her," Raul said before dismissing him by returning his attention to his laptop.

Zander was seething and terrified as he headed out of the office. Being raped to death was a horrific way to die. While he'd never witnessed it—he wasn't sure he'd be able to stand by and let it happen no matter the consequences of whatever mission he was on—he and his team had arrived too late to save three young girls from their fate on the final mission they'd performed before being captured.

The small, broken bodies, bruises littering their skin, and blood pooling between their legs from the internal injuries that had caused their deaths was another dark memory he carried with him.

One of many that prevented him from ever being a man worthy of a woman like Lucy.

It didn't matter that she currently hated him, that she might never forgive him for getting her dragged into this, he needed her to be safe and he *would* get her out of there.

Consequences be damned.

Even before he opened the door to the room she was being held in, he could hear her breathy moans of frustration as she was helpless to do anything about the arousal throbbing through her body. She needed release, and while he had been dreaming about her naked body spread out beneath him, his to enjoy as he wished, bringing them both unlimited pleasure, he couldn't touch her like this. Not when it was impossible for her to give consent.

The room was locked, and there were enough men in the building that Raul hadn't posted a guard outside her room. Should Lucy be able to get out of the cuffs and out of her room, there was no way she would make it out of the house undetected.

Grabbing the key from where it was hanging on a hook beside the door, he unlocked it and walked through, bringing the key with him so no one else could get in. After locking the door behind him, he drew in a deep breath before he could turn and face the woman he owed the world's biggest apology to.

Before he even got that chance, she was flying at him, her small body colliding with his.

Unprepared for her attack as he was, he lost his balance, and both of them crashed to the floor. Somehow, he managed to angle them so he took the brunt of the impact. Pain flared inside him from his injuries, but better him than her.

Even with her injuries, her hands bound behind her back, and her much smaller size, Lucy put up a good fight.

Too bad for her it was a fight she could never win.

Careful to hurt her as little as possible, but aware that there could be cameras in there which meant he had to put on a show, Zander wrapped a hand around her neck and lifted her up off the floor. Bound as she was, she couldn't claw at the hand on her neck as he pushed her up against the nearest wall.

Fear filled her blue eyes, but there was anger there, too.

That was good.

Anger meant survival.

Sometimes, it was the difference between life and death, and he prayed she was going to hold onto it.

With her face level with his, he leaned in and asked for forgiveness as he pressed his lips to hers in a bruising kiss. Then with his mouth millimeters from hers, he whispered the word that would change everything.

CHAPTER EIGHT

January 24ᵗʰ
  10:13 A.M.

"WHAT DID YOU JUST SAY?" Lucy demanded as she abruptly stopped struggling.

"Blessings," Zander repeated.

Did he mean …?

No.

That was impossible.

But …

His blue eyes met her gaze and held it, and although it was hard not to get distracted by the color she knew wasn't real, she could see him willing her to understand.

Unless she was reading him wrong.

A distinct possibility given that it was hard to focus on anything with this clawing need still raging inside her.

Only … he didn't look like he was trying to play her.

The hand around her neck was gentle, his fingertips lightly caressing her skin, and he'd lifted a knee, bracing it between her legs so that she was mostly balanced on his knee rather than hanging by her throat. He was making no effort to cut off her air supply or even impede it in any way, and he had said the code word.

A code word that everyone connected to Prey was aware of. It was a play on words of sorts, substituting the word prey for its homophone pray, and then using a word that went with the homophone. All Prey employees were aware of it, and it was meant to be used in case you were ever approached in the field by someone, you could then easily identify them as an ally instead of an enemy.

But why did Zander Madden—who had never worked for Prey—know the code word?

"Look, I know you have no reason to believe anything I say, but I need you to hear me out, both our lives depend on it," Zander said.

As much as she wanted to hear his explanation for why he was walking around alive and well when his sister had buried him, and why he was buddies with a notorious weapons trafficker, it was hard to think of anything else but the desire inside her that only got worse with him so close to her. The feel of his massive thigh between her legs, pressed right up against her wet and aching center was too good, and she rocked her hips, creating the tiniest amount of friction that made her moan in delight.

Gritting his teeth he lowered her to the floor. "Don't do that, sassy girl."

Crying out at the loss of minimal contact, Lucy threw caution to the wind and thrust her hips forward in a silent plea, wishing her hands weren't bound so she could grab his wrist and force his hand to soothe her suffering. Maybe it wasn't fair of her, they didn't know each other well, but at least they did know each other, and she'd wondered if he was undercover somehow, so learning that he was—which was

the only explanation for him knowing the Prey code word—
meant he was a good guy.

If a good guy brought her relief, she wouldn't have to hate
herself as much.

"I can't, baby," he murmured although he looked torn.

"I need you to." Begging was absolutely not beneath her at
the moment, not with Zander.

"You can't consent," he reminded her. "And I won't be the
guy who assaults you while you're vulnerable."

"You'd be the guy saving me." Letting her forehead drop
forward to rest against his chest, she whimpered and rode
out another wave of excruciating arousal. "It's awful, Zander.
So bad. I hate those men so much, but I was so close to
pleading with them to touch me. Anything to relieve this
pressure. I feel like I'm about to explode and not in a good
way. Please. Help me."

"Baby," he said, voice tortured. "You don't even know why
I'm here, and you hate me."

"Not hate," she clarified. "I know that you know the Prey
codeword which means Eagle knows what you're doing.
You're undercover, and while I'm not going to lie and say I'm
not furious with you for hurting your sister, who I love like a
sister, I know you have a reason for it. Please, I'm ... begging
... I'm literally begging. I can't stand this any longer, I'm
going to lose my mind."

Shame filled her and she kept her head down as tears
leaked out.

The promises she'd made to herself to never beg for relief
were broken now.

Just because it was with a man she trusted—well mostly
trusted—only made it a little bit better. It still hurt to know
she wasn't as strong as she believed herself to be.

"Oh, baby." A finger hooked under her chin and Zander
took a step back and nudged until she was forced to meet his

JANE BLYTHE

eye. "I can't touch you, not when you're like this, but I have an idea."

An idea?

Hope sparked inside her.

She'd take anything she could get right now.

Grabbing her arm, he guided her over to the other door. This one she knew led to a bathroom, but it was kept locked unless one of the guards came in and allowed her to use the toilet. With the same key he'd used to enter her room, Zander unlocked the bathroom door and led her inside.

As soon as he'd closed the door behind them, he pulled out a knife and cut the zip ties binding her wrists. Pain immediately blossomed in her broken arm, and up through her shoulders as blood flow was allowed to return.

So very gently, Zander took her bad arm and carefully eased it forward and then began to massage it, helping with the horrendous pins and needles sensation. Once he was done, he repeated the process with her good arm, and Lucy felt her body relax under his ministrations. He might not be touching her where she needed him, but he was touching her, and the human contact felt so nice.

"Do you need help getting your clothes off?" he asked as he finally released her.

Eyes snapping open, she looked up at him. "Clothes off?" Was he going to ease the ache of arousal that lived inside her?

"Shower massager," he said, nodding at the shower behind them. "My bathroom has one, I was hoping yours would, too. I can't touch you, Lucy. Not because I don't think you're the most beautiful woman I've ever laid eyes on, not because I haven't craved you since we first met, it's because I've done enough things that weigh on my conscience and this can't be one of them. But I can't watch you suffer either. I thought it would be a good compromise."

It was perfect. "I think I love you," she murmured.

88

Zander laughed and he looked so wonderful, all relaxed like that, that her heart swelled in her chest. Before her stood a man who she somehow knew instinctively was broken in a lot of ways. Whatever he was doing here clearly wasn't easy for him, but she knew without him having to say it that he was risking a lot by helping her in any way.

While Zander turned the shower on and adjusted the temperature, Lucy tried her best to get out of the jeans and sweater she'd been stuck in for the last several days. Seeing her struggling, Zander came back to her and helped her ease the sweater off, being so careful of her broken arm that tears stung her eyes.

When he knelt in front of her to slide the jeans down her legs, he looked up at her. "I need you to play along with me, Lucy, can you do that? I will get you out of here alive, I swear it to you, I won't lose anyone else, but to do it I need your help."

The way he mentioned not being able to lose anyone else made those tears stinging her eyes begin to roll down her cheeks. There was such raw pain in those few words. Whoever he'd lost it had been devastating to him, and there was a big part of her that wanted to soothe his pain despite her lingering anger toward him for his lies.

"I'll do whatever you need me to do," she assured him. It was a promise that was hard to make in some ways because she didn't know what he needed her to do, but easy in others because Zander was her only hope of living through this ordeal.

"I'm going to need you to pretend that you're giving me the formula," he warned as his large hands splayed her hips and he picked her up and placed her in the shower.

"I can make up something that sounds like it could be real to buy time." Lucy took the shower massager when Zander handed it to her, and was half relieved, half disappointed when he turned his back to give her privacy. She'd just stripped naked in front of him without embarrassment or inhibition, would have let him have sex with her if he wanted, and throughout everything, she'd always felt a connection to this man.

Your friend's brother.

Who's currently undercover.

Who you have no idea if he intends to reveal himself as being alive when this is over.

The reminders ran through her mind as she adjusted the setting on the shower head and moved it between her legs, no longer able to wait to get some relief from her drug-induced arousal.

As soon as the spray hit her throbbing bud, everything else fled from her mind. After so many hours hovering so close to the edge, every muscle in her body went taut then a powerful orgasm ripped through her almost immediately, leaving her crying and shaking in relief as she sunk back to rest against the wall in exhaustion.

But at the back of her mind was a soft whisper that she still wished it had been Zander who had made her orgasm.

* * *

January 24TH

7:38 P.M.

NEVER HAD the hours ticked by so slowly.

It felt like time was moving backward, if it was moving at all.

Zander was on edge and was surprised he was doing as good a job at hiding it as he was.

So far, nobody seemed to guess that he was planning on

busting the new toy out of there in a couple of hours at the most. In fact, he was currently the most popular guy there because he'd gotten "intel" out of their toy.

The fact that it came at a huge cost to him and Lucy didn't matter to anyone else. They didn't even know that the intel he'd passed along to Raul was fake. It would take time for them to figure it out. Raul had scientists of his own that he intended to take the formula Athena Team had created and make the drug for him. Those men or women would realize as soon as they started working on the drug that the formula was nonsense. Close enough to fool anyone on a quick read-over Lucy had assured him, but not once they started actually making it.

Which was fine.

All he needed was to buy them time until nightfall.

As soon as it was dark, he was going to make his move.

Unfortunately, that meant they had to last the remainder of the day playing things up as though Zander was still helping Raul, and Lucy was a terrified prisoner awaiting her death. Which would likely come as soon as his scientists verified the drug, but by then they'd be long gone.

Although she had agreed to the plan, Zander knew Lucy was indeed a terrified prisoner. There was little to no acting required on her part to pull this off. But as scared as he knew she was, she was so brave. Not once had she complained, she'd listened to what he told her he needed her to do and done it. The questions she'd asked had been insightful, and while she had deferred to him as the expert there, she had offered her own input, but in the end, agreed with whatever he thought best.

There wasn't anything more he could have asked of her, she'd given him everything, and it killed him that she still had to suffer.

Casting a glance at where she was standing in the corner.

Dressed once again in the clothes she'd been wearing when they crashed, no one would be able to tell that she'd spent close to two hours in the shower earlier getting herself off until the drug was basically out of her system. Her hair was still a mess, her face was still dirty, and her cheeks still flushed.

More fear and embarrassment than arousal this time, though, since he'd given her a minimal shot of the drug. Raul had had his men administer it every four hours so she'd had two doses since this morning in her room. But he'd been the one to inject her, and he'd squirted out most of the drug before it hit her system, so whatever was in her bloodstream was nothing compared to what had been there before.

"You want another beer?" one of Raul's men asked.

"Yeah, sure," he agreed, although he had no intention of drinking it, just like he hadn't drunk any of the others he'd been holding in his hand the last hour or so.

When the other man stood, Zander had no choice but to stand as well. All afternoon he'd done his best to keep Lucy in his line of sight so he could monitor her safety. There was still a no-touch rule in place, but that didn't mean someone wouldn't decide to test his luck and play with Raul's new toy a little early.

But he couldn't outright refuse to go to the kitchen with the man without looking suspicious.

So even though he could feel her scared eyes on his back as he left the room, he didn't look back. It killed him because her fear was a tangible thing that seemed to fill the room, but keeping them both alive until he got her out took precedence over offering her a molecule of reassurance in this moment.

"Heard you got to play," the man said as they strolled through the hall to the kitchen.

Swallowing down the bile that threatened to burn his throat, Zander pasted on a smarmy smile. "We had a thing going in the jungle, used it to my advantage. This works magic," he added, grabbing his crotch.

The man laughed like assaulting Lucy was hilarious instead of a sadistic crime. But keeping cover often required you to do things that repulsed you. No stranger to undercover work from his years in Delta and the almost twelve months he'd been playing this role, Zander was able to force a natural-sounding laugh past his lips.

"Women all the same, yes? They are weak, let their bodies control them. Their words may say no, but their body always say yes. I cannot wait for my turn. She as hot in bed as she looks?"

Already, the other man was growing hard, and Zander quickly shoved open the fridge and pulled out a beer. It was either that or grab the man around the throat and squeeze the life out of him.

"Hottest I ever had," he replied, knowing that was the absolute truth even though he'd never touched her. Keeping his back to her while she was in the shower, moaning and crying out her release, had been hard. But Lucy deserved her privacy and his respect, she'd been through enough and he wasn't going to add to it by ogling her as she orgasmed over and over again.

If he ever got the chance to have a willing and consenting Lucy in his bed, he would consider himself the luckiest man in the world.

But it was more than he had a right to hope for.

After everything he'd done, he didn't deserve even a drop of happiness or a moments peace from the guilt that plagued him.

The other man was laughing and talking about all the things he wanted to do to Lucy when it was his turn with her, and Zander was doing his best not to snap the man's neck as they walked back into the living room.

Immediately, his gaze swept to the corner where Lucy was standing, on display for the men to look at, or get off to, or whatever they wanted.

Only the corner was empty.

"Take this, man, gotta go," he mumbled, no longer caring about his cover as he shoved his beer into the hand of the man beside him and hurried back into the hall.

Lucy was gone.

Had Raul come for her?

Did he already know that she'd lied about the formula and that it wouldn't make the Reactivator for him?

Surely they needed more time than that. Lucy had assured him it should take at least a couple of days before Raul's scientists knew they'd been conned, and it had only been hours since he'd strolled into Raul's office like he was top dog and handed over the fake formula.

Just like Lucy had trusted him and his expertise, he trusted hers. If she said it would take a few days, then he believed her, so if it wasn't Raul who had taken her then who?

She knew the plan, and it was to keep pretending he was who he was pretending to be and she wouldn't do anything to mess it up by trying to escape on her own, that he was certain of.

Which meant the only other explanation was that one of the men had decided he was done waiting.

If one of Raul's men had violated Lucy, all bets were off.

Already, he was prepared to throw his undercover gig under the bus to get Lucy out of there alive, to hell with the consequences.

Nothing would make him happier than to kill one of these men.

There was already so much anger raging inside him, and Lucy being assaulted would be the proverbial straw that broke the camel's back, setting him off, unscrewing the lid, and letting all that fury explode out.

"Don't, please. Stop!" Lucy's voice echoed through the hall as he approached French doors leading to a paved patio area.

The unbridled terror in her voice was the match that lit the fuse.

For eighteen months, he'd been living with anger that had no outlet. The helplessness he'd felt as he was forced to watch the slow, agonizing executions of the men on his team had filled him with something dark and ugly, something that was slowly consuming him.

If he didn't let it out somehow it would destroy him.

Lucy was a speck of light in that darkness calling out to him. An anchor that was keeping him from being completely swept away.

Now someone wanted to touch a woman he felt down to his bones was his even though he knew, in reality, he could never have her.

Nobody touched what was his.

Without conscious thought, Zander ran down the hall and threw open the doors.

The sight before him unleashed that dark beast of rage and he made no attempt to rein it in as he launched himself at the man with his hand down Lucy's pants.

CHAPTER NINE

January 24th
   8:00 P.M.

ONE SECOND, she was out on the patio, one of Raul's men gripping her bicep in a crushing hold while his other hand fumbled its way into her pants.

The next, a shadowy figure was flying at them.

When it connected with them, it knocked both her and the man assaulting her to the ground.

Pain zinged along her broken arm and battered body at the impact, but honestly, by this point Lucy was so used to being in pain that it barely even registered.

Not when there were other more important things to worry about.

Like the fact that Zander was currently beating a man to death right in front of her.

Violence had never been part of her life. She'd been lucky to grow up in a family where they were comfortable, not well off necessarily, especially with five kids, but her parents had good jobs and were able to provide everything their family of seven needed. School had been tough because of her epilepsy, but it hadn't been physically dangerous in any way. And her work at Prey was mostly lab work with occasional field trips with some of the guys.

No danger.

No violence.

Nothing like what she had experienced over the last few days.

Nothing like what she was witnessing right now.

There was so much anger rolling off Zander as he delivered blow after blow to the man who had assaulted her. It didn't seem to register to him that the man had long since stopped moving, that he was nothing more than a bloody pulp of flesh, likely already dead.

If they were found like this by any of Raul's men, it would be game over. Zander's cover would be blown, they'd discover in a day or so that the formula she'd given was a fake, and they would both be killed.

Despite a little lingering anger toward Zander for lying to his sister and hurting her by pretending to be dead, Lucy didn't want him to die. Whatever his reasons—he'd shared only that he was here because his team had been murdered and he wanted to catch the people responsible—for faking his death, they ran deep, she could see the pain he was in. He needed this mission to be successful if he was going to have any chance at healing.

Scrambling on her backside toward the two men, Lucy tentatively reached out a hand and laid it on Zander's back. He was in the zone, focused only on unleashing his anger, and he might not react well to her touch, but she sensed his need for a connection in this dark moment, so she trusted her gut and left her hand there.

"It's okay, Zander. He's dead now. He can't hurt me or anyone else," she whispered soothingly. With her heart hammering in her chest, and her fear that they could be discovered at any second, it wasn't easy to cling to calm, but Zander needed her, and he'd been there for her earlier when she needed him so it was only fair that she return the favor.

"He touched you," Zander growled as his fist slammed into the man's head again.

"Yes, but you stopped him before he did anything more than put his hand in my pants," she assured him. Only by a second, she'd felt the man's finger prodding at her entrance right as Zander had come flying out of nowhere. "Please stop. I'm scared, Zander."

Making the admission wasn't easy because she had clung to the idea that she was strong enough to survive this ever since those men found her in the jungle. Scratch that, she'd been playing the strong game ever since that alarm went off in the plane and she realized they were going to crash.

But it was just that.

A game.

Because she was nowhere near as strong as she believed herself to be.

Right now, she needed someone. Needed the only person around who she trusted. That person was Zander. He was risking everything to get her out of there alive and she didn't want him to lose his life because of it.

Unresolved anger aside, Lucy ... felt something for this man. Always had. And while she had no idea if there would ever be a time when they could explore it, at the very least, she wanted to know that he was alive and living his best life, whatever that looked like for him.

"I need you," she added, uttering the words aloud that she hated down to her very soul. After spending an entire life-time adamantly denying that she needed anyone, in this moment, she had no choice but to admit that she was vulnerable.

Like those words flipped a magic switch, he froze mid-strike. With his fist still in the air he looked over his shoulder at her. There was confusion on his face as he stared at her. "You … need … me?" he asked like the words were foreign.

Inching closer, she swept her hand up his back to his shoulder, allowing her fingers to betray her shaky emotional footing by curling into his T-shirt. "Yes. I need you. Please stop. He's dead, you saved me. I just want to get out of here."

There were still hours to go before they were going to make their escape, and with blood all over his clothes and dotted on his skin, plus his torn knuckles, she had no idea how Zander was going to maintain his role. But the thing was despite everything, she trusted this man. Yes, he lied, but she was sure if she knew the whole story she would understand why, this undercover job was taking a massive toll on him, and deep down he was a good man. A trustworthy man. One you could rely on.

"We should leave now." His hand moved to grab hers, pulling her to her feet along with him.

"We can't. It's not midnight." Midnight was the plan. Once the guys passed out drunk, he was going to sneak her out and into some tunnels that supposedly ran from the house out into the jungle.

"Don't care. Not having you hang around here a second longer. I won't risk that happening again," he said fiercely. It was clear by the expression on his face that Zander had switched into warrior mode and was running scenarios in his head.

"I can handle it," she said, although she had to swallow a lump of fear to get the words out. If it meant them both surviving, she would handle anything she had to.

Eyes softening, Zander pulled her closer, snuggling her against his hard chest as one of his hands cupped the back of her neck and the other arm wrapped around her waist. "I'm not going to let you get raped just to buy us a few more hours, baby. As soon as I get you out of here this role is blown and the op is over. A couple of hours earlier isn't going to change much."

Lifting her hands to place them on his pecs, she shook her head as she looked up at him. "I can't let you ruin your mission for me. I'm just one person, whatever you're doing here is more important." It sucked to say the words, but they were true. What was her life in comparison to the hundreds or thousands that would be saved if Zander's op was successful?

Darkness flared in his eyes and then the next thing she knew, his mouth was branding hers in a fiery kiss. "Don't say that again, Lucy." There was a warning note in his tone that confused her. She'd always sensed that the attraction she felt wasn't one-sided, but she'd never thought there was more to it than that.

But the way he said that made it sound like there was more.

Something that ran deeper than chemistry.

"But—"

"I've been doing this for almost a year. I have enough intel gathered to lead us to the men we were looking for, the group that killed my team. I was hanging around because I wanted to be part of the takedown. But ... vengeance isn't more important than your life."

Emotion swelled in her chest. That was so sweet of him to say, however, she couldn't help but feel that this vengeance was something he needed. "Zander, that's so sweet, and I appreciate it, but I understand ..."

"You don't. Because I don't even understand it. For eighteen months all I've been able to think about was getting my revenge on the men who tortured and killed my brothers. I would have sworn it was all I needed, only now I know there's something I need more than that. I need to know you're safe."

Without giving her time to process any of that, Zander started moving, pulling her along with him as he reclaimed his grip on her hand.

They headed away from the house, out into the dark jungle. Zander moved purposefully, confidently, like he knew exactly where he was going and what he was doing. Since she had nothing of value to offer, she just followed.

As he led her down into a tunnel, Lucy was suddenly swamped by a sick feeling she was unfortunately well acquainted with. It was hard to explain, kind of like you were riding a rollercoaster, only the rollercoaster was huge, going right up to the stars, and the sickening feeling in her stomach matched it. A headache creeped into the back of her skull as well, and combined there was no way she could ignore the warning signs. Despite this being the absolute worst timing possible, there was no denying the inevitability of it.

Some time within the next twenty-four hours she was going to have a seizure.

* * *

January 24th
9:02 P.M.

Barely an hour had passed since he killed the man assaulting Lucy and fled with her.

The more distance they put between them and Raul's

house, the safer he should feel, but for Zander, it seemed like the opposite.

Something was wrong with Lucy. That much he was sure of. There was a lethargy about her that had him on edge.

Of course, after the ordeal she'd been through it was normal that she have an adrenalin crash. Hopped up on the arousal drug as she'd been for the last thirty-six hours or so, he doubted she had gotten any meaningful sleep, and before that she'd been in a plane crash and hiked, injured, through the jungle.

Totally normal that she would be exhausted and lethargic.

Should be nothing to worry about other than the basics of dealing with the fallout of shock.

But it was more than that.

He knew it in his gut. Felt it.

"You doing okay?" he asked for what had to be the hundredth time since they'd first entered the tunnels, and he'd sensed a change in her.

"Hmm? Oh ... yeah ... fine," Lucy mumbled. There was a flatness to her voice that he didn't like one little bit, and he wanted to growl out his frustration only he was afraid he'd scare her if he did.

There was no way to hide the anger that lurked inside him. She'd seen it with her own eyes. Watched as he killed that man with nothing but his fists. He would have sworn it was impossible for her to feel anything but terrified of him, and yet ...

She'd told him she needed him.

Needed him.

How was that even possible?

Didn't she know how dangerous he was?

Didn't she understand the myriad of sins he had committed?

Didn't she get that he could never atone for those sins?

Why did she believe he could save her when all evidence pointed to the contrary? He hadn't saved his team and gave them only a fifty-fifty shot of getting out of Mexico alive.

Less if what he suspected was going on with Lucy was true.

Stopping, he turned to face her, placing his hands on her shoulders. When she stared stubbornly at his chest, he sighed and hooked a forefinger under her chin, tilting her face up until she had no choice but to meet his gaze.

"You're lying to me," he said softly, keeping his voice gentle so she knew he wasn't angry with her. While she might trust him to get her out of this mess alive, that was as far as it went. Even though he knew it would take time to gain her trust, Zander couldn't deny that he wished she would give it to him.

"We have to keep moving," Lucy said, her gaze skittering away but not before he saw the fear lurking in her baby blues.

"We're almost to the end of the tunnels," he assured her. If he hadn't had to modify his speed for her, they'd already be out in the jungle. Not that he was blaming her or upset with her about it. Lucy was giving him everything she had to give and that was all he could ask of her.

"But they have to know we're gone by now, they'll be looking for us," she protested.

"I doubt Raul is aware I know about the tunnels, he'll be looking in the jungle around the house."

"When he can't find us there, he'll check the tunnels."

"Probably. But we'll be further away by then."

"Only if we keep moving."

"We'll go as soon as you tell me what's wrong. I know you don't trust me, Lucy, but I'm here and I'll help in any way I can." If she needed to talk through what had happened, he'd listen, if she needed to cry she could go right ahead, if she needed to scream at him he'd stand there and take it.

"I don't not trust you, Zander." Her tone was serious, and she met his gaze squarely so he knew she was telling the truth.

"Then let me help."

"You can't help," she said softly.

"Whatever you need I'll give you." Lucy was the only person other than his sister who brought out this protectiveness in him. Of course, he'd joined Delta to try to make the world a safer place, but that was only one reason, and not even the top one. Earning his parents' love and respect had been number one, proving to them—and maybe himself, too —that he could do it was another.

But Lucy reminded him of the importance of men like him doing what they did.

There were a lot of monsters in human skin out there, and while there would always be another one pop up for everyone you eliminated, at least you were doing something, saving someone in the process.

"This is one thing you can't give me, Zander. No one can."

Heart stuttering in his chest, he asked the question he'd dreaded since he noticed the change in her. "Your epilepsy?"

"Yeah," she whispered, sounding so defeated his chest ached. "It's not well under control at the best of times. But I haven't taken my medication in days, and whatever was in the drug Raul was giving me will likely react badly with my system, a lot of medications do."

"You think you're going to have a seizure soon?" When he'd first met Lucy and learned from Scarlett that she had epilepsy, he'd read extensively on the topic. Why he wasn't completely sure, it had just seemed like important knowl-edge to have. He knew that epileptics could sometimes tell when they were going to have a seizure. The prodrome stage could be as much as a few days before a seizure, followed by the aura stage. He needed to know if Lucy knew which she was in so he knew how best to act.

"I know I am. I'm sorry," she quickly added. "I know the timing sucks big time, but if one is coming there's nothing I can do to stop it. Even if I had my meds I wouldn't be able to. At best, they offer some control over it."

It didn't sit well with him that she felt like she needed to defend a condition she had zero control over. Had her family or childhood friends made her feel like she was somehow less because she had a medical condition?

Still holding her chin, he pinched it lightly to make sure he had her attention. "Don't be sorry, baby," he ordered, a command in his tone because he wanted to force her to see herself the way he saw her. Fierce, brave, strong, loyal, beautiful, and intelligent. Lucy was an amazing woman, and the fact that she'd been battling a condition since she was a toddler only made her that much more amazing.

"It's not great timing."

"It's not," he agreed. No point in lying about it. A seizure now would slow them down as they'd have to stop, there was a chance of complications, and Lucy would be weak and exhausted after it. But it was what it was. "I'm going to carry you for a while. We can go faster that way, put as much distance between us and them, plus it will let you regain a little strength that you're going to need if you can rest for a bit."

Without giving her time to argue—because he absolutely knew his stubborn, independent girl would argue—he scooped her into his arms and began jogging through the last of the tunnels.

Instead of arguing, Lucy wrapped her arms around his

neck, rested her head on his shoulder, and gave the sweetest of sighs as she snuggled closer.

The puff of warm air against his neck shifted something in his chest.

Loosened the ropes he'd tied around his heart to lock it away and protect it.

What was she doing to him?

Zander knew he couldn't keep her even if she was willing to try a relationship with him, but he now knew what it was like to crave the same things his sister had all their lives. A place to belong, unconditional love, happiness, and peace.

Minutes after he'd picked up Lucy, they came out of the tunnels and into the jungle. Despite the late hour it was still muggy, and the final rays of sunset lit the sky. Running with Lucy in his arms was still easier than going at the slow pace her weak body had dictated.

Maybe thirty minutes later, Lucy suddenly went completely tense in his grip.

"You need to put me down," she said, voice tight.

Quickly locating a clear space where she wasn't going to hit something, he knelt and laid her down on her back. "I got you, babe."

Lucy gave a small nod then her entire body went stiff. He could almost see her muscles stretching before all of a sudden, she began to jerk. Since he'd read up on epilepsy and seizures, Zander knew not to try to hold her down, but it went against every instinct he had. She was hurting her already bruised and battered body with each jerking movement, and he wanted to pull her into his arms, hold her still, and cushion her limbs.

The best he could do was pull off his T-shirt and bunch it up, placing it under her head to at least cushion that as she continued to jerk as her muscles spasmed.

It seemed to go on and on.

Seconds ticked by so slowly, and a full two minutes passed before she finally sunk down against the ground.

After checking she was breathing, he rolled her onto her side since she was still unresponsive. Then Zander did the only thing he could. He prayed that God wasn't going to take from him the only woman he'd ever wanted.

CHAPTER TEN

January 24th
 9:58 P.M.

"Did I pee?" Lucy asked as awareness came trickling back in.

Please don't let her have soiled herself.

Of all the things she hated the most about having epilepsy, it had to be the fact that when she was having a seizure, she had zero control over her body.

Zero.

Over anything.

Not just her limbs which jerked about, but her bladder and her bowels as well.

For the rest of her life, she would never forget what it was like to be a six-year-old having a seizure in the classroom, the cries and screams of her peers as she slowly woke up again, only to then smell it.

Poop.

The unmistakable stench of poo.

It had been humiliating, and she'd begged her parents not

to make her go back to school afterward. But her mom had insisted that any kid who would tease her and call her poopyhead because she had a medical condition was not someone she should want to be friends with anyway.

Not untrue, but people wanted to fit in. Never more than when you were a first grader just starting out in what was going to be a long journey through school, and all you wanted was to be like the other kids, have friends, and be included in the games.

Over the years, there had been a couple of other times when she'd had a seizure in a public place. Once in a grocery store, which she'd never gone back to afterward, choosing to travel another ten minutes in the other direction to go to a different one. Once in college, where at least her peers had been respectful about what had happened, although she'd noticed afterward none of them could quite look her in the eye again.

Lucky for her, stubborn was her middle name. Her desire to prove to herself and everybody around her that she could still live a full and active life was all that had prevented her from becoming a recluse.

That, and the people she had surrounding her now.

In the years that she had been at Prey, she'd had a couple of seizures, one where everything inside her had come right on out, but the way her team and the guys had responded was everything she'd always needed. They didn't coddle or embarrass her, and they didn't treat her any differently afterward.

Their reactions had actually made her strong, practical, tough girl persona crack, and a flood of tears rush out.

Of all the times she could have lost control of either her bladder or bowels during a seizure, this one time seemed like it would be the worst. Zander was a man she was attracted to. On a deeper level than appreciating his smoking hot body. Lucy had no idea what that meant, if there was any sort of future for them, or what Zander's plans were after he finished his op.

None of it mattered, that connection was there, and she didn't want to humiliate herself in front of him. Didn't want him to be like so many others who treated her differently because of her epilepsy.

A hand smoothed down her back, then settled on her hip, tucking her closer against the big body she was draped over. "No, babe, you didn't."

"Did I ... poo?" she asked, squeezing her eyes tightly shut as tears of frustration and mortification burned.

"No, baby."

A sigh of relief had her sinking deeper into Zander's embrace. "Good."

"Not sure I agree with you there, sassy girl."

"Huh?" She lifted her head to look up at Zander's strong jaw and deep brown eyes. "Why would it not be a good thing?"

"Because it means you're dehydrated and starving. Think you can eat something?" he asked as he held up a canteen to her lips.

After swallowing several mouthfuls, Lucy was about to shake her head. It seemed she'd moved beyond the hungry stage and well into the too nauseous to think about food stage instead. But then she thought better of it. Her body was in dire need of fuel, and they weren't somewhere safe where she could wait until she felt better before eating.

"Yeah, I can eat." When she took the offered protein bar and her fingers fumbled to open the wrapper, Zander took it back, opened it for her, then held it to her lips. Warmth spread throughout her as she took a bite. He was taking care of her, and it was so sweet. When her parents tried to take care of her it always made her feel helpless, but with Zander it just made her feel all gooey and soft inside like a chocolate chip cookie straight out of the oven.

For a few minutes they just sat in silence, him feeding her a protein bar, and then another when she finished it, her just soaking up the feel of the muscled arms around her.

Here like this, even with the threat of Raul and his men, Lucy felt safe and protected. Zander might have made choices she didn't have all the information to understand yet, but he was a good man and she could see that those choices had hurt him.

"You took the contacts out," she said, cupping his jaw and trailing her fingertips through the stubble.

"I thought …" Zander hesitated looking unsure, and her heart swelled with more emotions than she could name.

"Thought what?"

"That maybe you liked my real eyes better," he finished, sounding completely unsure of himself.

A small smile curled her lips up. "I do. With the blue eyes you just don't look like … you."

Darkness shuttered his deep brown eyes, and she ached to wipe away whatever had put it there. "Lucy …" he started slowly. "I'm not … I'm … I'm not good for you." A hand palmed her cheek for the briefest of moments, caressing her skin before withdrawing. "I'm not good for anyone."

"I disagree."

"You think Scarlett would disagree?"

"Your sister doesn't understand why you would lie to her, let her think you were dead."

"You don't either," he reminded her.

That was true, he hadn't told her what had happened to him beyond the fact that his team had been murdered and he was out for revenge against the people responsible. But she knew that Eagle knew what he was doing, and she knew he'd given up that revenge for her.

Which was really all she needed to know.

"I know you saved me when you didn't have to," she said softly. "I know you didn't watch me in the shower when that drug was in my system, when most guys would have snuck glances at a woman getting herself off. I know you risked a lot when you didn't give me the whole dose of the drug. And I know you gave up something important to get me out of there and gave up your chance at vengeance."

"You're more important," he whispered like the words were as much a surprise to him as they were to her.

Their eyes met, something passed between them, something powerful, something that was pulling them closer like an invisible string ran from her heart to his. It was the strangest sensation and nothing she had ever experienced before.

Years of daydreaming about Zander couldn't have prepared her for what it felt like to be in his arms, his eyes on hers, this powerful emotion building between them.

When his head dipped and he leaned in closer, her lips tingled in anticipation of a kiss she was sure was coming.

But at the last moment, he pulled back. "I don't want to hurt you," he murmured.

"You won't. You wouldn't. You took care of me while I was having a seizure and afterward. You knew what to do without me having to tell you." Most people freaked after witnessing a seizure but not Zander.

"I researched the condition after I met you and learned that you had epilepsy," he admitted, making that warmth in her belly surge until it was almost burning hot. But burning in a different way than the arousal drug earlier. This heat was soothing, comforting, and reassuring. It was like somehow knowing for certain that everything was going to turn out okay.

"Thank you." He might have pulled back before kissing

her, obviously because he had doubts about them—well, doubts about himself she suspected—but she had no such doubts. Framing his face, she tugged it down and feathered a kiss to his lips.

For a second, Zander just sat there, then a growl rumbled through his chest, and the next thing she knew his mouth was devouring hers. The kiss was steamy and powerful. Zander took full control of it, shifting her on his lap and angling her head to give him better access.

The kiss felt like a promise only she wasn't sure what he was promising.

To get her home safely?

To tell her what had happened to him?

To give this weird connection between them a chance?

And what did she want it to mean?

* * *

JANUARY 25ᵀᴴ

12:16 A.M.

KISSING HER HAD BEEN A MISTAKE.

A big one.

Because now how was he supposed to walk away from her?

Zander was still wondering about that hours later as he held a sleeping Lucy in his arms.

Problem was, despite knowing it was a mistake as he did it, there was no way he could have stopped himself.

There was something between them. Always had been. He'd known it from the moment he met her. He'd liked Ella and Cassie, but he hadn't been compelled to go home and think about them every spare second. Hadn't gotten himself off to thoughts of them. Hadn't pictured them in his head when he'd been sure he was going to be tortured and murdered.

Only Lucy.

She was the only woman who had ever made him believe in the same things his sister did.

Until her, he'd thought Scarlett was crazy for being so determined to find love. Love didn't exist. Or at least, not the kind that filled songs, books, and movies. The kind of love his twin believed in was make-believe, it was what people convinced themselves of so they didn't have to live out an otherwise lonely existence. It certainly wasn't his experience with love.

Yet Scarlett had believed in it wholeheartedly.

While he'd thought it made her naïve and possibly even a little weak and needy, he now realized it made her strong.

So much stronger than he'd ever been.

Because she'd somehow known the truth despite the fact that love hadn't been part of either of their childhoods. She'd understood so much more about the world than he had, and he was ashamed now of all the times he'd rolled his eyes at his sister's attempts at finding love.

It might have been a rocky road for her, but Scarlett had found her other half, and maybe … maybe he might have as well.

A glance at the sleeping woman in his lap filled him with completely unfamiliar emotions. But they felt nice. They felt right.

But no matter how right they felt, it didn't change anything.

Didn't undo what had happened to his team, didn't change the fact that darkness lived inside him now, didn't mean he could reach out and take the happy ending that could be waiting for him with Lucy.

She was so damn trusting. Despite his lies, despite what she'd been through, despite everything she believed in him.

So sweet.

So naïve.

She had no idea of the kind of man he was. Of what he had allowed to happen.

"Zander?" Lucy's sleepy voice whispered his name as she stirred.

"Go back to sleep, baby." Unable to resist, he dropped a kiss to the top of her head.

"Can't, we need to keep walking." Although she desperately needed the rest, she was already pushing herself upright with a determination he knew wasn't going to be squashed.

"We can wait a little longer for you to rest some more." If he carried her and ran, they could make it to the extraction point in time and still let her sleep for another hour or so.

"Not if we want to stay ahead of Raul's men. They'll know better than us where the nearest towns are."

"We're not heading for a town, we're heading deeper into the jungle, the opposite way to where they'd expect us to go."

"Then how are we going to find a way to get home?" Lucy looked exhausted by the prospect of hiking for so long and through such thick rainforest, and he realized he'd never briefed her on the whole plan.

"We're hooking up with a team that Eagle is organizing to get us out," he told her.

Confusion filled her blue eyes. "Prey? How would they know where we are? I mean, other than knowing we crashed somewhere in Mexico?"

"I called them. I had a phone in my backpack, it survived the crash." Sighing, he dragged his fingers through his hair, knowing he had a lot to confess. "Luce, I was never going to let Raul get his hands on you. When I heard what happened with Scarlett, I made contact with Eagle. Explained that I was using the weapons dealer to bring down a terrorist group and would hand over all intel when I was done. Eagle knew that you were going to need to go back to Mexico to get more of the plant you were using so he asked me to fly the plane."

Lucy was staring at him with wide eyes, and he couldn't read what she was thinking so he just kept talking."

"He was worried about you and knew that if anything went wrong, I knew of a safe place to take you. We crashed close to Raul's house, that's why I couldn't let you go off on your own. My handler was about fifty miles or so away from where we went down. That's where I was taking you. I was going to have you hide out there with him while I went back to Raul to finish my mission. That way I could tell him you were gone when I woke up after the crash, and I had no idea where you were."

Lucy stared at him a moment longer then glowered at him and punched his arm. "You terrified me, ghost man. You could have just told me all that from the beginning."

"I didn't want you to get close enough to me to know any of that. I … didn't want you to hate me more than you already did when you learned the truth about what I was doing. It's not a pretty story, Lucy. And one that was bad enough that I would put my sister through hell just to do what I could to fix it in any way possible. After I was shot, and I realized you'd been taken, I called Prey. I knew if I called my handler, he'd tell me to stick with the plan. That your life was an acceptable sacrifice for the greater good, that you'd just be another casualty of war. But I couldn't let that happen. Not to you. Never to you."

The very thought of Lucy not being alive filled him with ice-cold dread.

It was like being asked to live out the rest of your life with a piece of yourself missing.

"So, I called Prey instead. I told them to give me forty-eight hours and arranged an exfil site. I thought I could get to Raul's and get you out within that timeframe. If we got out early we'd hide in the jungle, if I needed more time I could call them again and tell them. But I knew that you were more important than any mission. More important than revenge."

Softness and empathy filled Lucy's eyes, and instead of asking the questions he dreaded answering, she pressed herself closer, drawing his head down until their foreheads touched. "Thank you. I told you that you were a good man. I know the world we live in, know the evil that exists, and I don't know what happened to your team, but I know that life is always a better choice than death. Thank you for choosing my life over revenge."

"My team would have had my head if I didn't save you," he murmured with a rueful smile.

"They would? How would they even know about me?"

"Because they knew there was a woman I was interested in, they just didn't know your name. They all would have loved you. You're so strong, so brave, and so tough. You do what has to be done and you don't complain about it, you just do it. I miss them so much. I know I'm doing the right thing but ..."

"But you wanted to avenge them," Lucy finished for him.

"They wouldn't want that. Not if it meant sacrificing you, but I can't help but feel like I'm letting them down all over again."

After a pause, Lucy's hold on him tightened. "What happened to your team, Zander?"

The dreaded question.

One he knew she would ask sooner or later.

There was an easy out. All he had to do was tell her it was classified, and yet this was Lucy, and she'd been dragged into this mess. She deserved an answer.

"Just another terrorist who wanted power and a big death toll. My team had solid intel on where he was hiding out in Syria. We headed in. Turned out the government had under-estimated him and the number of men he had willing to fight and die with him. We were outnumbered, overpowered, and captured. They chained us up in this large open-roofed courtyard. The sun and heat were brutal. They didn't give us any water. In the middle of the yard was a table. One by one they took my men, chained them to it, and started killing them. Chopped off fingers, toes, ears at first, then moved on to hands and feet, then arms and legs. They put salt on the wounds to help them heal faster, plus it hurts like hell. I watched all seven of them bleed out in front of me."

Zander had to pause to still the nausea swelling inside him as the images flashed through his mind in rapid succession.

"Slow deaths. Agonizing deaths. Their screams ... damn, I still hear them inside my head, I don't think they'll ever go away. The terrorists promised if I gave up the intel they wanted they'd make the deaths quick, but I couldn't do it. Not that my men wanted me to. I wouldn't give them the reaction they wanted. Wouldn't yell at them or lose my cool, on the outside anyway, because inside I was dying along with my brothers. I thought I was going to die there, too, but a team of SEALs came in just before it was my turn on the table and got me out."

Furious.

That's how he'd been with those men.

He'd wanted to die by that point, and they were taking away the only thing that might give him any relief, any peace.

"You have to understand, Lucy," he said a little desper-ately. "I *wanted* to die. I *wished* I had died there with my men. That's why when I was approached with a plan to catch the men responsible for my teams' deaths I had to take it. I was dead inside anyway. This was all I had. A chance to at least avenge the deaths of seven good men. So, I agreed to fake my death and pretend to have gone rogue. There was intel that Raul Castillo was going to be making a weapons deal with the head of the terrorist cell. Zafir Mostafa. I need him dead. I need him to pay for what he did. I was prepared to sacrifice anything, including letting my sister believe I was dead, to get that. It was all I've lived for the last eighteen months."

"But you gave up that vengeance for me." Lucy sounded completely awestruck by that as though he hadn't just told her how he was responsible for the horrific deaths of seven brave soldiers.

"He'll still pay, I just won't be the one to hand out his punishment." A sacrifice that was more than worth it. Lucy had to live. Quite simply, his soul needed her to be alive, to be safe.

"Zander?" Lucy asked softly. "What happens next? What do you do after he's dead?"

That was a question he had no answer for.

Because he hadn't planned on living.

He'd planned on taking out the terrorist and as many of his followers as he could and going out with them.

Now ...

He had no idea.

CHAPTER ELEVEN

January 25th
  12:47 A.M.

SHE'D NEVER UNDERSTOOD what a broken heart felt like before now.

As Lucy and Zander walked hand in hand through the jungle toward the extraction point, Lucy could feel her heart cracking inside her chest.

While he hadn't offered any answer to her question, she knew what it was without him having to verbalize it. Instead of answering, Zander just told her that it was time to go, gave her water and another protein bar, and helped her stand and led her off into the jungle.

As much as she wished she was wrong, she knew what Zander's plans had been. Maybe still were.

He hadn't expected to live past his plot for revenge.

Killing the man responsible for taking his team from him was the only thing keeping him going in the aftermath of such a horrific ordeal.

Hearing him tell her what he'd been through, what those poor men had suffered, it had taken every bit of self-control she had not to burst into tears, or throw up. If it wasn't for the fact that she sensed Zander's need to feel her arms around him, to have her support and comfort, she would have fallen apart.

But she couldn't.

Zander needed her and she was going to be there for him.

How could she not after everything he'd done for her?

He was giving up the one thing he needed because of her. There was no way to repay him for that. If it wasn't for him, her life would already have been forfeit. She had no doubt that what he'd said was true, and whatever agency he was working with would have ordered him to allow her to be killed if it meant getting their man.

The greater good and all that.

But Zander had put her first and that filled her with both warmth and dread.

Because the answer to the question she'd asked him was a simple one. There was no what happened next. For Zander there was no next. There was never going to be a next. He had planned to join the rest of his team in death.

And nothing had changed.

If it had, if he wanted to live now, if he wanted to give this thing between them a chance, then he would have told her so.

The fact that he hadn't told her meant he still intended to die.

Whether he was going to commit suicide or was still going to try to go back and be part of the takedown once he knew for sure she was safe, Lucy had no idea. But she knew he didn't want to live without his team. The guilt he felt—misplaced though it was—was more than he could bear, and she didn't know how to help him, how to shoulder some of his burden.

Or if he'd even let her.

There was something between them, they both knew it, both acknowledged it, but that didn't mean either of them knew what was to come.

Lucy was having a hard enough time figuring out what she wanted. There was a part of her that wanted Zander, craved him, but she was wary of allowing herself to think too much about it because she was pretty sure it wasn't what Zander wanted.

"Here, this is where we'll wait," he suddenly announced, breaking the stifling silence that was every bit as oppressive as the humidity.

"Okay," she agreed, allowing him to lead her to a space where he thought they could safely wait until the helo arrived. It seemed that Zander had been prepared for any scenario because he'd had a pack hidden at the end of the tunnel. It had canteens of water, water purification tablets, protein bars, MREs, weapons and ammo, and night vision goggles. Since there was only one pair, she'd had to hold onto him and allow him to do all the leading.

Not that she minded. She trusted him.

After hearing what he'd been through there was no way she could blame him for his choices.

Was she still upset that one of her best friends had been hurt? Sure. She wished there had been a way for him to do what he needed to without hurting Scarlett in the process. But he was thinking of nothing else at the time other than surviving the only way he knew how. Revenge was all that had kept him going, and he'd latched onto it with a tenacity that still made her marvel at how he had been able to set it aside for her.

A different kind of need filled her now.

In a way, it was like the arousal drug in that it was all-consuming and difficult to control. It sent fire licking through her veins, and she knew there was only one way to quench that fire.

Only this time it was something she wanted.

There was nothing against her will happening inside her body.

If she was never going to be able to have Zander for real, if he wasn't in a place where he was willing to give her a chance, to give them a chance, then she didn't want to pass up this opportunity.

It could be all she ever had.

There was a better than even chance that as soon as they got home, he was going to disappear, and if that happened, she wanted to have this memory to hold on to.

Maybe there were the last remnants of the drug in her system, giving her a confidence she wouldn't otherwise have possessed, because she didn't hesitate to reach up and grab his shoulders the second he settled them under a rocky outcrop like the one they'd slept in that first night in the jungle.

Drawing him down, he was unresistant, but also didn't participate as she touched her lips to his. If he didn't want this then she'd stop, but she felt his need as surely as she felt her own, and she knew he wanted this every bit as much as she did.

It might be all either of them ever had.

After a couple of seconds, she felt his control snap, and then he was lifting her up, hauling her against him, the bulge in his pants nestled against her throbbing center as he kissed her until there was no air left in her lungs.

"Are you sure this is what you want?" he asked against her lips.

"Positive."

"Lucy, I can't promise anything. I want to, but ... I'm not in a good place right now and I won't drag you down with me."

"You'd never drag me down," she told him, positive of that. Zander was struggling, and he wasn't the only one who had lived through a horrific ordeal. What had happened to her at Raul's house would live in her head forever, and right now, it felt impossible for it not to affect everything she did from here on out.

But with Zander she was safe.

That thought was all that was in her head at the moment.

Nothing else.

She wouldn't let anything contaminate this beautiful moment.

"I'm not asking for promises, all I'm asking is that you don't shut me out. Let me be there for you. I know what it's like to feel alone, and I'm not at all comparing having epilepsy to living through what you did, but you feel enough for me to save my life, so please feel enough for me not to shut me out. I'm here for you, Zander."

As soon as the words were out of her mouth, his lips were back on hers. While he didn't say anything she felt his gratefulness, his awe, and his appreciation in the kiss that reached down inside her body all the way to her soul.

Pressing her back against the rock, he balanced her with one hand on her backside while his other found its way inside her pants. Despite what had happened earlier, nothing but desire fanned to life inside her as he ran a finger across her wet center.

There was a desperation she knew they both felt, and Zander didn't hesitate to nudge his finger at her entrance. He teased it a little first, rimming around it before slipping just the tip in. His thumb found her bud, and when it glided across it, she already felt pleasure beginning to build inside her.

After all the orgasms in the shower, and only small doses of the drug in her system after, Lucy would have sworn there was no way her body could orgasm again for days. But already it was quivering inside her.

"Zander," she moaned as his finger sank all the way inside her, grazing that spot that had little pinprick stars dancing in her vision.

"You're so tight, babe, so perfect," he murmured, then began to kiss and nibble at her neck.

With nimble fingers, he simultaneously worked her inside and out, all while taking her weight with his other hand, and never before in her life had she felt so utterly secure. Didn't matter that they were in the jungle, being hunted, that they were both scarred and a little broken inside, in this moment everything was perfect.

Just as she felt herself beginning to climb the ladder of pleasure, Zander's fingers withdrew. A protest fell from her lips, and Zander's hearty laugh kept her hovering on the ladder, not falling completely back down again.

"Hold on, babe, want to be inside you when I come. Do I need a condom? I'm clean, haven't had sex in ... I don't even remember how long."

"I'm clean, too, and on birth control. I don't want anything between us, Zander." Not a condom, not his trauma, and not her own. No barriers, she wanted to feel the full ramifications of this connection that tied them together.

"I've never gone in without one, I'm glad you're my first," Zander whispered as he unzipped himself and pulled his very impressive length free.

Feeling what he'd left unsaid, that she would be his first and likely only, Lucy refused to let it take her out of this moment. Zander wasn't lost to her yet, and she was going to do everything she could to hold onto him. All he had to do was let her, she'd do the rest.

Let me in, Zander.

The silent plea echoed through her mind at the exact moment that Zander shoved her pants down, removing them, and then slid inside her in one smooth move.

His pace was fast, near frantic, and Lucy wrapped her legs around his hips, drawing him deeper, and her arms around his shoulders, holding on as he slammed into her over and over again. Once again, his hand moved to her bundle of nerves, working it hard, giving her exactly what she needed.

She was flying up that ladder, the pressure inside her growing, it consumed every single part of her body, her heart, her mind, and her soul. Tying them all together in a knot she didn't even want to untangle. Drawing in Zander's soul as well, binding it to hers in a way that could never be completely undone.

When she finally reached the top of that ladder and tumbled off it, pleasure so strong that her cries would have woken the whole jungle if Zander's mouth hadn't claimed hers again, rushed through her.

The feel of Zander hitting his own release, feeling the evidence of it squirting inside her, was an almost magical experience. Lucy felt claimed, marked, and she wondered if he felt that, too.

Would he be able to walk away from her after this?

Would she be able to let him?

* * *

JANUARY 25TH
1:10 A.M.

. . .

BEING INSIDE HER FELT PERFECT.

Zander wanted to hold onto this moment and never let it go.

Here he felt peace, a lightness that he hadn't felt in eighteen months. Sex with Lucy didn't mean everything was going to be okay, it didn't solve his problems, erase the darkness inside him, or mean he could have a future with this amazing woman. But it did mean that for one blissful second, everything inside him had stilled and he'd been able to live in the moment.

It should have been a mistake because walking away from her would be hard, and he wasn't sure he could or even wanted to, but he couldn't make himself see this as anything other than the perfect joining together of their bodies. Two halves of a soul reconnecting in a way that would forever be something special no matter what the future held.

If she hadn't uttered the most content little sigh and nuzzled her face against the side of his neck, Zander would have been tempted to ask her if she regretted sex with him. If it had been a spur-of-the-moment decision based on the adrenalin rush of their situation, or the lingering effects of the drug.

But it wasn't.

He felt her pleading with him even though she didn't speak.

Her words echoed in his mind. Asking him to let her be there for him.

Could he do that?

Was it fair to do that?

Surely, saddling her with the darkness that consumed him, the anger and guilt that ate at him constantly, wasn't fair.

Yet she said it after she knew the truth, knew about the stains on his soul. She knew that he'd gotten seven good men killed and yet she was still there, still wanted him, still let him take her without the barrier of a condom between them.

What had he ever done to deserve a woman like this?

Nothing.

That was the answer to that question.

Reluctantly he shifted, sliding out of her, and lowering her to her feet. Her arms lingered around his shoulders for a moment before she let go and stiffened her back, prepared to let him go if that was what he wanted.

But it wasn't.

Not at all.

What he wanted was to hold onto this woman forever. But he was scared. It sucked to admit it, made him feel weak like a coward, but the last thing he wanted to do was cause Lucy pain.

Would she see it that way? Or would she think his pushing her away was because he didn't want her?

"Thank you for giving me that, baby," he said as he knelt and rifled through his pack for the wipes he kept in the first aid kit. Taking them, he began to clean up the evidence of what they'd just done. Wiping his cum off her legs almost felt like erasing their connection, but then Lucy's hands rested on his shoulders and that connection surged again.

"Don't thank me, Zander. I wanted that, too. I needed it. This thing between us is confusing, I've never felt anything like it before. I don't want to play games, that's not my style, I'd like for you to give us a chance, but if you're not ready yet, then I can wait."

Startled, his head snapped up to look at her. Kneeling as he was in front of her, his eyes were level with her chest, and this time he took her chin and tilted it down to meet his gaze. "You'd wait for me?" he asked, confused. Why would she offer something like that when he'd told her he couldn't make any promises. It wasn't that he didn't want to, it was just the damn fear again. It was crippling and he hated it, but he didn't know how to get out from under its crushing presence.

Her brow furrowed adorably. "Of course I would. You feel it, too. I know you do so don't bother pretending otherwise."

That sass had him smiling, or maybe it was just because he loved how straightforward she was. Never would he have to guess what his girl was thinking. "I wouldn't pretend otherwise. It's just, there's darkness inside me, Lucy. And I don't want to contaminate you with it."

"Isn't it my choice what I get "contaminated"," she made air quotes as she said the word, "with? I'm a big girl, and I've lived through a lot of uncertainty. I know that it might not work out between us, I know that even if it did, something could steal our happiness away from us. But one thing that living with epilepsy has taught me is to cherish the good moments. I'm willing to risk losing you to have you, the only question is, what are you willing to risk?"

Before he could tell her that there wasn't anything on Earth he wouldn't risk for more moments with her like the one they'd just shared, he heard something.

Something that had the hairs on the back of his neck standing on edge.

Quickly he straightened, pulling Lucy's jeans on and zipping them, then righting his own clothes. "Shh," he breathed out the sound, touching a finger to Lucy's lips because he could sense her confusion. "We're not alone."

Nodding so he knew she was ready to follow any orders he gave, he slipped on the backpack, righted the NVGs, and took her hand. There was someone out there, Raul's men searching for them, but he also heard the sounds of the approaching helo. All he had to do was get his girl onto that chopper.

If he had to stay behind to make sure she got out of there safely then he'd do it.

Anything to get her home alive.

Pulling her in for a quick kiss, he then led her out of their little hiding place. They only had a couple of hundred yards to cross to the point where the helo would pick them up, they should be able to make it without being seen.

Given that he was a weapons dealer, Raul had access to all kinds of weapons, including those that could take down a helo. But the man also had no idea that Zander wasn't who he said he was, that he wasn't a rogue Delta Force operator, and that the intel he was gathering to bring down the terrorist would also lead to Raul himself being captured. There was no reason for the men searching for them to have anything other than guns on them because they didn't know he was waiting for an exfil, they thought it was just him and Lucy alone out there.

The sounds of the helo got louder, and he snatched Lucy up and threw her over his shoulder, ignoring her pained grunt as he took off at a dead sprint to the spot where the rope would come down. A rope that would get his girl out of the jungle and back home where she belonged.

Going for speed over everything else, the sounds gave away his position and bullets began to fire at them.

Thankfully, it appeared that the men weren't wearing NVGs because their accuracy sucked, and as the helo appeared in the sky, Zander was already closing in on the pickup spot.

"As soon as the rope gets down, I'll buckle you in. You cover your head with your arms, keep it tucked against your chest on the way up," he ordered Lucy.

"You're coming with me, though, aren't you?" The tremor in her voice about killed him.

"After you go up, I'll have my turn."

Small hands clutched at his T-shirt. "No. We go together. I can't lose you already, Zander. Don't make me. Together. We go together."

More gunfire split through the night, but this time it wasn't just coming from behind them but from above them, too.

"I'll be safer with you on the rope with me," Lucy said, tightening the screws. "Up there alone I'm like a sitting duck. But with your cover fire, and the guys on the helo covering both of us, I have a better chance of making it without getting hit."

"You don't play fair, do you, sassy girl?"

Lucy grinned. "Not when your life is at stake."

Since he couldn't argue with that, he nodded, and when the rope came down, he made quick work of buckling her in, then snapped himself in and gave a tug.

In the next second, they were sailing up into the air. Shots fired all around them and as they hit the top of the tree line they were so exposed that he fired every bullet he had at the spot where the shots had been coming from.

No way was he letting his woman get hit.

He hadn't been able to save his team, but he damn sure wasn't failing the woman who owned the keys to his heart.

It seemed to take forever, but then hands were grabbing him, pulling him into the safety of the helo. Lucy was pulled in as well and the second they were unbuckled from the rope she was throwing herself into his arms.

Her slim body shook, and her cheeks were wet as she pressed her face against his neck. At first, he thought she was crying out of fear over almost being shot, and the shock of surviving an ordeal she likely thought she wouldn't.

But when she spoke he realized he was wrong.

"Thank you for coming with me, thank you for at least being willing to give me this. I won't ask you for promises,

Zander, but I'm making you one. I'm here. Right here. For as long as you'll let me be. I'll wait, I'll give you space, or not, whatever you want. I'm just here. For you."

Curling his arms around her, he pulled her into his lap, uncaring of the fact that they had an audience. How could this woman possibly be making him promises after what she knew about him?

Could he find a way to extinguish the darkness that raged inside him? Or if he let Lucy in, would it wind up destroying her along with him?

CHAPTER TWELVE

January 25th
2:32 A.M.

HE PICKED HER.

Lucy was still smiling about that when they finally started their descent onto the landing pad on the top of Prey's building.

She knew she still had a long way to go convincing Zander to give them a chance, to prove to him that he would never knowingly hurt her, but at least she had this. Because for a moment there, she knew he had been all ready to sacrifice himself in the jungle to get her on that helo. For some strange reason, she seemed to be able to sense what Zander was thinking even when he didn't verbalize it, or even give it away with his expression. So, she'd known he was going to stay behind, and allow the men to capture him if it meant getting her up onto the helo and safe.

But she didn't want him to sacrifice himself.

Even though she knew he felt like he did, he had nothing

to make up for. What had happened to his team was nothing short of tragic. It was horrific, the thought of anyone dying that way was almost too much, but each one of those men understood the lives they had chosen. She wished they had made it home alive, that help had come sooner, but what had happened was not Zander's fault.

How did she make him understand that?

Could she?

Or was she being majorly naïve?

Regardless, she wasn't giving up on Zander. Not now. Not ever.

He was a warrior who fought for his country, fought to get rid of evil, and fought to make the world a safer place. But right now, he needed her to fight for him. He needed her to be the same kind of warrior he was, strong and brave, tough and smart. It might be the biggest battle of her life, but she was ready and willing to fight it.

Because if she was successful then the payoff would be more than worth it.

She was absolutely counting it as a win that Zander had held her the entire flight. The SEAL team who had come in for them was the same one that had helped to save Scarlett just a week or so ago when she had been kidnapped by Raul Castillo the second time. She didn't know the guys on Blake "Rocco" Wise's team very well, but she liked them. They were smart and fair, they hadn't judged Scarlett by the false evidence against her, and it was partly because of them that her friend was still alive.

Other than when the guys had been tending to their injuries, giving her fluids, antibiotics, and painkillers, she'd been in Zander's lap. Even when she was sitting on her own seat, he'd been scowling at whichever one of Rocco's team was touching her, even if it was just checking her pulse, cleaning and bandaging wounds, and setting up an IV.

Now the IV was gone, a Band-Aid on the inside of her elbow covering the tiny puncture wound, and they were all waiting to land. As excited as she was to get back home because she had been so sure that it would never happen, she was apprehensive, too.

Right now, she had Zander, but what happened when they landed?

Would he stay?

Leave?

Did he have a choice?

If whoever he was working for called him back in, he would have to go, she understood that. But she was also hoping that Eagle Oswald—founder and CEO of Prey Security—had enough sway to have Zander stay and help them take down Raul, since he likely had more intel on the man than they did. Maybe something he knew might even point to the identity of the mole at Prey.

When the rotors stopped spinning and the guys all stood, Lucy did, too. She was surprised, but pleasantly so, when Zander took her hand and laced their fingers together. Hand in hand, they stepped out of the helo onto the roof, and almost immediately, three figures were rushing toward them.

The next thing Lucy knew, she was being wrapped up in the embraces of her team. Ella, Cassie, and Scarlett were all crying, all talking over the top of one another as they asked how she was, where she'd been hurt, what had happened to her, and if she was okay.

Since there was no way she could answer all those questions at once, she simply held onto them and soaked up the feel of their hugs. For someone who wasn't much of a crier, she was a little surprised to find a fresh wave of tears tumbling down her cheeks. Maybe the toll of the last week was catching up with her. A hot shower, a call to her family to hear their voices, and comfort food were all high on the list.

But Zander was on the list, too.

Time with him when he wasn't undercover and lying to her, where they weren't in danger and running for their lives, when they could just be together and get to know one another, that was what she wanted. And she definitely wouldn't say no to another round of amazing sex.

When she realized she was no longer holding his hand, and that he'd taken a few steps back as though he didn't belong here by her side, Lucy gently extracted herself from her friends' embraces.

"I'm okay," she assured them. "I have a whole ton of bruises, a broken arm, probably some cracked ribs, and all I want to do is sleep for about a month. But I'm alive, and it's all thanks to Zander."

As though they'd all forgotten he was even there, everyone's attention suddenly shifted to him, and she could feel his uneasiness even though his stiff posture didn't alter. She knew that the last her friends had heard, she was on a plane with Scarlett's supposedly dead brother, and they all wondered if maybe he was somehow involved in everything that had gone down with Scarlett, the mole, and the weapons dealer.

"Zander was undercover," she quickly explained. She had no idea what they knew and what they didn't, and she didn't want anyone looking at him with suspicion. While he would never tell anyone or say it out loud, their accusations would hurt him. Already he blamed himself for the deaths of his team, and having people place more blame on his shoulders when he was already carrying such a heavy burden would be more than he could handle.

"We heard," Cassie told her.

"Eagle caught us up on the fact that Zander was working to bring down a terrorist cell," Ella added.

Scarlett said nothing. She was too busy glaring at her twin brother.

Tate Laurier, a SEAL whose team had been called in to help locate Scarlett when she had been kidnapped the first time and was now dating her, stepped up beside her and took her hand.

"Don't say anything you'll regret," Tate said softly to Scarlett, but it was clear from her expression that she wasn't listening. Scarlett was a sweet woman, one who Lucy had long since admired because she went after what she wanted and didn't get deterred when there were bumps along the way.

But right now, Scarlett wasn't thinking clearly.

Grief and betrayal were hard to deal with, and when they came from the one person who had always been there for you, who you loved so much, it was even worse. Then add in that she'd been framed as a traitor and almost lost her life because of it, and Lucy worried it was too much for her.

"He didn't have a choice, Scar," Lucy said, moving so she was between the brother and sister. While maybe her loyalty should be to her friend and team member, she felt too much for Zander to allow him to take more hits than he already had, even if that meant protecting him from her friend's anger. Anger she understood but knew that once Scarlett heard what had happened to her brother would fade away.

At least, she hoped it did.

Because if it didn't, Lucy wasn't just going to be fighting against Zander's guilt driving a wedge between them, but Scarlett's anger as well.

Ignoring her, Scarlett glared at her twin. "You let me believe you were dead. When I called Mom and Dad to tell them you weren't, they said they already knew. You told them the truth, Zander, yet you lied to me. How could you do that? Didn't you care that you were hurting me? Shutting me out and joining the military to get Mom and Dad to love you was one thing, I didn't understand it, but I didn't want to lose you completely over it. But letting me believe you had died, that's something I can't get over."

"Scarlett," Lucy warned, taking another step closer to Zander so she was by his side. Because she wanted everybody to know where she stood, she reached out and took his hand. Surprised faces looked from her to Zander to their joined hands. Even Zander looked down at them as though he couldn't quite believe she would be so blatant about their teeny, tiny, little possible fledgling relationship.

But playing games wasn't her style. She'd told him that and promised to be there for him. Did he not think that meant standing up for him with his sister?

"You need to listen to him," she told her friend. "Once you hear what happened, you'll understand why he had to do what he did. I don't like that he hurt you, I told him that, but I do understand."

Anger crackled in the air, arcing from Scarlett to her brother. "If you think I'm ever going to understand how my own twin brother could let me suffer thinking that he was dead, then you're crazy."

With that, Scarlett turned and stalked away, leaving pain flowing in waves off the man standing beside her.

* * *

January 25th
2:54 A.M.

He'd lost her.

The only family he'd ever really had.

That thread that had always tied them together as twins snapped as Scarlett walked away from him.

Zander had never intended to tell his sister he was alive, not after how his parents had reacted. Branding him a failure, they had reiterated every single thing he'd been feeling about the ordeal. His guilt, his remorse, and his anger. How could he face the only person whose opinion of him mattered when the people he'd been trying so hard to please had confirmed his worst fears about himself?

That was the moment he'd known he was done trying to earn their love.

Quite simply they didn't have any real meaningful love to give.

Then he'd been approached to go undercover and never expected to come out the other side alive. What was the point in making his twin mourn him twice?

Now, though, he's lost her.

Lost his sister, and he was pretty sure he was never getting her back.

Fingers squeezed his, and then lips brushed a kiss to his jaw. "She's angry right now. She loves you a lot and your death hit her hard. I don't say that to make you feel bad, I know why you did what you did, but she doesn't. All she knows is you chose a job over her. Again. She just wants your love, she wants back the brother she remembers from when you two were kids," Lucy told him.

"I made a mistake trying to get my parents to love me. They aren't worthy of my love, my respect, or anything else. If I'd picked Scarlett and my relationship with her over them, none of this would have happened." He wouldn't have joined the Army, wouldn't have made it to Delta, and maybe the lives of his teammates would have been spared.

"You can't think like that, Zander. You're good at what

you do, I can attest to that, and in Delta, you saved so many lives and stopped so many people who would have done unspeakably evil things. I'm glad you're the man you are, I just hate my friend got hurt along the way. But that doesn't change the promise I made you. I'm here for you. I'm not going anywhere."

Her words were so confident, her intent so clear, that he couldn't not grab her and drag her close so he could kiss her. "Thank you. You're more than I deserve, Lucy Elrod."

The smile she shot him was pure sass. "I'm going to remind you that you said that," she teased.

"So, you guys are … together?" Ella asked, her green eyes full of curiosity.

"Because that we did not see coming," Cassie added.

"We're seeing how things go, but yes we bonded out there," Lucy replied, giving him the option of an out if he wanted one.

Since he was in no position to make plans for the future, he merely maintained his grip on Lucy's hand as they all headed for the lift that would take them down to the conference room.

Well, the rest of them would go there, but Lucy had to go to the hospital. Her arm needed to be x-rayed so doctors could see if it needed surgery. And she should be properly checked out after her seizure as well. He knew she had epilepsy and didn't necessarily go to the hospital every time she had a seizure, but given the drug she'd been pumped full of, he wanted her to be thoroughly examined.

"One of you needs to take Lucy to the hospital," he said to Ella and Cassie as they all got into the lift.

"I'm not going to the hospital," Lucy protested, sounding aghast at the prospect.

"Your arm, babe," he reminded her. Unsure if she wanted

her friends to know she'd had a seizure, he didn't mention that.

"Can wait until the debrief is done. I'm not leaving you alone here without backup." The way she said it made it clear arguing was going to be futile, and a big part of him didn't want to anyway. That she was so determined to be there for him and have his back had a delicious warmth spreading through him.

"As soon as it's done, you go to the hospital." That was non-negotiable. After everything she'd been through, she needed a doctor, not just a medic. Those guys were trained to deal with gunshot wounds and things, keeping a patient alive until they got to a doctor, so as grateful as he was to the SEALs, he still needed to know his girl had been seen by someone with a medical degree.

"I'll go if you go. You did get shot remember."

Actually, he'd forgotten all about the wound. It was nothing more than a flesh wound. He'd lost a bit of blood but now he was fine. Still, he wasn't going to argue against a reason to spend more time with Lucy. When everything felt so up in the air and unsettled it was nice to have something solid to hold onto.

"We'll go together," he agreed.

"Aww, you two are really very cute," Cassie said, watching them with curiosity. The youngest member of Athena Team was a verifiable genius. Despite her high IQ, Cassie had an innocence that made her incredibly endearing. While he'd been attracted to Lucy from the beginning, he'd felt more of a brotherly vibe with Cassie. And the least connection of all to Ella, although the woman was sweet and a talented musician.

"We're not cute," Lucy said, making a face that made the rest of them laugh.

"You are," Ella agreed. "I can't believe that first Scarlett and Tate fell in love, and now you two are ... bonded from your experience," she finished although it was clear she'd been going to say they were a couple.

Even though he wanted to claim Lucy in that way, making sure everybody knew she was his and he was hers, he wasn't ready to take that step yet. He had to be sure that the darkness curled inside him ready to spring out like it had when he'd caught that man assaulting Lucy was not going to be a threat to her.

"Bonded," Lucy echoed, and from her expression she was completely satisfied with that description for now.

By the time they reached the conference room, everybody else was there. Eagle Oswald himself, the team of former SEALs who now ran Prey's East Coast office, Rocco's SEAL team who were going to be sticking around until Raul and the mole were in custody, and Scarlett and her boyfriend.

Much as he'd love to be able to go to his sister, make her smile like he used to do when they were kids, tickle her till tears of laughter rolled down her cheeks, or make silly jokes until he had her giggling and forgetting what had made her sad in the first place, he couldn't do that anymore.

It wasn't his place.

The distance between them was his own fault. Enlisting had been the first step, and it had all culminated in the lie about his death.

There likely wasn't a bridge on Earth long enough to breach that distance now.

"You should talk to her," Lucy said quietly, following his gaze. "Once she understands she'll get over her anger. She loves you, Zander."

That he believed.

It just wasn't enough.

Not for the mistakes he'd made. It was asking too much of his twin when he hadn't given her anything in return for so long. Not since childhood. They'd been thirteen when they were first split up, and looking back now, it was the beginning of the end. If they'd stayed together in foster care, he likely wouldn't have been able to break her heart by joining the military.

"Talk to her," Lucy said again.

"Okay," he agreed, it wasn't like it could make things worse.

Drawing in a breath, he released Lucy's hand, even though it felt like being out in the ocean and letting go of your life preserver, and crossed the room to where his sister stood with her arms crossed and a frown on her face. But beneath the anger he saw her pain. She wasn't trying to be mean to him, to hurt him, she'd just grieved him and then learned she'd been lied to. Of course she was angry, it was only natural. He just had to pray that one day she could understand he hadn't wanted to hurt her, he'd just thought she was better off without him in her life.

"Scar, can we talk so I can explain?" he asked.

"I don't want to hear anything you have to say," Scarlett said, unshed tears shimmering in her eyes. Then her gaze shifted to something behind him, and he knew she was looking at Lucy. "And if I lose someone I care about because you come between us, I'll never forgive you for that either."

The threat to end whatever it was he had with Lucy hung between them. It hurt that his sister would try to take away the only thing he had when she already had so many people who loved her, but he had to remind himself that she was acting out of her own hurt.

Still, it latched onto his doubts and compounded them. If he wasn't good enough for his own twin, how could he ever hope to be enough for a woman like Lucy?

CHAPTER THIRTEEN

January 25th
  4:38 P.M.

IT FELT like something was missing.

So much so that Lucy kept looking around her living room to see what wasn't there even though she already knew what it was.

Zander.

That was what was missing.

They'd parted ways after the hospital. Not parted on bad terms at all. They'd exchanged numbers, they'd kissed before she got into Ella's car, and he got into his truck which someone had dropped off for him.

The only thing they hadn't done was make concrete plans about when they would see each other again. As much as she'd wanted to ask, she hadn't wanted to push. Zander was dealing with so much, and Scarlett had been there, glaring at him, and she knew he needed time on his own to process.

She just wanted to be there for him.

JANE BLYTHE

But she knew she couldn't force him to let her be.

If there was one thing she understood, it was being independent and wanting to handle things yourself. This was the first time she'd really been on the flip side of that and it sucked. It definitely gave her insight into what her family had felt all these years when she'd pushed them away because she needed so badly to cling to her independence.

Still, she could be patient. Because Zander was worth it.

It didn't mean she didn't wish he was there though.

When a small sigh escaped, she knew that one of her friends was going to zero in on it. They'd been great as she knew they would be. After the debrief, they'd gone with her to the hospital. They'd stayed while she was examined. When she'd been discharged, they drove her back to her place and stayed with her.

It was nice.

She appreciated it.

But it was Zander that she craved.

Only four days had passed since the crash, which was completely weird because in those four days Lucy felt like she had lived an entire lifetime. So much had happened, she had been so fundamentally changed by what she'd lived through, she wasn't even the same person anymore.

In that time she'd grown so close to Zander. It was completely crazy because there had been a solid day that they hadn't even been together, which was a quarter of that time. And another quarter of that time she'd been unsure if Zander could be trusted and was actively looking for a chance to get away from him, going so far as to try to kill him.

The other half of the time it had felt like it was the two of them against the whole world.

Those were the moments that had bonded them so closely.

Closely enough that she ached to have him there by her

148

side. His presence would comfort her, make her feel safe, and she didn't want to sound like an ego, but she believed her presence would help him, too.

Fingers clicked in front of her face, and she blinked and looked over to see Cassie watching her with concern.

"You doing okay, Luce?" Ella asked.

"Yep." Although her fingers were convulsively stroking through Cotton's curly poodle hair. "Painkillers are doing their job, I'm clean and in fresh clothes, and I'm thrilled I don't have to have surgery. I'm happy to be home," she said, throwing in a smile for good measure.

That was all true of course. The shower had been heaven and she'd washed her hair three times and her body four, thankful for the waterproof brace on her arm. It wasn't until the water began to run cold that she'd been able to drag herself out. Her favorite leggings and oversized hoodie, along with a pair of fuzzy socks, made her feel more like herself, and she really was glad that surgery wasn't on her upcoming schedule. Cotton had followed her around everywhere, even lying on the bathroom floor while she bathed, and the dog's presence was comforting in and of itself.

"I don't think she was asking if you were clean or in pain," Cassie said.

"How are you *doing*?" Ella repeated her question. "This is us. We're a family, the four of us, you can tell us anything."

Usually, she would agree that was true.

But talking about Zander with Scarlett felt weird. She understood why her friend was angry, she knew the kind of life Scarlett and Zander had lived as kids, and knew the bond they shared. But she also knew Zander, and how badly he'd suffered watching his friends die and how deeply it had affected him.

There was no doubt in Lucy's mind that Scarlett wouldn't hold onto that anger for long. She was too sweet, and she loved her brother too much. She'd even seen her friend approaching a doctor at the hospital to ask about her brother's injuries when she thought nobody was watching.

That wasn't what was bothering her. What was bothering her was whether Scarlett would be okay with her and Zander being a couple.

More than that, would Zander?

He liked her, but she knew he was on the fence about taking things any further. His demons were screaming in his ear that he was no good for her, no good for anyone, and he had to be alone as his penance for his sins. It wasn't true, but she had no idea how to convince him of that. Especially if he wouldn't even give her a chance.

"It's Zander, isn't it?" Scarlett said flatly. Tate shifted a little closer to her and Scarlett immediately leaned into him. It was kind of weird seeing the two of them together. Their relationship was about as new as it could get, and most of the time they'd spent together, had been hiding out from both law enforcement and Raul Castillo's men, so she wasn't used to seeing her friend and this man together.

"I hate to sound like a broken record, but you need to talk to him," Lucy told her friend, snuggling Cotton closer so she could press her face into the soft fur. She was so happy that Scarlett had found a man who had her back, who would be there for her, give her that sense of belonging she had always craved, and the acceptance she deserved, but she also knew her friend still needed her brother.

More than that, Zander needed his twin.

While Scarlett had Tate, Athena Team, and Prey, Zander had nobody in his corner right now other than her, and he needed more. Deserved more.

"He told me what happened, and when he did, I understood why he felt like he had no choice but to do what he did," Lucy continued. In the briefing earlier, Zander had not gone into any detail on what had happened to his team beyond saying they'd been killed, and while she didn't want her friend to hear the gruesome details she knew that Scarlett was going to have to if she was going to get past this.

When Scarlett began to pick at her cuticles, a sure sign she was stressed, Tate reached over and grasped her hands, stilling them, then entwining their fingers together. "I'm scared," she whispered.

"Of what?" Lucy asked. The only way to fix a problem was to acknowledge it. You couldn't fix what you didn't know was broken.

"Losing my brother for real," Scarlett admitted. "If I listen to him then I have to accept what he tells me. I have to understand. I have to forgive him for letting me believe he was dead."

"Why is that a bad thing?" Lucy asked without judgment. She'd known Scarlett for years, and there truly was nobody else on Earth with a bigger heart, she just wanted to understand what Scarlett needed from her so she could provide it and the siblings could reconnect.

"Because if I forgive him, then I have to admit how much I love him. How it doesn't matter that we grew apart in foster care, and that a wedge was driven between us when he joined the Army, I always loved him. I always will. He's my brother, my twin, my other half. Sorry, Tate," Scarlett said with a small smile as she looked up at her boyfriend. "If I have to admit that nothing could make me stop loving my brother, no matter what he does, no matter any mistakes he might make, no matter how noble he believes he has to be, then I have to risk losing him all over again. I couldn't survive that. I know I couldn't."

With her admission, Scarlett began to cry, and Tate immediately wrapped his arms around her, holding her close.

Watching the couple, Lucy felt her own eyes tear up. She wasn't usually much of a crier, but lately, she'd shed so many tears, and she was starting to admit to herself that tears weren't necessarily the weakness she had always believed them to be. They were real, they were an outpouring of emotion, and they were part of life.

Over the years she had proven herself strong enough and capable enough to do whatever she set her mind to. So why did she keep feeling the need to maintain her independence to the point where she was uncomfortable sharing her emotions with the people who cared about her?

This should be a safe place. Her family should be a safe place, all the people in her life loved her and would never put her down because of her condition. This was what Zander should have right now. What she had gone through was nothing in comparison to what had happened to him and his team, and yet here she was, surrounded by people, while Zander was alone.

That broke her heart because even the toughest of warriors should have his team at his back. And these people in her living room with her would be his team if he'd let them.

But she feared he wouldn't.

And alone she wasn't sure he could fight his demons and win.

* * *

JANUARY 25TH
10:26 P.M.

LONELINESS WAS HITTING him hard tonight.

Which was stupid because Zander had been on his own for a long time.

As a kid, the only person in his life who had truly been on his side was his sister, but they'd been separated at thirteen when their grandparents died and their parents refused to come home and take care of them. Foster care was tough, but he hadn't been abused, just more of what he'd gotten at home, neglected and ignored. Without his twin there to lessen that ache he'd learned to deal with it alone.

It wasn't until he joined the military that he finally found the family he'd always known was missing, and the sense of belonging that Scarlett had always talked about.

For as long as he could remember, his twin had been a romantic at heart. While he used to try to make her laugh when she was sad, she always tried to convince him that love existed when he shut down.

There had never been a time when he believed in the kind of love she talked about.

Not until the day he'd met Lucy.

Something had shifted inside him that day, and even though he had never intended to do anything about it, even less so after his team was killed and he faked his own death, those feelings had always been there.

Now after they'd spent time together and he knew how amazing she was, it was even harder to stay away from her.

If she was here right now, snuggled on his lap, the sense of peace, of quiet, that she'd given him would be back.

Instead, the darkness roared inside him.

Ordering him to do things he knew he shouldn't.

Throw caution out the window, damn the consequences, and go back to Mexico and track down Raul Castillo, make him pay for what he'd done to Lucy. Get to the location he knew the weapons deal was going to take place and get the vengeance his team deserved.

Pick up the weapon that sat on his coffee table and end things the way they should have ended in Syria.

Zander knew he wasn't supposed to have survived that ordeal. He was supposed to have died along with the rest of his team. Knowing that had made deciding to fake his death and take the undercover job so much easier. Because he'd never intended to return alive.

If he couldn't die with the men he considered his brothers, then he could at least die taking out the men responsible for their horrific deaths.

But he had survived.

And fate had placed the only woman to ever stir up emotion inside him right back in his path.

He didn't regret his decision to put Lucy and her life and safety first, not for a single second, it was the right thing to do, and the only decision his teammates would have respected, but it left him feeling ... lost.

What happened next?

How could he expect Lucy to take on him and his demons when she had her own to battle? How could he expect his sister to be okay with him dating one of her best friends when she hated him? How could he be with Lucy when he had absolutely nothing to offer her?

What if he dragged Lucy down into the darkness with him?

What if he destroyed her because he couldn't control the darkness?

It felt like too big a risk and yet already being without her was hell.

So many times at the hospital he'd ached to ask her out on a date. Something completely normal, pizza and a movie, maybe grab some ice cream after, it didn't matter that it was winter, in his opinion, it was never too cold for ice cream. But underneath the urge was an undercurrent of fear.

His life was far from uncomplicated.

Eagle Oswald had helped him get things sorted out with his superiors and he wasn't going to face any disciplinary action for leaving early. They all agreed that as soon as Raul's scientists found out Lucy had lied his cover would be blown anyway. Given who Lucy was, who she worked for, and the potential of the drug to save so many lives, they had also agreed that she was an important asset who shouldn't be lost.

But that didn't mean he knew what happened next.

Legally, he was dead, he'd kept a house and a truck under an alias. At the time he hadn't known why, just that it had seemed like a smart idea. Did he have himself declared undead or stick with an alias? What was he going to do for work? He had some money stashed away but not enough to live on forever. Would he be offered another undercover job? If he was, should he take it or find something else to do?

And how would Lucy fit into all of that?

Just because she'd promised to be there for him didn't mean she wanted to date him. Maybe all she wanted was to be his friend, or worse, maybe she just felt sorry for him after what had happened to his team, and indebted because he'd gotten her out of Raul's house alive.

Neither was what he wanted.

When he fought down the darkness enough that he was able to be honest with himself about what he wanted, he could acknowledge that he wanted it all. Wanted a chance to date Lucy, get to know her properly, and see if he could fall in love with her. He wanted marriage and kids, wanted the whole big fairytale that Scarlett had always dreamed of and managed to find with a man who seemed to love her like she deserved.

But when the darkness was screaming at him louder than he could ignore, that was what got to him the most.

Scarlett deserved to be loved. She was sweet and kind, she

was true to herself and what she wanted. She was brave and strong. She deserved the world and the only man he would approve of for his twin sister was one who would give it to her.

Lucy deserved to be loved as well. All her life, she had been fighting to show the world that she wasn't defined by her condition, could do anything she set her mind to, and was strong and capable. And she was. She'd survived the hell Raul had put her through, and she hadn't just lived her life, she'd flourished in it. A successful scientist working for a prestigious company, doing good, and finding time to push her limits and have fun. She also deserved the world and he wanted to give it to her.

How could he though?

Because he didn't deserve to be loved.

Joining the military had broken his sister's heart and pushed away the only meaningful family he had. Then he'd allowed that distance between them to grow and hurt his twin all over again. After which he'd delivered the final nail in the coffin of their relationship and allowed her to believe he was dead.

What kind of brother did that?

Then today he'd let Lucy down as well. After lying to her and almost getting her killed she'd still been prepared—more than that, *willing*—to give him a chance. It had been clear in the way she'd looked at him as they'd kissed goodbye at the hospital that she wanted some kind of assurance that it wasn't goodbye. That she would see him again, or at the very least, he'd call or text.

As much as he'd wanted to give her that reassurance he couldn't.

Because he wasn't sure that he had what it took to give her the world. To give her the life she deserved. To love her without condition. To never fail her.

After all, he'd failed the seven men he'd been responsible for that day. Men who were family, brothers born of blood. Their deaths would forever be on his conscience, forever weighing him down with guilt he didn't deserve to be set free from. What happened in Syria was a stain on his soul that he knew sooner or later would contaminate everyone around him.

Maybe it was better that Scarlett hated him.

That hatred could keep her alive, keep her safe from his demons.

Safe from him.

Lucy might not hate him, but he could still keep her safe from him and away from his demons by taking himself out of the equation.

There was not a single doubt in Zander's mind that both his sister and the woman who had somehow managed to grab hold of his heart and make it her own would be better off without him.

He'd done what he needed to do.

Whether he was part of it or not, the date and time of the weapons deal was now in the hands of his superiors. A team would be there when it happened, and the group responsible for slaughtering his team would be stopped, either killed or captured. His team would be avenged.

What else was there left for him to do?

Eyeing the weapon still laid out on the coffee table in front of him, Zander reached out and picked it up. The weight of it in his hand was comforting, and knowing that he could extinguish both the darkness inside him and his ability to hurt the people he cared about with a single bullet filled him with a sense of peace.

CHAPTER FOURTEEN

January 26th
3:20 A.M.

HER HEAD SNAPPED in the direction of the door.

It sounded like someone was out there.

Lucy kept one hand tangled in Cotton's fur while her other trembled as she tentatively reached for the weapon sitting on her coffee table. Just because she knew how to use the gun, and just because she had a permit to own it, didn't mean she was in any way comfortable around it. Scarlett was the only one on their team who was actually confident with guns, and that was only because her parents had insisted she learn to shoot as a small child, in preparation for the life they had planned out for her. A path she hadn't wound up walking down.

Maybe she imagined the sound?

There were no more sounds, and there was no reason for anyone to be at her front door anyway.

Prey wasn't taking any chances with her safety or anyone

else's on Athena Team. Scarlett was with Tate so she was safe, and a few guys from the SEAL team who had helped rescue Scarlett were helping out by watching over her house and Ella's and Cassie's. She liked Mark "Bubba" Wright, who had been the one to disarm the bomb intended to kill Scarlett and whoever was close enough to her at the time. Trusted the man, too. He was a nice guy, married to Zoey, and while she hadn't met the woman, Lucy knew what it took to make a relationship work with a man with a job like Bubba's so she knew Zoey was a strong woman.

She was safe with Bubba out there, but knowing it and *knowing* it were two different things.

Even though it was three in the morning she had yet to make it to bed. There was too much going on in her mind to be able to settle down and sleep. Out in the jungle it had been about survival. There was no time to think about what had happened to her and the myriad of ways it had changed her.

But now …

Now there was time to think.

Too much time.

And she had no choice but to start attempting to process it all.

At least her inability to sleep might work to her advantage now. Because if there was someone out there, and they had managed to get past Bubba, then they would be expecting her to be upstairs in her bed, not in the living room with a poodle and armed with a weapon she was scared to use but absolutely would if she had to.

Another sound had her jack-knifing to her feet, causing Cotton to lift a head and shoot her an offended look. Too bad her dog was about as far away from a guard dog as you could get.

That was something.

Someone.

There was no use pretending that there wasn't someone on her porch, someone who would likely be inside in seconds, a minute at the most.

Panic swelled inside her, and her sweaty hands snatched up the gun, holding it pointed at the door.

Ready.

Just when she was about to shake herself into spontaneously combusting there was a knock on her door.

A knock?

What kind of intruder announced themselves first?

None.

Maybe it was Bubba?

She thought if he needed her for any reason, he would have texted first to let her know what the problem was then come in so he didn't scare her to death. He was lucky if she didn't put him into an early grave for scaring her like that.

A rebuke was right on the tip of her tongue as she set the weapon down and unlocked her door, opening it, but it got stuck before it could fly out.

Because it wasn't Bubba who was standing there.

It was Zander.

Took a moment for that to register. Zander was there. On her front porch. Knocking like he thought she would be up at three in the morning.

There was a hesitancy to his stance that she hadn't seen once when they were in Mexico. Then he'd been so sure and confident. It had been infuriating when she wasn't sure he could be trusted, but reassuring once she knew he was on her side.

Now his uncertainty just made her sad.

This was exactly why she'd missed him so much these last few hours. She knew he needed her, and she needed him, too.

Without allowing herself to think about what she was doing, she stepped forward and wrapped her arms around

Zander's waist, pressing close and resting her cheek on his chest, right above his heart so she could hear its steady rhythm.

When his arms moved to wrap around her, Lucy couldn't hold in a content sigh. This was perfect, this was exactly where she wanted to be. For the first time in hours, she felt the weight lift off her shoulders and her muscles relax.

Not just her. She could practically feel the tension melt away from Zander.

"I'm sorry for coming around so late, but I didn't think you'd be asleep." His voice rumbled through his chest, and the cadence of it washed over her with a soft touch that soothed her and made her feel like maybe everything could be okay.

"I wasn't asleep," she assured him.

"Is it ... okay that I'm here?"

Again, she was struck by the doubt in his voice. As if she would have wanted him anywhere else. If it was up to her, he would have come home with her after the hospital. "Of course it's okay. I missed you," she admitted. It might have only been hours since she'd last seen him, but it felt like days had passed.

"Thank goodness, because I missed the hell out of you, babe." With that, he tightened his grip around her waist, lifted her off her feet, and carried her back through the door. After locking it behind them he carried her over to the couch.

Cotton lifted her head to give them both an annoyed look but otherwise didn't move.

"Don't mind Cotton, she's the epitome of lazy. She'll be more interested in you after breakfast," Lucy said.

"Pretty dog," Zander said as he sat down and set her on his lap, and Lucy felt her cheeks heat as she realized that she liked sitting on a man's lap. Well, this man's lap anyway. It had always seemed kind of juvenile to her, sitting on some- one's lap like you were a five-year-old. But when she sat on Zander's lap, all she could feel was safety, it was like being wrapped in her very own security blanket.

It wasn't until she realized that Zander's muscles had stiffened again that Lucy realized something was wrong.

Quickly she scanned the room but nothing was there, and Cotton had gone back to sleep.

Looking up at Zander, she saw his gaze was fixed on the weapon lying discarded on her coffee table.

"I was scared," she said by way of explanation. "I know Bubba is outside, but I needed it to feel safe."

His arms tightened around her until it was just shy of painful, and his fingers gripped her chin in an unyielding hold. Lucy had no idea what was going on, but there was an almost wild look in Zander's brown eyes. "Tell me that's all it was," he demanded, the thread of fear in his voice setting off an echoing explosion of fear inside her.

"That's all it was," she told him, not really sure what he was asking her.

Then it hit.

Zander was asking her if she'd been sitting up tonight, alone and scared, traumatized by everything that had happened to her and contemplating suicide.

There hadn't been a single second where she had contem- plated taking her own life other than those first hours at Raul's house where she'd planned to try to kill the weapons dealer even if she had to end her own life to do it.

Why would Zander even be thinking that's what she was going to do?

Unless ...

Was that how he'd spent his night? Sitting at his place with a weapon in his hand, wondering whether the best way forward was to just end it all?

Breaking free from his hold, Lucy scrambled to bring him closer. "Zander, I wasn't going to kill myself, but were you?"

His eyes shuttered, and he slid her off his lap and stalked to the other side of the room, dragging his fingers through his dark hair.

He didn't get to run away from this.

From her.

This was why he'd come here, wasn't it? Because he needed someone to reassure him that if he wasn't around he would be missed. That he mattered.

Well, he *did* matter, and she would do whatever it took to convince him of that.

"Zander?" she prompted, going after him. When she placed a hand on his muscled bicep, he shrugged it off, still refusing to turn around and look at her. "Answer me, Zander, were you thinking about committing suicide? Is that why you came here?"

Ever so slowly he turned to face her. His expression was tortured and there was a hopelessness in his eyes she never wished to see again as long as she lived.

He looked so desolate, and there was a distance between them even though there were mere inches between their bodies.

"Were you thinking of killing yourself, Zander?" she asked softly.

Her heart cracked into a million pieces as he uttered his one word response. "Yes."

* * *

JANUARY 26TH
3:27 A.M.

. . .

Zander could have lied.

Told Lucy that he hadn't spent the last few hours staring at a picture of him with his team taken shortly before they left on that fateful mission. It was taken at one of the guy's houses, and they were having a cookout, laughing and being silly, enjoying the moment of perfectly normal life because they knew how quickly their circumstances could change.

Little did they know how badly and how quickly.

Three weeks later, he was the only one of the eight men in the photo left alive. Four women left widows, six children who would grow up without their fathers.

Looking at that photo, knowing what had been lost because of his refusal to follow his gut, and his overconfidence in believing his Delta Force team was more skilled, more intelligent, and more determined than their enemy.

Gone now.

No way to get them back.

And one very easy way to join them in death.

Told her that it was her he was worried about and not himself.

Anything to get the look of fear out of the wide blue eyes that stared up at him.

But he couldn't do it.

Because when he'd been sitting in his dark living room, the photo in one hand, weapon in the other, there had been a tiny pinprick of light shining at the back of his mind. A voice echoing in his ears.

"I won't ask you for promises, Zander, but I'm making you one. I'm here. Right here. For as long as you'll let me be. I'll wait, I'll give you space, or not, whatever you want. I'm just here. For you."

"I'm here for you. I'm not going anywhere."

Lucy's words.

Her promises.

They were the only string keeping him tied to the world

of the living and they'd tightened tonight, drawing him here. Bringing him to her because as badly as he didn't want to drag her down into the darkness, without her light he was already lost.

Dropping his forehead to rest against hers so he didn't have to see her expression of terror any longer, he whispered, "Yeah, babe. I thought about it. Came close to doing it, but I couldn't. Because of you."

Knowing the pressure he was putting on Lucy wasn't fair and only made him feel worse. They might have known each other for a few years, but only ever at a distance. She was Scarlett's friend, and he was Scarlett's brother. Attraction might have simmered between them from the beginning, but chemistry didn't build relationships, it was merely a stepping-stone to get you started.

There had been no meaningful talk of the future. They'd exchanged numbers but at the time he hadn't been sure he'd ever call or text. They were at the very beginning of something that might lead to a future or might crash and burn.

Yet here he was, resting his very life on Lucy's shoulders.

"Didn't know where else to go," he admitted softly.

Arms wrapped around him, holding on with a strength that belied Lucy's small stature. "You came to the right place. You came to what you knew was a safe place. And you believed in me, Zander. You trusted me. You didn't think I was incapable of giving you what you needed, or that I wasn't strong enough to hold you up. You just came here. To me. I can't tell you how happy I am that you did."

Her words surprised him. They were so immediately accepting of the fact that he'd done the right thing, and joy that he had seen her for the strong, capable woman that she was.

Something inside him eased a little. His heart had known

this was where he had to be even if his head had tried to talk him out of it.

"It might not be fair, babe, but I ... need you." The words felt foreign on his tongue. He was supposed to be a warrior, but even a warrior had a team at his back, and he was in desperate need of a team.

"You have me, Zander." Lucy pulled back enough only to be able to look up at him, her arms remained locked around his waist. "Always. Even if things don't work out between us, I will always be here for you. Always. No matter what. Any time, day or night, you can come here, and I'll give you whatever you need. Thank you, for not taking you away from me."

Those words and the accompanying tears shimmering like diamonds in her blue eyes had him clutching her to him, lifting her feet off the floor so he could just hold her. "You would miss me if I wasn't around?" That seemed crazy since things had only progressed between them in the last couple of days, but he needed to know that despite everything he'd done, someone would care if he wasn't around.

In answer Lucy crushed her mouth to his, kissing him with a passion that branded his heart. "Don't ever ask me something so stupid ever again. Of *course* I would miss you. I want a chance to explore this thing between us. I'm not going to push you because I know you're dealing with a lot, but it doesn't change what I want."

"Even knowing what I allowed to happen?"

"Even knowing you believe you're responsible for what happened," she replied, arching a brow to make sure he noticed how she phrased it.

As if he'd missed it.

"Even knowing there's a darkness inside me I'm not sure I can control?"

"A man who can keep his back to a woman orgasming over and over again for over an hour, knowing that if he wanted to, she would have said yes to sex is one who has impeccable control. I'm not afraid of you, Zander. Maybe I was when I didn't know whose side you were on, but not anymore. Not ever. I'm so glad you came tonight."

"I am, too," he admitted. "I thought maybe it wasn't fair to put this on you because you've already been through so much."

"Yeah, I have," she agreed. "And right now, I don't even know which way is up, I haven't even begun to process anything, but I know that when you're here I feel grounded. I'm not a balloon floating up into space because you're holding the string. Will you make love to me, Zander?"

There was nothing on earth he'd love more than to bury himself inside this woman and allow her light to soak into him, soothing the damaged pieces and giving him hope that maybe one day life might seem bright again.

Or maybe bright for the first time ever.

With Lucy, all things seemed possible.

Since she had her legs wrapped around his hips, he placed one hand beneath her backside while his other palmed her cheek. "Are you sure, baby?" Sex wasn't why he'd come there tonight, and in Lucy's own words she hadn't even begun to process what had happened to her, the last thing she needed was him taking advantage.

"If I wasn't sure I wouldn't have asked." Her smile was soft and warm, and he loved the way it made him feel.

"I don't think I have it in me for slow and sweet this time around," he warned her. There were too many emotions raging inside him.

"Take me however you want me."

Those words were a precious gift and one he treasured as he balanced Lucy's weight with one hand, shoved down his pants and boxers enough to free himself, and then pushed Lucy's yoga pants and panties out of the way.

While he couldn't give her slow and sweet, he was already rock hard and aching, he wasn't going to take her without making sure she got off at least twice.

"Hold onto me, babe," he ordered as he lifted her up and set her on his shoulders so her legs hung down his back and her center was spread open and ready for him to devour.

"Zander, you can't—" Lucy's words cut off, turning into a moan as his hands gripped her tight backside and his tongue darted out to swipe across her already wet core.

"Yeah, I can," he said, smiling as another moan tumbled from her lips as his tongue nudged at her opening.

Licking and nipping, he alternated between thrusting his tongue inside her tight, wet heat and playing with the bundle of nerves that quickly had her body beginning to quiver as pleasure built inside her. There was no better sound in the world than hearing his woman in the throes of making love. It was the sweetest sound and matched only by the sweet taste of her on his lips as he ate her as though he were starving.

And he was.

Starving for love that had been denied him as a child.

It was freeing to admit he wanted everything his sister had always believed in, everything he thought he could find with the woman seconds away from coming on his tongue.

Taking her bud between his lips, Zander sucked hard, raking his teeth over the sensitive bundle of nerves, and Lucy came on a scream.

Her internal muscles were still quivering when he lifted her down and buried himself inside her in one thrust.

Their eyes met, hers hazy with pleasure, cheeks tinted the prettiest shade of pink, and held as he began to rock his hips, building a steady pace that would soon have them tumbling over the ledge together.

Together.

Such a beautiful word.

But not more beautiful than his girl.

Taking her mouth, he kissed her slowly, sensuously, pouring into it all the words he didn't know how to say aloud.

Working her bud with his thumb, he held onto the orgasm ready to explode inside him, waiting until Lucy was ready to join him. When he could feel her teetering on the edge he pressed hard with his thumb, deepened the kiss, and Lucy let go. He did, too, and they fell together, locked in a world of pleasure, a world where everything was perfect.

Hope and fear warred inside him.

Because while Lucy offered him a future brighter than he could ever have imagined, there was somebody out there who was prepared to play games with her life. He couldn't allow himself to forget that it had to have been the mole who messed with his plane, because it hadn't been Raul or his men.

So long as the mole was out there, Lucy was in danger, and there was a chance that his life would remain cloaked in darkness forever.

Without Lucy, there would be no light.

CHAPTER FIFTEEN

January 26th
9:31 A.M.

"WE'RE LATE," Zander said as they walked through the front doors of Prey.

"Mmm, yep. A whole one minute," Lucy teased. Actually, she usually hated to be late. Her parents were the kind of people who left more than enough time to make it somewhere at least fifteen minutes early, and then left another thirty minutes or so before that. As a kid, they'd spent so much time sitting in the car waiting for an acceptable time to go inside wherever it was they were going that they were all experts at car games.

Today, though, she didn't care about being late. Because she wouldn't have traded the hours she and Zander had spent together for anything. They'd managed a couple of hours of sleep in her bed, tangled in one another's arms. Then showered together and made waffles for breakfast.

Those moments were even more precious because not

only were they getting to know one another and starting to make memories together—good memories rather than those of running for their lives in Mexico—but they could so easily not have happened.

She'd come dangerously close to losing Zander before he was ever even hers.

Never would she take for granted a single second with this man who held her hand like it was the most natural thing in the world.

There was still a chance she could lose him. He was battling his demons the best way he knew how, but Lucy knew he was struggling, doubting himself and his place in the world. All she could do was be there for him and hope and pray it was enough. Despite what Zander thought, the world wouldn't be a better place without him in it. He was not responsible for what happened to his team, and of course, there was a darkness inside him after living through an ordeal like that.

Already, she could feel tendrils of darkness inside her own soul, and she hadn't suffered half as much as Zander had.

But they were home, they were safe, and they were together, and for now that was enough.

"One minute now." Zander threw a quick glance at her. "But by the time we get in the lift, and get up to the third floor, and then into the conference room—"

"We'll be maybe four minutes late at the most," she finished for him.

"Lucy!" Dora Hibbert came out from behind the reception desk and threw her arms around her in a crushing hug. While definitely a sweet woman, Dora had a habit of being a little too touchy feely, Lucy knew it sometimes made the guys, who were all happily married, a little uncomfortable. "I'm so glad you're okay. I was so worried when I heard that your plane went down, and then hearing that you were captured." Dora shuddered. "So awful. I'm so glad you're home safely now."

"Thank you, Dora." Lucy returned the woman's hug. Despite her over-demonstrative personality, and the fact that she was the hub of office gossip, they all knew that without Dora, things would not run so smoothly around here. "This is ..." she trailed off, realizing she'd been about to introduce Zander as Scarlett's brother, but call her selfish she wanted to introduce him as hers. Only her what? "My ..."

"Boyfriend," Zander supplied, and she stared up at him in shock. Was he ready to call himself that? It was what she wanted, but she was surprised he'd said it like it was no big deal, especially after what he'd been considering last night.

"Oh." Dora looked confused as she glanced at their joined hands. "I thought you were Zander Madden, Scarlett's brother."

"He is," Lucy said.

"Oh," Dora said again, this time with a hint of reproach like Lucy was doing something wrong by dating her friend's brother.

Was that how everybody else saw it?

Did they think she was betraying her friend by going out with Zander?

She sincerely hoped that wasn't true because she wasn't giving Zander up. Not for anybody, not even Scarlett. Zander needed her, and she needed him, too.

"We've got to get upstairs, Zander doesn't like to be late." She shot him a teasing smile so that he knew she was okay with Dora looking down on her, nothing was making her walk away from him. She'd made him a promise and it was one she intended to keep.

When they got into the lift, she could sense Zander emotionally withdrawing, and since she was having none of that, she literally threw herself at him so he had no choice but to catch her. Once he did, Lucy wrapped her arms around his neck and her legs around his waist, wrapping her smaller body around as much of his as she could.

"Don't pull away from me, Zander. I don't care what Dora thinks. I'm here for you. Not because I have to be, not because I owe you since you saved me, and not because I feel sorry for you, although my heart does break for what you've been through. I'm here for you because I want to be, and because there's nowhere else I'd rather be."

When he smiled and she felt some of the tension ebb out of his body, she relaxed, knowing she'd gotten through to him. "Do you read minds, sassy girl?"

"Yep, sure do," she teased, and then because she couldn't be this close to him and not kiss him, she leaned in and brushed her lips across his.

Framing her face with his hands, his fingertips swept across her cheekbones. "Thank you doesn't seem to be big enough for how I feel about you being here for me."

"I said the same thing to you when you saved my life, and you told me there were no thanks necessary," she reminded him.

"You really are a sassy girl, aren't you, babe?"

"Only with you," she whispered, which was absolutely the truth. Serious, that was the word most people would use to describe her, but with Zander she felt freedom not to have to prove herself. If he didn't believe in her, he wouldn't have come to her when he was at rock bottom.

"That you feel free to be yourself with me means more to me than you can ever know," Zander whispered back, and then his lips were on hers and he was kissing her in the same way he had last night, like he was pouring his whole heart into it. Was there anything better than when someone kissed you with their whole being?

"Eww, my eyes, why are you two making out in the elevator?"

The voice had them both breaking the kiss and turning to find Grayson "Chaos" Simpson standing in the open lift door grinning at them. The man was a top-tier prankster who loved nothing more than making the lives of everybody around him his playground as he looked for ways to outdo himself. From the grin on his face, he was obviously pleased to have been the one to break up their kiss and embarrass them.

"As if I haven't had to watch you and Juliet make out a million times," she tossed back as Zander set her on her feet and reclaimed his hold on her hand.

"Hey, that's because we're adults, and you two are still kids," Chaos said.

"There's not even ten-years difference in our ages," she reminded him as they all headed for the conference room.

"Ten years is a lot, kiddo." Chaos ruffled her hair as he walked along beside her making her take a swing at his shoulder and miss when he dodged out of the way.

"You are impossible, I don't know how Juliet puts up with you, and now you have two little munchkins you're training to be just like you. Poor Jules."

"My woman loves me and the fun I bring into her life," Chaos said with another grin, and it was absolutely true, the couple was madly in love, and their two little boys were adorable, even if the three-year-old was following in his daddy's jokester footsteps.

"Nice of you to join us," Owen "Fox" LeGrand said as the three of them entered the room. Although her boss didn't look angry with them, he did look stressed. Not a good thing.

Actually, everybody looked stressed. The rest of the guys who ran Prey's East Coast office along with Fox and Chaos, Ryder "Spider" Flynn, Eric "Night" McNamara, Logan

"Shark" Kirk, and Charlie "King" Voss, all had tense expressions. As did Rocco's SEAL Team who were also in the room. Decker "Gumby" Kincade, Beckett "Ace" Morgan, Cole "Rex" Kingston, Forest "Phantom" Dalton, and Bubba.

The tension in the room quickly wiped away any joy she'd felt in the elevator a minute ago. Something bad was going on.

"Told you we were going to be late," Zander leaned down to murmur in her ear, and since she knew he was trying to get her to relax, she forced out a breath and calmed herself.

"I don't think they care," she murmured back. "What's going on? Is it bad news? Did we find the mole?" That would be both good and bad news. At least the threat would be over, but they'd all have to face the fact that someone who had worked with them had betrayed them.

"No news on the mole. Or Raul Castillo," Fox added.

"Then what?"

Fox's dark eyes shifted to Zander. "The weapons deal went down last night, right when and where your intel said it was going to."

Zander didn't relax or rejoice at the news because they both knew something else was coming.

"But?" Zander asked.

"But Zafir Mostafa's younger brother was able to escape with a handful of men before their camp was raided," Fox informed them. "Zimraan wasn't among the dead or those taken into custody, and word is, he's out for vengeance against the man he believes to be responsible for his brother's death."

Fox didn't have to name names.

The Syrian terrorist wanted revenge against Zander.

* * *

JANUARY 26TH
    12:19 P.M.

HIS HEAD WAS STILL REELING from everything they'd discussed at the meeting.

Zimraan Mostafa was out to avenge his brother's death and he was placing the blame squarely on Zander's shoulders.

That meant he wasn't safe.

Worse than that, it meant Lucy wasn't safe.

As far as he could tell there were only three options. One, he hunt down the Syrian terrorist himself. Two, go into hiding and just disappear, something that was absolutely doable, if he wanted he could just fall off the face of the Earth and nobody would ever find him unless he wanted to be found. Or three, he stayed there, watched Lucy's back, protected what was his, and trusted that Prey had his back.

Trusting anyone was hard after what he'd been through. Just because it wasn't betrayal, just faulty intel that got him and his team captured, it didn't mean he hadn't lost faith in the system. His faith in everything, most importantly himself, had been shattered.

Running was what his brain was urging him to do. The darkness inside him as well. It whispered insidiously that he couldn't protect Lucy, that he'd fail her just like he failed the rest of his men.

"We can do this, Zander. We have your back. All of us. I know you lost your team and having another one must be terrifying, but these guys are some of the best, just as skilled as your guys were. Prey will be there for you, every step of the way. Please don't run. Trust us, or at least trust me, to have your back."

Looking down at Lucy, at her imploring blue eyes, there was no way he could say no to her.

"I'll stay, baby. But I think you're the only one here who wants to be on my team." Zander couldn't help but feel like the others were only tolerating him because of Lucy, looking down on him for betraying his sister like he had.

"No," she said, shaking her head so firmly her blonde locks went swishing about it. "Absolutely not. If Eagle didn't trust you, there is no way he would have let me get on a plane with you. And if these guys didn't trust you, then you wouldn't be here. Trust me on that. Prey is a family, and *you* are part of that family. Because you're important to me, sure, but I'm not the only one who you're important to."

When Lucy looked over his shoulder to the other end of the long conference table, Zander reluctantly shifted so he could follow her gaze.

Scarlett was sitting there along with Tate, and all throughout the meeting she'd been shooting him looks he couldn't decipher. Zander no longer knew how to read his twin sister's expressions, even though it used to be as natural as breathing.

"Every single one of these guys knows you were in an impossible situation. They all understand why you faked your death, and I don't think any one of them could say they wouldn't do the same in your situation. You should know," Lucy added, "that Tate had your sister arrested because he thought it was the right thing to do under the circumstances."

"He did what now?" Zander growled, making Lucy chuckle.

"Everyone makes mistakes, Zander, because we're all human. Go talk to your sister, she misses you, and she's scared of losing you again, it's why she's pushing you away."

"Did she say that?"

"Yeah, she did. Go."

With a nod, he slowly pushed away from the table. Scarlett watched his approach, only looking away briefly when Tate whispered something in her ear and dropped a quick kiss to her lips.

Since she didn't tell him to get the hell away from her, he pulled out the chair beside her and took a seat. The SEAL guys had left about ten minutes ago as had the Prey guys, so it was only him, Lucy, Scarlett, Ella, Cassie, and Tate left in the conference room. The others had gathered down near Lucy and no one was looking at him and his sister, and he appreciated them giving the two of them some space.

"I'm sorry, Scarlett," he said. It didn't seem like enough for what he'd put his sister through, just like it hadn't seemed like enough this morning when he'd been with Lucy. But it was all he had to give her. There was no going back and doing it all over again. What was done was done, and they all had to live with the consequences of his choices.

"I don't understand why you'd tell Mom and Dad you were alive but not me." The raw pain in his sister's voice tore at his heart, ripping off the scabs of wounds that were only just beginning to heal and making them bleed freely all over again.

Somehow, with the two of them, it always came back to their parents.

Just because they'd never been physically abused didn't mean there weren't a lot of scars littering both of them. They'd been neglected, lived with strict rules, and been pushed to do things most kids their age had never heard of, like learn to fight hand-to-hand combat, shoot weapons, use a knife, and survivalist training. They'd been shoved into the foster system, and both of them had learned over and over again that their parents didn't love them.

Dragging his hands down his face he met his sister's eyes,

his eyes because while they might not be identical twins, couldn't since they were opposite genders, they were carbon copies of one another. No one could mistake them as strangers, they looked as much like siblings as it was possible to look.

"It wasn't like that, Scar. I swear it wasn't. My team and I were captured. We were kept in the hot sun, chained up in a dusty courtyard. One by one, they killed my team in front of me. Cut their bodies to pieces while they were still alive."

Scarlett gasped, a hand flying to her mouth.

Part of him wanted to censor what he was saying, but he knew she had to hear it to understand.

"We were there a week. They killed one man every day. They took pleasure in their pain, wanted to punish me for not giving up intel, and refusing to beg and plead for our lives. I carry the pain my men suffered on my shoulders. I never expected to survive. They didn't feed us and gave us only enough water to keep us alive, by the time we were rescued, I was in bad shape. I didn't want to live, fought the team that was trying to save me because I wanted my blood to spill in the same place my team's did."

"Zander." Scarlett's hand covered his, squeezing tightly, and he felt and heard her pain. They were twins, they shared a bond not many people could understand, they were tied together from their very conception.

"I didn't call Mom and Dad, Scar. They're my parents, I'm not married so they're considered next of kin. The military notified them not me. They reiterated every single doubt and fear I had, told me I was a terrible soldier and I should have died with my team. I couldn't face you, Scarlett, I couldn't take the chance you would feel the same way. That would have broken me."

"Oh, Zander, that makes me so much madder at you and breaks my heart all at the same time." The next thing he knew his sister was fighting her way onto his lap, wrapping her arms around him and holding him close. "I'm your twin sister, I love you, for so long it was just the two of us against the world. I would *never* say those things to you. Ever. How could you think I would?"

"Wasn't in a good place, Scar. I wasn't thinking clearly."

"I wish you didn't care so much about what Mom and Dad think about you."

"I don't. Not anymore." He'd learned the hard way not to bother trying to earn their love. "When I was approached about the undercover op, I didn't want you to have to mourn me twice, so I just left things as they were. Plotting my revenge was the only thing that I could think about, and I believed you were better off without me in your life anyway."

"I'm not better off without you, Zandy. Not ever."

Lucy had said the same thing to him, and when he glanced over he saw her watching him and Scarlett with a smile.

"You really like her, huh?" Scarlett asked, following his line of sight.

"I do. A lot. Is that okay?" Zander wasn't sure he could break things off with Lucy for anyone, not even his twin sister.

"It's more than okay. I love Lucy, she's like a sister to me, and if you two wind up getting married, then one day she really will be my sister."

That made him laugh. "One day at a time, Scar. One day at a time." For now, that was a good mantra. It would take time for him to heal, time for Lucy to heal, too, and they weren't in any rush. They had the rest of their lives to be together. "So, am I forgiven?"

"Are you planning on putting me through thinking you're dead again?"

"No, Scar, I learned my lesson. Family is what's most

important. Real family not the kind that's yours only through DNA. You, Lucy, that's what's important to me, I don't ever want to lose you."

"You won't, Zandy. And Lucy will be good for you, I think you'll be good for her, too. I'm happy for you, for both of us, we both managed to find someone despite our example of relationships and love growing up."

They had both been lucky, but someone was threatening his family, and he didn't take kindly to threats. Zimraan Mostafa, Raul Castillo, and the mole at Prey were all going down.

CHAPTER SIXTEEN

January 26th
  4:42 P.M.

"You didn't have to come with me, but I'm really glad you did," Lucy told Zander as he opened the passenger door of his truck.

"No place else I'd rather be," he said as his large hands circled her hips, and he lifted her up and into the seat.

That earned an eye roll. "Yeah, I totally believe you. Because sitting in a doctor's office for almost two hours is everybody's idea of a good time."

A grim lit up his face. "Okay, so it was the company not the location that was perfect."

There was a lightness to him that hadn't been there before. It was obvious that making things right with his sister had helped a lot, but she also wondered if it was knowing he had a team at his back again that eased some of his anxiety.

Being undercover must be hell.

Besides the obvious that you were never able to relax, that you had to remain "on" at all times or risk getting found out, you were all alone. There was nobody to watch your six. Nobody to take a turn being on guard so you could get some proper sleep. You had to do and say things that were not only distasteful, but downright disgusting in order to maintain your cover. And there was not an end necessarily in sight. A job could last days, weeks, months, or even years. For Zander, it had been eighteen months of pretending that he was a rogue former Delta Force operator who had faked his death and gone to the dark side.

It hurt to think of Zander alone and hurting, believing he had nothing to live for and nobody who would miss him when he was gone. To know that his plan had always involved him ending his own life at the end when he finally got justice for the team he had loved and lost.

"Babe?" Gentle hands brushed featherlight caresses across her cheeks, and she blinked to make Zander's worried expression come into focus. "Where did you go just now?"

Since they had already decided there was going to be no more lies or half-truths between them, she lifted her good hand and grasped his wrist. "Just thinking about how much you went through and how glad I am that you're not alone anymore. You have Scarlett, and all of Prey, and you have me. I don't ever want you to feel alone again."

A smile transformed him from handsome to downright sinfully gorgeous. "Babe, can I tell you a secret?"

"Mmhmm."

"As long as I have you, I can't ever be alone again. Want to know why?"

"Is that a trick question?" she sassed.

"No, babe." The grin slid from his face, and he got all serious. "It's because you're here." Taking one of her hands, he pressed it to his chest, above his heart. "I don't know how you got in there, but I'm glad you did. And because you did, I'll never be alone again."

Because when Zander was around, emotions she didn't usually have any problem controlling just bubbled up and insisted they be expressed, tears flooded her eyes, making Zander's handsome face go all blurry. "No one has ever said something that beautiful to me before."

Another smile lit up his face. "Good. I don't want anyone else saying beautiful things to you again. That's my job now."

Again with the sweet words. He was killing her here. It wasn't like she had been avoiding looking for a partner or that she was against the idea of falling in love, and she even believed that love existed, she'd seen it in her parents growing up. It was just that maybe, deep down, she'd believed that she would never meet someone who would see her as strong and capable, who could handle her condition and the limitations it placed on her.

Because no matter how many times she insisted to others and to herself that her epilepsy didn't control her life, there were a lot of ways it did in fact impact a lot of what she did and the choices she made.

But Zander looked beyond that.

He just saw ... her.

"Your job, huh?" she asked, hoping he meant that and wasn't going to disappear as soon as all of this mess, hers and his, was sorted.

"Hoping I don't get fired." Unlike last night, there was no doubt in his eyes this time around, no uncertainty, somewhere along the way over the last few hours he seemed to have just accepted the fact that they were together.

Now it was her having the doubts.

The doubts weren't about whether or not she wanted to be with Zander and give this relationship a real chance, they were about external factors. Raul Castillo, the mole, the terrorist's brother who wanted Zander dead, his own demons that while temporarily quietened could come roaring back to life and steal him from her.

But today she wasn't going to worry about the future, she was just going to enjoy this moment when everything with Zander was fresh and new. It was exciting, getting to know someone who was already so important to her, and she didn't want to miss any of it because she was worried about problems that right now, she couldn't fix.

"I don't think I have any plans to fire you anytime soon, Zander."

His smile was magic, and the kiss he dropped to her lips made her body tingle and her toes curl.

When he pulled back, she mewled a protest. She could quite happily spend the rest of her life kissing Zander.

Actually, she'd love to spend the rest of her life kissing Zander.

The man knew how to kiss, and she absolutely loved how he poured so much emotion into it. All the things they hadn't talked about yet, she felt with each stroke of his tongue. They were both falling hard and fast and it was as scary as it was exciting.

"Can I take you out to dinner?" Zander asked.

"Like a date?"

"A proper date. No jungles, no sleeping in caves, no plane crashes, and no armed gunmen. Just a guy taking out the most beautiful girl in the world."

His sweet words made her blush. She was hardly the most beautiful woman in the world. Her hair was twisted up into a messy bun, she wasn't wearing any makeup, and she was dressed in jeans and her favorite old hoodie, with a simple pair of white sneakers on her feet. While clean, she still kind of felt like the same bedraggled waif she'd been out in the Mexican jungle.

"I'd love to go out to dinner, but I'm going to need to go home to shower and change," she said, already running through outfits in her mind. Outfits that would make her look even half as pretty as Zander seemed to think she was.

"You look perfect just as you are."

"Are you patronizing me, Zandy?" she demanded, deliberately using Scarlett's childhood nickname for her brother because she knew she'd get a reaction out of him.

As predicted, his eyes narrowed and he leaned in close, his hands braced on either side of the doorframe as he crowded her. "What did you call me, sassy girl?"

"You prefer ghost man instead?" she asked with a sweetly innocent smile. While she knew the nickname had bothered him at first, she also knew that things had changed and it wouldn't hurt him any longer. It was weird, but in a good way, being able to read someone so clearly.

"You're going to pay for that one, baby girl." With that, his hands moved so fast they were nothing but blurs, and then they were on the sides of her stomach tickling her.

There was only one way he could know that she was ticklish, and her friend was going to pay for passing along that little tidbit to her twin brother.

"Stop!" she squealed as she squirmed in her seat, laughing hysterically as she tried to squiggle out of the way of Zander's relentless fingers.

"Not so funny now, are you, sassy girl?" Zander teased as he continued tickling her.

"Okay, okay! You win, I won't call you Zandy anymore!"

"Oh, that was too easy, baby girl. I thought you'd put up so much more of a fight." Zander's fingertips caught the tears of laughter streaming down her cheeks.

"I only promised not to call you Zandy, I'm sure I can think up plenty of other fun nicknames," she said, throwing him a grin.

"You think you're so smart don't you? You're going to be a challenge every step of the way, aren't you, my sassy girl?"

"The best things in life are always a challenge," she shot back.

Smoothing a stray lock of hair off her cheek, he tucked it behind her ear, then palmed her cheek. "You couldn't be more right. And I think I just found the best thing I could ever have hoped for."

With those sweet words his lips met hers, searing them with a claiming kiss that stirred up fire in her body. Lucy felt the same way, she'd been given something so special in this man and she didn't want to lose it.

Please, God, don't let anyone—not even Zander himself—take him from me.

* * *

JANUARY 26TH
8:59 P.M.

LUCY WAS GIGGLING as he unlocked his front door, and honestly, Zander couldn't think of a more beautiful sound.

All afternoon her smile had just grown and grown.

The date he'd planned had been simple and fun. They'd been through some heavy stuff in the last week, and he wanted this to be the complete opposite. While he had every intention of making their next date super romantic, this one had just been about letting go of all the stress they were both carrying.

First, he'd taken her to an indoor trampoline park where she'd wowed him with her ability to flip and turn like she'd been doing it all her life. Lucy had admitted she'd taken gymnastics as a kid, after a lot of begging and pleading on her part because her parents were worried that she might have a seizure while in the middle of performing on the beam or bars. Even though she said she hadn't done any gymnastics since she quit when she was fifteen, she was still really good.

Next up was skateboarding. While she claimed she'd never done it before, Lucy had picked it up quickly and even mastered a couple of easy tricks. Skating had been his dirty little secret as a kid. It wasn't something his parents and grandparents approved of, since in their minds it had served no practical purpose. But he'd done it anyway, saved his allowance and bought the skateboard, and kept it hidden in a back corner of the shed, since he was in charge of tending to the garden nobody else went out there anyway.

The woman never ceased to amaze him with her skills and ability to pick things up quickly. What had taken him weeks as a preteen to master, Lucy had managed in just a couple of hours.

He also loved that she hadn't cared that he didn't take her to a fancy restaurant. She was perfectly content with pizza and soda, sitting in his truck watching the waves crash on the shore. Every time he looked at her, Zander wondered how he'd gotten this lucky because he sure as hell had never done a thing in his life that made him worthy of Lucy Elrod.

Now he had her home and with her twinkling eyes and bright smile there was no way he could resist dragging her into his arms a second longer.

"You're stunning, do you know that?" he whispered against her ear as he swung his door shut and pressed her up against it.

Her sharp intake of air and the widening eyes were enough to know she was every bit as anxious as he was to be alone.

"I'm not ... bad to look at ... I guess," Lucy stammered, a

hint of doubt in her beautiful eyes. It was clear his girl still had a tendency to think less of herself because while with the best of intentions, her family had continuously made her feel lacking and not completely capable.

A growl rumbled through his chest because he didn't like the idea of Lucy doubting a single thing about herself. From her face to her body to her brain, she was a perfect ten out of ten. There was not a single thing lacking in her.

"Nobody disrespects my woman. Not even my woman," he warned as he nipped at her neck and then swirled the tip of his tongue over the reddened flesh.

"Mmm, do that again," Lucy murmured, tilting her head to the side to give him better access.

"You like my mouth on you, baby girl?" he asked, taking a step back and smiling as Lucy mewled a protest.

"Yes," Lucy said, voice gone all heated and needy, the sound sending every drop of blood in his body running south.

"Then you strip and let me see every inch of that perfect body."

There was a flare of surprise in her gaze, but it was quickly replaced by desire that only added fuel to the fire raging inside him. The only thing in the world that could quench this fire was the woman standing before him.

Hands trembling a little, Lucy moved them to the hem of her hoodie and pulled it up and over her head, then dropped it to the floor beside her. A delicate lace bra in the prettiest shade of pale blue that matched her eyes cupped both of her perfect breasts, holding them the way his hands longed to. Already he knew how receptive those nipples could be as he sucked them into his mouth and played with them with his tongue and teeth.

A small moan fell from her lips, and he saw a tremor

rocket through Lucy's body, and he smirked, loving how he could affect her with just a hungry look.

"You wearing the matching panties, babe?"

"I guess you'll have to wait to find out," Lucy sassed as she kicked off her sneakers. This time he was the one to groan because he already knew the answer from the amusement dancing in her eyes, and he couldn't wait to see her standing there in nothing but scraps of blue lace.

With excruciating slowness—which he knew was precisely the point because his sassy girl gave as good as she got—Lucy hooked her thumbs into the waistband of her jeans and inched them down her legs. By the time she finally stepped out of them he was regretting his decision to ask her to strip for him because he could have had her out of those clothes so much quicker if he'd done it himself.

But it was worth the wait.

She was worth the wait.

It felt like all his life he'd been on hold waiting for her to come into his life. At the time, he hadn't felt like anything was missing, but now he knew he'd been walking around with a gaping hole that this woman had filled.

Filled so completely that he felt whole for the first time ever.

"See, stunning," he said as he took a step closer and cupped both breasts in his hands, enjoying the slight weight of them resting in his palms.

"You make me feel stunning," Lucy whispered. "I know my body is okay, I work hours at the gym to prove to everyone I'm strong and capable, and I've had men tell me before that I'm beautiful ... but I'm not sure I ever really felt it until now. Until you. The way you look at me, that makes me feel stunning. It makes me feel gorgeous inside and out."

"Because you are, baby girl. Absolutely gorgeous and stunning and beautiful inside and out." Pulling her delectable body up against his, he ground his hard length against the apex of her thighs. "Ever been skinny dipping?"

Her eyes widened, and her cheeks pinked, and the tip of her tongue ran across her bottom lip as she shook her head.

Dragging his thumb along the path her tongue had just trailed, he asked, "Want to go skinny dipping with me, babe?"

"Skinny dipping?" Lucy squeaked and he could guess that her good girl persona had never done anything like that before. It was one thing to hunt down adrenalin pumping sports to prove to people—and yourself—you were capable, it was another to take risks like the one he was asking her to take with him.

"I've got a pool in the backyard. It's beautiful like a trop-ical oasis. It's the reason I bought this place even though I didn't think I'd ever use it. I was going to find a way to give it to my sister. There are ferns and a rock waterslide, and a pretty little waterfall. Take this risk with me, babe?"

When Lucy nodded her agreement, he knew she'd just given him the most precious gift possible.

Her trust.

Something he didn't deserve but would treasure forever.

Making quick work of stripping out of his jeans and shirt, he then turned Lucy around and crowded against her back. "This soft skin of yours is going to look so delectable with the moonlight glistening off droplets of water." He murmured the words against the spot where her shoulder and neck met, then dropped a kiss to it.

"You do know it's winter, right? It's going to be freezing," Lucy said, looking over her shoulder at him through heavy-lidded eyes.

"I can guarantee I'll keep you warm, babe. The heat between us is going to make steam, I promise you."

She laughed and he undid her bra and let her breasts spill out into his hands. The laugh turned into a moan when he kneaded the small mounds, tweaking her nipples until they hardened into little pebbles beneath his ministrations.

"Just so you know, babe, I'm keeping this underwear," he whispered in her ear, touching a featherlight kiss to her earlobe before trailing a line of kisses down her spin as he knelt behind her. When he pulled the lacy panties down her legs, revealing the two perfect round globes of her tight backside, he touched kisses to each cheek, then stood, scooping her into his arms as he did.

"I can't believe I'm doing this," Lucy said with a giggle as he carried her through the dark house and out into the yard. It was a beautiful winter night. The sky was a clear, inky black, and a million stars scattered across it, sparkling like diamonds.

"I can. You're so brave and strong, you face everything life throws at you with such determination and pragmatism. You're an inspiration, sassy girl. My sassy girl."

His.

And he was never letting her go.

No one was going to take her from him. Not Zimraan Mostafa, not Raul Castillo, and not the mole at Prey.

Possessiveness filled him as he carried them to the edge of the pool. "You know the only way to do this is to jump right on in."

The warning was the only one she got before he jumped into the deep end.

Seconds later, freezing water surrounded his entire body.

In his arms, Lucy squealed as the cold water enveloped her as well, but she made no move to try to get out of the pool.

Swimming through the water, Zander stopped in the opening of the little cave with water sprinkling down on them from the waterfall that hid it. As predicted, the moonlight reflected on each droplet of water that ran down Lucy's creamy white skin, and he brushed a few droplets off her face as he cupped her cheeks in his palms.

"Don't think I can wait another second to be inside you, babe."

"Thank goodness, because I'm about ready to come just from you looking at me."

Chuckling, he gripped Lucy's hips, lined them up, and slid inside her in one thrust. "Touch yourself, baby girl. Make yourself come."

Lucy's good hand moved to where their bodies joined, finding her bud and circling it as her braced arm rested on his shoulder. "Move, Zander, let me feel you moving inside me."

Not needing to be told twice, his lips found hers as he thrust in and out of her. His pace increased as he felt them both getting closer to reaching the peak, growing almost frantic as Lucy began to buck against him as her orgasm shimmered into existence.

The second she cried out, and her internal muscles clamped around him, he let go. Let pleasure take over, sweeping through him with the force of a tornado, leaving him feeling physically drained but emotionally full.

With the heavens smiling down on them with the myriad of twinkling stars, Zander sent up a silent prayer as he snuggled his girl close.

Don't take her from me.

Don't make me lose her, too.

I can't survive losing has as well.

CHAPTER SEVENTEEN

January 27th
   7:53 A.M.

"WE'RE NOT GOING to be late this morning," Lucy said as they drove toward Prey's offices. She made the comment more to break the silence than for any other reason.

Something had changed when they climbed into the car this morning.

It wasn't like there was distance between them. They'd already made love twice this morning. Once she'd woken with Zander's head between her legs, then they'd had a little fun in the shower. The good and playful mood continued through breakfast and when they got out to the car. After helping her up into her seat, Zander had kissed her like he hated the idea of taking her away from his place where they could just make out whenever the urge arose.

But as soon as they'd begun driving, he'd started to be off.

Stopped chatting, gotten all serious, and from the

hundreds of glances he'd given the rear-view mirror it didn't take a genius to figure out why.

They were being followed.

At least that's what she suspected although Lucy was a little too cowardly to ask for confirmation. After everything she'd been through, it didn't seem unreasonable to want to stick her head in the sand and refuse to believe that anything else was going to go wrong.

Because her biggest fear was that she couldn't handle anything else going wrong.

So sticking her head in the sand it was.

For a few more minutes anyway.

"Nope, won't be late today," Zander said, although his strained tone made it clear he was making an effort and not at all in a teasing and jovial mood.

"I'll have to thank your sister and Tate for looking after Cotton last night," she continued, making another attempt at pretending nothing was wrong.

"Mmhmm."

Cursing this feeling of helplessness that blanketed her, she hated that all her life she had worked so hard to prove to everybody, and mostly to herself, that she wasn't useless. Most of the time it worked, she made sure her environment was one that remained nearly constantly under her control. But this wasn't under her control. This was so far out of her element that she may as well be shooting off in a rocket into outer space.

If life had taught her anything, it was that being prepared and informed worked best at keeping fear and anxiety away.

To that end, she placed her palms on her knees and straightened her fingers out when they wanted to curl into impotent fists. Then she drew in a breath, attempting to drag in as much strength and calm as she could muster before breathing out slowly, purging her body of tension and stress.

She could do this.

Already she'd survived a plane crash, a hike through the jungle, and being held captive and drugged. If she could do that, she could handle a simple car ride through the city.

"Zander?"

"Hmm?" He tossed her a quick glance before returning his gaze to the road.

"Are we being followed?"

"Truth or lie?"

Truth or dare had been her least favorite game as a teen because guaranteed one of the kids would wind up asking her about her epilepsy if she picked truth. And if she picked dare, they would usually just make her tell them about her epilepsy anyway. That, or they would dare her to kiss a boy or something like she was some freak who nobody would want. But she'd had her first kiss when she was eleven, behind the large tree in front of her church one Sunday morning.

Although, why that was important at the moment she had no idea.

Swallowing down the urge to ask for the short-lived comfort and reassurance a lie might bring, she forced herself to make the right choice.

Really the only choice she could make. If they were being followed, the last thing Zander needed was her freaking out or panicking. That was only going to make matters worse.

"Truth."

"Yeah. Picked up about ten minutes after we left my place. Not sure how they knew where I lived, that house isn't in my name."

"Does someone at Prey have the address?" Lucy assumed they did since she was sure Eagle would have made sure somebody was watching the house last night as another line of protection for both her and Zander.

"Yeah, Eagle asked. Said he wanted security on you."

While she was sure Eagle had mentioned security for both of them, she didn't push the issue, it didn't really seem relevant right now. "Then the mole must have it. They must have passed it along to Raul Castillo and he had some of his men lying in wait for us." It was what he'd done a few weeks ago with Scarlett, kept sending men after her until he got her back in his clutches. The man was nothing if not predictable.

Sooner or later, that would catch up with him and lead to his downfall, but not soon enough to save her and Zander from whoever was following them.

"Wish I hadn't sent away the protection detail this morning. I made a mistake, I thought that nobody outside of Prey had the address. Eagle said he was only going to allow a small number of people he was sure he trusted have the intel."

"The mole has proven themselves to be pretty intelligent so far. They likely have a backdoor into the system and hacked it to get the intel." At least she hoped that was what had happened because the alternative was that one of the people she trusted one hundred percent to have her back was actually working against her. "What's the plan?"

"Try to lose them and get to Prey. Then once I get you there keep you locked away in a room where only I have the key to the door."

Since he said it so seriously, she actually managed a small laugh. "I don't think we can count on a simple lock to keep the mole out."

Zander swore and she felt bad for reminding him of that. But the truth was, with the mole situation at Prey there was nowhere safe for her or their team. And besides, she wasn't the only one in danger. Zimraan Mostafa blamed Zander for the raid that got his brother killed and had sworn vengeance, so really Zander should be locked away along with her.

"Once we get to Prey, we'll be safe," she assured him, reaching over to place a hand on his thigh. "The mole can't really make a move while we're there without exposing themselves."

"That's what I'm counting on because I need you safe, baby girl. Can't lose anyone else I care about. I already lost my team, I came so close to losing my sister, and then I almost lost you in Mexico several times over."

"You'll keep me safe, Zander," she said softly, believing that with all her heart. While he wasn't invincible or a super-hero, Zander was smart and well trained, he would do everything within his power to protect her and that was all she could ask of him.

Making what sounded like a scoffing sound of disbelief, Zander said, "We'll be at Prey in less than three minutes. All I need from you right now is a promise that you'll do what I tell you when I tell you to do it."

"Promise." An easy one to make. This was Zander's area of expertise not hers, and the last thing she wanted to do was put both of their lives in danger because she thought she could actually offer him assistance.

The remainder of the ride was tense. Neither of them spoke, and as much as Zander kept looking in the rear-view mirror, she kept looking out the side mirror. While she couldn't pick out the vehicle that had been following them, she had no doubt that if Zander said it was there then it was there.

Seconds felt like hours and minutes like days, but eventually, they turned into the street Prey's building was located on and Lucy let out a sigh of relief.

"When I park out the front of the building, I want you to wait for me to come around and cover you. Then we walk to the door without looking back. Got it?"

"Got it," she acknowledged.

As soon as he turned off the engine, Zander was out of the car and rounding it to come and get her. Nerves were beginning to get the best of her, and fine tremors began to ripple through her body. All she wanted was to get inside behind the bulletproof glass where both she and Zander would be surrounded by a whole bunch of highly trained men.

Out here felt too exposed.

The feeling only intensified as Zander opened her door and helped her out. Keeping his big body between her and the road, they'd gone no more than two steps toward the building when chaos erupted around them.

Gunshots began to fire in all directions, and a black van roared up beside them. Men poured out of it, coming toward them.

Zander fought and fired his weapon.

She did the best she could with nothing other than her bare hands.

But there were too many of them.

Pain exploded inside her head and the next thing she knew, the world was cloaked in darkness.

* * *

JANUARY 27TH
  11:23 P.M.

PAIN POUNDED INSIDE HIS HEAD.

It flared between his temples making nausea swell in his stomach.

It was pure reflex and not conscious thought that had Zander rolling to the side and vomiting onto the ground instead of all over himself.

With a groan, he sank back down, feeling weak and shaky.

Not a good thing.

Because while his body ached and his brain throbbed, his memories were completely intact.

They'd been ambushed and abducted.

Not just him.

Lucy had been with him, taken alongside him, and now he was going to be forced to watch her be tortured and murdered just like he'd watched his team.

He had no idea how he knew that, but deep down in his gut, something told him it was true.

If he wanted to find a way to save her, he had to open his eyes, gather as much intel as he could, and pray for a miracle.

It wasn't rocket science to know that the miracle was really all that was going to work.

Last time he would have died along with his team if they hadn't been rescued. Why should he believe that this time was any different?

Why should he believe that rescue would arrive at all let alone in time?

In time to save Lucy at least.

Because if he watched her die and then was rescued, he didn't want to live. He wasn't even sure that vengeance would be a strong enough motivator to keep him alive. Already he'd learned that there were more important things in life than revenge. For eighteen months it had kept him alive, but the best decision he'd ever made was letting go of it for Lucy's sake.

She came first.

Before everything.

Including himself.

This time around, he wouldn't be holding back, wasn't going to be silent, if there was a way to talk their abductors into letting Lucy go and taking his life instead then he would gladly take it. Whatever pain he suffered before his life was over would be well worth it if it kept his girl alive.

"Zander?"

The weak call of his name from the woman he was well and truly prepared to die for was enough to drag his weak and uncooperative body out of its haze.

His eyes snapped open and immediately he wished they hadn't.

Given Raul Castillo's stubborn streak and inability to let things go even when he was pursuing something that was no long in his best interest, Zander had expected to find himself and Lucy back in Mexico, prisoners of the weapons dealer.

But this sure as hell wasn't Mexico.

There was no jungle. Instead, around them were the rocky mountains he remembered far too well. Scenery that was forever burned into his mind's eye along with the stench of blood and the echoes of agonized screams.

This was Syria.

They hadn't been taken by Raul Castillo, they'd been taken by Zimraan Mostafa.

How was it possible that the brother of a Syrian terrorist cell had been able to find him on the other side of the world within hours of the raid that had killed his brother and broken up the cell?

Simply put, it shouldn't be possible.

While in theory there was a chance that Zimraan might have been able to track him down, it would have taken both time and money. Given that the cell had been raided and most of their men killed with a few captured, money should be an issue. But even if Zimraan still had access to money, how had he managed to get the location of both Zander's house and Prey so quickly?

And how had the man even known that Zander was associated with Prey?

He'd been Delta Force before his team's capture and subsequent deaths, no affiliation with Prey, although he had worked a joint mission years ago with one of Prey's teams. But there was no possible way that a young Syrian wannabe terrorist could know that he was working with Prey to help bring down a feared weapons trafficker.

Unless ...

Was it possible that the mole at Prey had somehow managed to make contact with Zimraan and sold the intel?

If so, why?

What could they possibly have to gain by having him and Lucy abducted and murdered?

It was one thing to sell off the Reactivator, the drug that Lucy, Scarlett, and their team had been working on. The drug would give soldiers a substantial advantage in the field so it was a definite game changer and could save thousands of lives. Selling it would have gotten the mole a bag full of cash, and that was something he could see motivating a person.

But this ...?

This wasn't about money.

This felt almost personal. Like the mole was making a decision that had nothing to do with money.

Which made zero sense. If the mole had a grudge against Lucy, Scarlett wouldn't have been targeted first. And how could the mole possibly have a grudge against him? He didn't work for Prey, and he'd only been assisting them for literally a couple of days, that was nowhere near enough time to have angered the mole to the point where they would have to go to all the trouble it would have taken to make contact with Zimraan Mostafa and sell him out.

"Zander?" Lucy called out to him again, this time her

voice was a little stronger and threaded with terror.

Turning his head toward the sound, he took in the place where they were being held. Like when his team had been captured, they were in a courtyard. There was dry, sandy dirt beneath him, and there were stone buildings all around the outside of the space. Light spilled out of a couple of windows, and since the courtyard was outside there was also the light from the moon and a few scattered stars.

It was like traveling back in time.

The only differences this time around was that instead of the heat making the space unbearable, the air around them was wintery cold. And instead of having seven highly trained men chained up with him, men who had signed up for the job and who knew the risks they were taking, there was one small, vulnerable woman.

A woman who meant something to him.

More than something, she meant *every*thing.

And she was going to be tortured and murdered because of him.

The thought left him paralyzed by fear.

Knowing what Lucy was going to suffer all because she'd believed in him and made him a promise to be there for them was a sour ball of agonizing terror sitting heavily in his gut.

He'd seen what these men did to women, watched first-hand as they raped girls. Brutally raped them to the point where he wasn't even sure the young women would have survived their injuries.

The death Raul had promised Lucy echoed in his mind.

Different sick monster, same horrific fate.

Because there was no doubt in his mind that Zimraan knew that Lucy was important to him. That the young man had plans to both physically torture her as well as sexually. That Lucy's death would be long and drawn out, she would beg for mercy, but there would be none to be found.

Like there would be no redemption for him.

Not after this.

Not with another death on his shoulders.

"You're scaring me, Zander." Lucy sounded borderline hysterical. Not a good thing because his woman was a rock, knew how to control her emotions, was the epitome of calm, cool, and collected, and she was rational and pragmatic.

But there was no way anybody could be rational when they woke up to this mess.

He felt the chain around his ankle and knew from experience that there was no way to break it or pry it free from the concrete it was embedded in, at least not with your bare hands. Lucy would be similarly chained up, and he could see the table waiting in the middle of the courtyard. This was a different place than last time, he knew that for sure because it was smaller, not big enough to chain up eight men, but the end result would be the same.

Bloodshed and screams and pain.

"Zander, are you dead? Please, if you're here, answer me," Lucy begged, and he could tell even from there, even in the dark, that she was crying.

As his gaze sought her out, he saw the small figure in the opposite corner of the yard. She was on her knees, trying desperately to wrestle with the chain binding her in place. It killed him to know that she was there because of him.

That he'd done this to her.

She'd promised to always be there for him, and it had signed her own death warrant.

"Please, Zander, I don't want you to be dead, please don't be dead."

Those words, accompanied by weeping, hurt worst of all.

Because before she took her final breath, Zander had no doubt that Lucy would be cursing the day she met him.

CHAPTER EIGHTEEN

January 28th
   6:18 A.M.

IT HAD BEEN A LONG, cold, terrifying night.

Lucy's head throbbed with a vicious headache from being knocked out when she and Zander were abducted, and she had no doubt that she had another concussion.

Not a good thing for any person to have two head injuries so close together, but for somebody like her, whose brain malfunctioned all on its own, without prompting, sending her into seizures for no identifiable reason, it was particularly dangerous.

But worse than the cold, worse than knowing what was coming, worse than the pain and the fear, was feeling Zander slip further and further away from her.

He could barely look at her and had uttered nothing more than the bare minimum to answer a direct question, although he'd ignored her at first when she'd woken up and begged him to speak to her so she knew he wasn't dead.

Those minutes when she wasn't sure if he had survived the initial kidnapping were the worst.

When he didn't answer her, she was positive it was because she'd already lost him.

Then finally, he'd told her he was alive. He'd told her who had taken them, although since they weren't in the jungle she'd kind of figured it out all on her own anyway. And that was about it. After giving her the briefest of rundowns on what would likely happen to them so she could be prepared, he'd just shut down.

She got it.

Really she did.

Already he blamed himself for the deaths of his teammates at the hand of Zimraan Mostafa's brother, and to be back there, with her, this was like reliving his worst nightmare.

So, while she understood his need to withdraw from her and start building emotional boundaries he wouldn't allow her to cross, it didn't mean it didn't hurt.

Because it did hurt.

A lot.

She was already losing him even though he was still alive, and at the worst possible time. She needed him right now, needed his comfort and reassurance even if it was in vain. And she knew that he needed her, too. He needed to know that she wasn't angry with him and didn't blame him. Whatever happened to them was not his fault. If she could take that assurance and force it into his brain, she'd do it in a heartbeat.

This was not Zander's fault.

He'd been doing his job when he and his team were captured, and he'd been doing his job when he gathered the intel on the weapons deal so Zafir Mostafa could be caught or killed. If the terrorist's brother had vowed vengeance that was not on his head.

But how could she convince him of that when he wouldn't even look at her?

As much as she wanted to beg and plead with him not to shut her out, that if she was going to suffer and die then she at least wanted to hold onto the connection they were forging, she didn't. Zander had to survive how he had to survive, and she couldn't demand that he put her needs above his own.

So, instead, she sat huddled in the corner, knees pulled up to her chest, arm wrapped around her legs, her body shaking so badly her muscles ached. They hadn't dressed to be outside in the cold since they would only be inside at Prey, and her jeans and sweater were no match for icy temperatures.

Her mouth was dry with that cottony feeling of dehydration, but she could do nothing about it. It wasn't like she was going to call out to the men inside the houses surrounding the courtyard. They didn't care if she was dehydrated or cold. They'd brought her there maybe because they knew she was connected to Zander or just because she'd been with him at the time, but whatever the purpose, she was there to be tortured and killed, her comfort was of little consequence to them.

Although she couldn't know for sure, she was pretty sure she hadn't been brought by accident. Somehow, Zimraan knew that she and Zander were a couple, and that was why she was there.

Which made it all worse.

There was no chance in hell that Zander wasn't going to blame himself for this.

Lucy ached to reach out and soothe him however she could. They could have spent the hours comforting one another, talking through what had happened, who could have leaked intel to the Syrian terrorist, anything to pass the hours so she hadn't had to spend them alone.

Now the first rays of sunlight were beginning to streak the sky, and Lucy could honestly say she had never felt this alone in her entire life.

With more light filling the courtyard, she could better make out Zander's huddled form in the opposite corner. His big body was curled in on itself and she knew everything would have been just the tiniest bit better if she could touch him. Offer comfort and take some comfort for herself.

Anything had to be better than this.

Clamping her teeth together was the only way to prevent herself from calling out to him. It hadn't taken her long to figure out that Zander didn't want to talk to her, that he was only going to give her the absolute bare minimum of answers, and after a while, she'd just given up trying to talk to him.

Shifting slightly, Lucy tried to find a more comfortable position even though she knew in reality there was none. Her body was still bruised and sore from the crash, and sitting on the hard ground out in the cold all night long was the last thing it needed.

Still, when a door opened, Lucy curled tighter in on herself, much preferring the cold, and thirst, and loneliness to whatever came next.

She wasn't the only one who had heard the door opening because Zander suddenly straightened and rose to his feet. The expression on his face was nothing short of fierce, and it made her shaking increase. She'd hate to have that look aimed in her direction. If ever there was a picture to go alongside the if-looks-could-kill saying this had to be it. In fact, she half expected daggers of fire to come shooting out of his eyes.

Half a dozen men came streaming out of the house, and it was only because Zander's gaze immediately zeroed in on one of them that she knew who Zimraan Mostafa was.

Barely more than a boy, the young man was only nineteen years old, but it was clear he looked up to his older brother and had believed in Zafir's fight because he wanted to continue it. Take over the reins and presumably attempt to carry out whatever the plans were once he finished on his personal mission of vengeance.

"You let the woman go, she has nothing to do with this, Zimraan," Zander said, his confident voice sending spikes of fear through her.

No.

She wasn't going anywhere.

She'd promised to stay by Zander's side no matter what.

It was a promise she intended to keep.

Only when she shakily pushed to her feet to tell him that he couldn't try to sacrifice his life for hers, he shot her such a hard look that she stayed right where she was.

Zimraan laughed like Zander had just said the funniest thing he'd ever heard. "I don't think so," he said in accented English. "An eye for an eye, isn't that the saying? You took away the most important person in my life so I will do the same for you. This is your woman, yes?"

When Zimraan turned to look at her, it took every ounce of strength she possessed not to cower before him. This man got off on inflicting pain and suffering, he wanted her to be afraid, wanted her to fear him and what he was going to do to her.

While she absolutely did, she also wanted to be strong for Zander, not make this any worse on him than it had to be. Already he was blaming himself, and if he had to witness her fear it would destroy him.

So, she stayed where she was, met Zimraan's dark gaze, and refused to flinch.

The young man's eyes narrowed in irritation, and he turned back to Zander. "My brother allowed me to watch what he did with your team, so I could learn and one day earn my position as his second in command."

"A real man doesn't take his issues out on a woman. Are you not a real man, Zimraan?" Zander asked as though he were trying to provoke the volatile terrorist.

Stiffening, Zimraan took a few steps toward Zander like he didn't know he was taunting a lion waiting to pounce. "I am nineteen. I am a man. And because you killed Zafir, I am now the leader of the resistance. We will annihilate your country. You think you can dictate to the world how every-body should live, but you will be destroyed."

With lightning-fast speed, Zander surprised her, Zimraan, and the others when he suddenly leaped, kicking out with his legs and sweeping the young man to the ground. Her warrior wrapped his legs around Zimraan's neck and began to squeeze the life out of the young terrorist.

Then the other five men descended on Zander, hitting him, kicking him, striking him with the butts of their weapons, and attacking him like they intended to kill him right here and now.

* * *

January 28th
  7:01 A.M.

Each blow felt like success because it was one less strike Lucy would have to take.

As long as he kept Zimraan's attention on him, Lucy was a little safer.

With his legs wrapped around Zimraan's neck, it meant his arms were still free and he was delivering at least as many hits as he was receiving.

Wasn't like he was going to win this fight, there were five of them to his one, and more men were spilling out of the houses, but at least he was going to deliver a message. Mess with what was his and suffer the consequences.

All night he'd ached to be able to hold Lucy in his arms, cocoon her cold body with his own, soothing at least one of her problems, but every time he glanced at her the realization that she was there only because of him hit so hard he could barely breathe.

In the end, he hadn't been able to look at her at all without his entire body freezing up on him.

After several minutes his body had received too many hits to keep fighting, chained up as he was. If he'd been able to get his hands on a weapon this would be a different story, but Zimraan's men were at least trained well enough to know to never give up your weapon no matter what. They had maintained firm grips on them while hitting and kicking him.

Too bad, because if he had gotten one, this would all be over.

He'd kill every last one of them, blow off his own foot if it was the only way to get free and get Lucy out of there.

But now a particularly vicious hit to his head had him loosening his hold on Zimraan and sinking down onto the dirt.

As soon as he was free, the young man, not really more than a boy, scrambled away, rubbing at the red marks on his neck.

Satisfaction gave Zander back a little of his strength.

While he might be outnumbered, he had proven to Zimraan and his men that even chained up he was a legitimate threat.

"You will not win, Zander Madden," Zimraan said as he shoved to his feet, swaying a little as he did so. "Just like you watched my brother kill your men, you will now watch me kill your woman. I love the sounds of a woman's screams, don't you? So pretty and melodic. Like a bird caught in a trap. I once caught a bird, ripped out every one of its feathers, then peeled off its skin until its little heart gave out and it died. I was six at the time and my skills have since vastly improved."

The psychopathic terrorist nodded at a few of his men who stalked across the courtyard to where Lucy was sitting.

To her credit, she didn't cower before them, instead, she stuck her chin out and looked up at them with contempt. The men sneered at her, and as they grabbed her and dragged her to her feet, they made sure to make their grips crushing if the brief flash of pain on her face was anything to go by.

Marching her over to where Zimraan was carefully remaining outside the circle of Zander's reach, Lucy's gaze darted to his, and for a moment, it shone with every emotion she felt for him before hardening as she looked up at the man who held their fates in the palm of his hand.

Zimraan gave him a wicked smile before turning his attention to Lucy. "You are a beautiful woman, yes?" he asked as he trailed a fingertip down Lucy's cheek and then across her bottom lip.

Zander knew what she was going to do a split second before she did it.

Even if there was time for him to tell her not to do it, he wasn't sure if he would.

Because they both knew they weren't walking out of here alive.

They would be tortured and then when Zimraan got bored and felt like he had avenged his brother's death sufficiently, they would be killed.

If his woman wanted to get in a little payback of her own, who was he to stop her?

Lucy's mouth opened, and her straight white teeth clamped down on the finger on her lip before Zimraan even knew what was happening.

The man's howl of pain was like music to both of their ears, and even as the terrorist jerked backward, grabbing her broken arm and twisting it up behind her back, Lucy gave a triumphant smile.

It felt good to be able to fight back even if you weren't going to be able to get yourself out of the situation. And Zander was glad there was still fight left in his woman because he was still going to take advantage of any opportunity that might prevent itself.

"I see you need to be taught your place, *woman*," Zimraan sneered. Then he looked to his men. "Take her to the table, I'm ready to get started."

Four men grabbed Lucy, pulling her over to the table as she fought against them. While her moves showed that she had been trained well in self-defense, unfortunately, you could do nothing when you were outnumbered. And Lucy was a woman, smaller and physically weaker by design, injured as she was she didn't stand a chance, but he was proud as hell that she fought with everything she had and landed several good strikes before the men had her lying flat on her back on the table with her wrists and ankles chained in place.

Wandering over to the table, Zimraan picked up a knife and held it with the point pressed to the tip of his finger. He must have pressed hard enough to break the skin because a small drop of blood was visible.

"I do like my women subservient, but there is something special about it when they scream, isn't there?" Zimraan asked, his tone conversational like they were discussing something as mundane as the weather. "I also like them covered in blood. There is something about the color of blood that I have always found soothing."

The young man was a pure psychopath, there was no other way to describe him. While Zafir had certainly enjoyed inflicting pain on others, there had been something more controlled about him. He was motivated more by the idea of money and power, whereas his younger brother seemed to be more led by his need to hurt other people.

It made Zimraan that much more dangerous.

A bloodthirsty person would go to great lengths to satisfy that craving, and Zander was already able to see how this was all going to play out.

"Blood is a curious thing, is it not?" Zimraan asked as he took the knife and used it to slice Lucy's sweater open from the bottom hem right up to the band around the neck. The young man peeled the material back exposing the creamy white skin of her stomach and chest. Thankfully, the bra she was wearing covered her breasts so she wasn't bared to these sick, twisted men, but it seemed like Zimraan wasn't interested in anything but his craving for blood.

Moving the knife, he pressed the tip to the base of her neck, and much like he'd done when he cut her sweater open, he dragged the tip down, following the same path, until it stopped just below her navel. Blood immediately began to bubble out of the wound, visible even to him from where he was sitting a good ten feet away.

Other than sucking in a breath as Zimraan had trailed the knife through her skin, Lucy hadn't made a sound or moved at all. The wound wasn't deep, probably wouldn't even leave a scar, or at least not much of one, but it still had to hurt, especially with the cold wind blowing against it.

"It looks like nothing more than thicker water, and yet it is so vital," Zimraan continued as he moved the knife, this time lying the whole blade sideways against the flesh on Lucy's stomach. Right how you'd hold a knife if you were preparing to skin someone.

Zander's entire body went taut with fear.

He was consumed with the need to save his woman, and yet he was powerless to do anything to stop this from happening.

Just as he'd been powerless to save his team.

"Without blood we die. So simple. Skin is also a curious thing, don't you think? It keeps our entire body together, holds everything in, and yet when removed, it seems so inconsequential."

With that, he slid the sharp blade with pinpoint precision through the skin on Lucy's stomach, removing a good-sized portion with the skill of someone who performed skin grafts for a living.

The scream that was torn from his girl's lips was a sound that would haunt Zander for an eternity. Dead or alive, that sound would forever echo in his ears.

CHAPTER NINETEEN

January 28th
  8:44 A.M.

WHOEVER SAID breathing through pain helped was an idiot.

Nothing helped this kind of pain.

Not a single thing.

It was just … there.

Kind of living inside her like it was a real being with its own thoughts and feelings. It ran from her wounds through her body, spending time in her stomach making nausea churn, then it would dart up to her head, into her brain, making it spin and spin like she was stuck on a carousel running at full speed that never stopped.

It made no difference if she tried to block it out, smooth out her breathing in an attempt to regulate it, it was just there, doing its thing, uncaring of the impact it was having on her.

At least it was quiet.

Zimraan had had his fun and disappeared inside to have breakfast with his men, leaving her and Zander alone out there. There wasn't really anything to talk about, he'd been beaten and she'd been skinned, and they were both scared, alone, and hurting. Talking about it wasn't going to change anything, and anyway, Lucy didn't think she had the energy to talk right now.

She just wanted to lie there, soaking up these moments of peace, even if they were ruined by pain because sooner or later Zimraan would be back.

How long did it take to skin someone alive?

Hours?

Days?

Weeks?

If he paused in between, went slowly, taking his time, only doing so much each day so he didn't throw her body into shock, could he keep her alive for weeks?

That was a terrifying possibility.

Just like Zander had warned her would happen, she was more than ready to start praying for death and she'd only survived maybe an hour or so of torture.

How had Zander survived the aftermath of living through something like this?

Her admiration for him went up even though she already thought he was one of the most amazing men she had ever had the pleasure of meeting. He was so strong and so brave. He was loyal and been willing to do whatever it took to get justice for the men he had served with. But he was also compassionate enough to put her life above what had been his only purpose for living.

If he was the only one to walk away alive again, Lucy prayed that he wouldn't shut Scarlett out this time, he was going to need his sister and her support to make it through this. Because the last thing she would want was for her death to destroy him. Zander deserved to be happy, he deserved to be loved, he deserved all the joy in the world, and if he couldn't have those things with her then she hoped he could find it with someone else.

Someone who could see just how special he was.

He was special.

Very special.

"Lucy."

The sound of her name startled her out of the hazy little bubble she'd somehow managed to float inside of, and her pain came roaring back. The cold against the wounds on her stomach, her chest, and her left breast made them sting like crazy, and the throbbing pain was more than enough to drive her insane.

"Luce, baby girl, answer me."

Zander sounded worried, and she wanted to soothe away all his anxiety. Pepper kisses to his lips, and smooth her hands up and down his impressive abs, anything so long as he didn't sound so tortured and lost.

"Come on, honey, let me know you're okay."

Yesterday, when they'd first woken up there, she'd called out to him like that several times before he finally answered. She'd begged and pleaded and wept, thinking that he was already gone, and now she wanted to answer, to assure him that she was okay, but she couldn't seem to make her voice work.

Curses filled the courtyard, along with the jangle of a chain, and she realized that Zander was trying to get to her even though they both knew it was impossible.

"I'm ... okay," she slurred, her voice much weaker than she would have liked. But she was dehydrated, hypothermic, and had open wounds. It was the best she could do at the moment.

"I'm so sorry, Lucy."

There was so much pain in Zander's voice that tears flooded her eyes, spilling over and trailing icy paths down her cold cheeks.

Why did this have to happen to them?

Why couldn't they have gotten their happy ever after?

Neither of them had even realized that they wanted one until they met each other, but now that they had, Lucy wanted it all. The whole white picket fence, big home with a pool, kids, and a dog, waking up each morning wrapped in the arms of the man you loved and going to sleep each night the same way, growing old with a partner by your side.

That should be their future.

Not this.

Not cold, and pain, and death.

She wanted to rage against the unfairness of it all, but honestly, she was too tired to bother.

But not too tired to offer what reassurances she could. "S'okay, Zander. Not your fault," she murmured sleepily.

Now that she thought about it the pain was dulling a little, being overtaken by exhaustion.

Her eyes were too heavy to hold open, and they drifted closed, the pale blue of the sky disappearing. The cold had worn out her muscles after hours of shaking and now they felt heavy, but not unpleasantly so. And with the pain fading a little, maybe she could finally get some sleep.

Sleep.

That sounded so nice.

Almost magical.

It would be so wonderful to just drift away for a while, away from this hell hole, just disappear into a nice, big, cozy hole of peaceful, inky blackness.

"Stay awake for me, baby. I need you to stay awake, can you do that for me?"

Zander's voice pierced holes in her little sleepy bubble,

dragging her further back into reality. She wanted to fight against it, let go of everything, but the fear in his voice was like an anchor holding her there.

"I'm awake," she mumbled.

"Good, good girl, you stay with me, okay? I know you're tired, and I know you're hurting, but I need you to stay with me. I know it's not fair, but I can't let you go yet, you hear me? I need to keep you with me. I'm so damn sorry you got dragged into this, baby girl. I wish like hell I knew a way to get you out, and I'll try, I promise you I'll try, but you have to do your part, okay? And that means staying awake, it means staying with me. I need you," he whispered the last part, but his words carried to her, and she pried her eyes open and turned her head so she could see him.

"I'm here, you have me," she whispered back.

Their eyes met.

Held.

So much flowed between them.

It felt like it was too early to even think about the L word, and yet she might never get another chance to tell Zander she was falling in love with him. Those weren't words she wanted to say with an audience, any audience, but especially Zimraan and his men, but they were alone now.

Just as she parted her lips to tell him how she felt, the doors to the houses burst open and at least three dozen men spilled out.

More men than had been out there before when Zimraan had taunted Zander, then had him beaten before torturing her with his knife.

Something was going on.

Something that had scared the young terrorist if the expressions on the faces of his men were anything to go by.

Since she didn't speak Arabic, Lucy couldn't pick up

much of what was being said, but then Zimraan began to speak and she learned what was happening.

"How did you do it?" Zimraan yelled at Zander. "How did you tell them where you were?"

Her ears perked up at that. Someone was coming? Could it be Prey? Had they somehow figured out where she and Zander were being held?

Was that too much to hope for?

Apparently, it wasn't because the sounds of gunfire filled the morning, and Lucy cried out in relief.

Someone was coming and it had to be Prey.

Zimraan shouted instructions at his men, most of whom seemed to be scurrying around like chickens with their heads chopped off.

In the commotion, it was hard to keep track of what was going on, and she startled when hands suddenly began to undo the chains holding her on the table.

When she looked up into Zimraan's cold, dead eyes, she knew that fate wasn't going to smile on her today.

"I'm not dying here today, I'm getting out of here alive, and you're going to make sure nobody stops me," the young man snarled before dragging her to her feet and pressing the blade of his knife against her throat.

* * *

JANUARY 28TH
    9:10 A.M.

WHERE WAS LUCY?

Zander couldn't see her through the crowd of men filling the courtyard.

Something was clearly going on, from what he'd been

able to pick up, a helo had just dropped a dozen men not far from the compound, and they were making quick work of approaching.

Although he had no idea how they'd managed to do it, the men had to be Prey. Somehow, they'd found the location of where he and Lucy were being held and mounted a rescue. It was the only scenario that made sense even if he didn't understand it.

All he had to do was keep himself and Lucy alive until Zimraan and his men were either dead or in custody.

He could do that.

He *had* to do that.

Because he wasn't losing his girl.

If Lucy was able to forgive him for getting her abducted and tortured, then he was going to hold onto the happy ending they both wanted and refuse to let go. If she couldn't find a way to forgive him, he'd completely understand and walk away without causing her any more pain.

It would kill him to do it and go against his every instinct to fight for his woman, but he'd hurt her enough, he wasn't going to make it any worse.

Right now, it was hard to see how Lucy could possibly forgive him for all of this, but he had to put his faith in the promises she'd made him. Ignoring the little voice in the back of his mind that whispered she'd made those promises before she'd been strapped to a table and had her skin peeled off.

Maybe it was ludicrous to believe he still had a chance with her, but right now, it was the only thing he had to cling to.

Protect his girl.

Keep her alive.

That was what he had to focus on, everything else could be sorted out later.

A cry of pain drew his attention.

That was Lucy's voice.

Lucy's pain.

Someone was hurting her.

Unacceptable.

Rage clouded his vision. Somehow, the saying about anger turning your vision red seemed to be true because it was like a haze of red suddenly filled the courtyard.

The beast inside him howled to be let out, confident it could do what it took to protect what was theirs.

For once he was grateful for that darkness because he needed it to survive. Lucy did, too.

She was counting on him, and he wasn't going to let her down.

He'd already failed her, failed his team, failed his sister, there couldn't be any more failure. Not when the stakes were this high.

So, he let out a growl of anger and kicked out at the nearest body.

Caught off-guard, the man stumbled and fell to his knees close enough for Zander to reach. Planting both hands on either side of the man's head, he jerked them sideways and heard the satisfying sound of the man's neck breaking.

Dropping the now dead body at his side, Zander snatched up the man's weapon and began to fire it.

Not expecting gunshots to be fired from inside the court-yard where they believed they were safe, men began to drop left, right, and center.

Screams of pain filled the air, along with the growing stench of blood.

But Zander didn't stop.

He didn't care that he had no cover, he fired at anything that moved, praying that somehow Lucy managed to avoid being hit. Vaguely, he was aware of some return fire, of bullets hitting the sandy dirt millimeters from his feet, and pinging off the stone wall behind him, but he was too focused to care.

Protect what was his.

Kill anything that got in the way.

That was all he cared about.

His own life was inconsequential. He would gladly give it up if it meant keeping his beautiful, brave woman alive.

By the time everything fell silent, Zander was breathing hard, and wavering on his feet. Too many hours out in the cold, with nothing to eat or drink, plus the head injury from being knocked out, and the likeliness that he'd been fed drugs to keep him out until he was brought to Syria was taking a toll on his body.

But his mind was still laser-focused.

There were dead bodies littering the ground of the court-yard, at least thirty of them, but there was only one person he cared about.

Only when his gaze fell on the table he found it empty.

Lucy was gone.

A whistle was the only announcement he got before black-clad figures entered the courtyard.

Without that whistle, he would have opened fire without thought, eliminating whoever it was.

But the whistle told him it was someone on his side.

Still, he kept the weapon in his hands, aimed at the dozen men who were cautiously entering the courtyard, their own weapons trained at the sea of bodies on the ground, no doubt searching for anyone who moved.

The only one left moving was him.

"Zander, you hurt, man?" a man asked, approaching him slowly. Despite the adrenalin pumping through his system along with fear for Lucy, he was able to identify the man as

Rex, a SEAL on the team who had been working with Prey to bring down Raul Castillo.

Giving a single nod, not sure whether his answer was truthful or not, he scanned the mass of bodies, still searching for the only one he cared about. But there was not a hint of the lavender sweater Lucy had been wearing when they'd been taken.

"Lucy," he said, seemingly unable to get more words out.

"Do you know where she is?" Phantom asked, coming up beside Rex.

"She was here. When the shooting started, she was here. There, on the table," he said, pointing to the table that was stained with her blood. Where was she? How had she gotten free and where had she gone? Was she hiding somewhere, scared by all the shooting?

"Start looking for Lucy," Rocco called out to the men, who immediately began walking amongst the bodies searching for the only woman.

"Lucy?" Zander called out, too wired to do anything about the desperation in his tone, and even if he could, he didn't care that these men knew how important she was to him. In fact, he wanted to stand on the mountaintops and scream it to the whole world. To let everybody know that Lucy was his, that someone like her would want to be with a man like him. "Baby, answer me! Are you hurt? Lucy, you can come out now, it's okay, please, baby girl, answer me."

This was his payback for being unable to answer her that first night, it had to be.

The terror pulsing inside him was karma, reminding him that at every turn he managed to fail the woman who held his heart in her hands.

"We'll find her," Gumby said, kneeling at his feet and using bolt cutters to snap the chain that bound him.

As soon as he was free, Zander began to help the others search through the bodies looking for Lucy.

With every one he turned over, he was painfully aware that Lucy could have been hit, that she could be bleeding out at this very second, or already dead.

No.

He couldn't allow himself to think that.

Not without proof.

Lucy had to be alive. She had to be. Because how was he supposed to go on without her?

"Where is she? Lucy, where are you? Why isn't she answering?" he demanded of no one in particular, all too aware of how close he was to falling apart. A few more minutes with no response from Lucy and he was going to lose it. Already he was wavering on the edge, a single misstep, and he'd be in full-on meltdown mode. Completely useless to anyone, including the woman who needed him.

"She has to be here," Bubba reminded him.

That was cold comfort given the SEAL team and the men from Prey appeared to be the only living people inside the courtyard.

If Lucy was in there then she was dead.

It was already too late.

He'd already lost her.

Something ripped open inside him, an invisible wound, one that tore through his heart leaving a shattered mess inside his chest. Lucy was gone and that meant she'd taken his heart along with her because it belonged to her.

Zander wished he'd told her he was falling in love with her when he had the chance. But he'd been a coward, felt like telling her he loved her was somehow going to jinx things, and was tantamount to admitting they weren't going to make it out alive.

Suddenly Rocco's eyes snapped to his as he listened to whatever was being said into his comms.

"What?" Zander demanded.

"That was the pilot, he says someone's approaching the helo," Rocco told him. "A man and a woman. Looks like it could be Zimraan Mostafa, and he's using Lucy as a human shield."

CHAPTER TWENTY

January 28th
9:19 A.M.

EVERY TIME A SHIVER rocketed through her body, Lucy could feel the blade of the knife pressed against her throat nick her skin.

Zimraan's arm was locked tightly around her chest, pressing painfully against the wounds he'd made.

Almost worse than the pain was the unrelenting cold. Hours of being out in it, the constant shivering, her muscles were aching, and honestly, without Zimraan holding her up and dragging her along with him, she was pretty sure she would have collapsed against the knife already and inadvertently slit her own throat.

"I will not be stopped," Zimraan roared in her ear, making her flinch.

They were walking—well, Zimraan was trying to run, but she was too weak, too cold, and too clumsy to keep up—

across the wide, open valley. They were practically sitting ducks out there, but Lucy was reassuring herself with the fact that the young terrorist's men weren't going to open fire on them, and if it had been Prey who had come to rescue them, they were too skilled to shoot randomly at them and risk hitting her.

Right now, it was Zander that she was most worried about. He'd been there in the courtyard when bullets started flying in every direction, and she was terrified that he'd been hit by one.

What if he was bleeding out right at this very second, all alone when she'd promised she would always be there for him?

Or, worse, what if he was already dead?

The very idea of him dying alone sent another shiver through her that, this time, had nothing to do with the cold.

"They will not kill me as long as I have you," Zimraan said, but she got the feeling the words were more for his benefit than as a threat to her. It was obvious he was afraid, he was young, inexperienced, had no idea what he was doing, and he needed to reassure himself that he was making it out of this alive.

Only she had no intention of letting that happen.

Ahead of them, she saw a helicopter sitting on the ground. It had to be the one that had brought in Prey and was waiting to take them all to safety.

As soon as he saw it, Zimraan picked up the pace, forcing her to find strength she didn't really have to keep up with him or risk having her neck split open and dying right there in a dusty valley in Syria.

When they reached it, he shoved her on board. "Take us out of here or I kill her," he warned the pilot.

The man looked at her, and she could see him debating his

options. He was wearing a headset, and she hoped he communicated with the men who had stormed Zimraan's compound. If he'd already alerted them, help was only minutes away. All she had to do was stay alive a tiny bit longer and she could go home.

Finally, the pilot nodded, and he started the rotors.

The roar hurt her ears, but held as she was there was no way for her to move her hands to cover them. The bite of the blade against her neck was a constant reminder of how precarious her situation was. One wrong move and her carotid artery could be sliced right open, and she'd be dead before anyone could do anything about it.

Just as they began to lift off the ground, she heard Zander scream her name.

Well, in reality she knew there was no way she could hear anything over the roar of the helicopter, but she felt him, and when she turned, she saw a dozen men running toward them. The man at the front of the pack was Zander.

Lucy knew it, felt it, even as her vision wavered and she couldn't see clearly.

Alive.

Zander was alive.

Rejuvenated by the knowledge, Lucy quickly ran through scenarios.

If Zimraan got her away from there then it would be all over. She'd be killed, she'd never go home, and never get to explore this thing with Zander. Without her, she was worried about what would happen to him. It wasn't out of a sense of ego it was just that he already blamed himself for what happened to his team, and then if she died at the hands of the same family, would he be able to survive it?

No.

She couldn't let Zimraan take her away.

With her on the helo there was no way the guys would be

able to shoot it down because she'd die along with the terrorist if they crashed.

But if she took herself out of the equation ...

Then they could do what had to be done.

A quick glance out the window showed they were barely ten feet off the ground. Not terrible odds, she would almost definitely survive that fall. The guys were too far away to be able to do anything, although they were quickly making ground.

This was her only choice, and delaying only increased the chance she would die.

"Jump," she yelled to the pilot, she didn't want his death on her conscience. If both of them jumped, it left Zimraan to decide between going over the side with them and getting caught or killed by the men on the ground, or crashing in the helo because she doubted the young man knew how to fly it. Even if he did, the second she was clear, Zander and the others would open fire on the helo.

Not needing to be told twice, the pilot jumped.

Startled, Zimraan lowered the blade enough that she was able to summon all the remaining strength left in her body and shove him to the side.

Then without a second thought, Lucy pretended she was just going sky-diving with a parachute safely strapped to her back, and threw herself out the helo door.

They'd risen another couple of feet, but she was still confident that she could survive the fall as she slowly dropped toward the earth. Time seemed to slow down, and her body felt weightless. If her parents could see her now, bloody wounds, half naked with her sweater flapping in the wind, jumping out of helicopters, they'd have a heart attack and insist that she live at home with them forever.

But she'd saved herself.

And there was a smile on her lips that was only wiped off

by the jarring thud of her body slamming into the hard, unforgiving ground.

Footsteps pounded toward her, and a second later, a body flung itself on top of hers.

Covered as she was, the explosion almost caught her by surprise.

Still, as soon as her brain processed that it had to be the helo hitting the ground, she let out a sigh of relief. Zimraan was dead. That meant Zander was safe.

The relief made her lightheaded.

Or perhaps that was shock.

Or cold, or pain.

Or even an impending seizure.

Take your pick.

Any or maybe all of them.

"Don't you *ever* do something so crazy and reckless again," Zander's voice was harsh with fear, but his hands as he eased her onto her back were so very gentle.

Blinking, she tried to clear her vision, but everything remained hazy.

Kind of ... distant ... removed.

She was here but she didn't feel like she was here.

Her body might have hit the ground, but her mind seemed to be still floating through the air.

"Lucy? Answer me, now! Are you okay?" Zander sounded panicked, and even though she really wanted to soothe him, she didn't seem to have control over anything. Not even her own body.

"Let me get an IV set up," Bubba said.

Even though she felt stuck floating in the air, it was like she was still able to look down on what was happening. It was a little fuzzy, but she could see Zander and Bubba kneeling beside her, Rocco and Gumby were standing protectively beside them. Rex, Phantom, and Ace were surrounding the pilot, and Fox and the guys running toward the flaming wreckage of the helo she'd just jumped out of.

Guess Zimraan really didn't know how to fly a helo.

Good.

She was glad he was dead.

He'd threatened the man she was falling in love with, made Zander live out his worst nightmare all over again, he deserved a lot worse than he'd gotten.

"What's wrong with her?" Zander asked, the panic in his voice growing. "Why won't she answer me? She's awake, her eyes are open, but she's not saying anything and looking right through me."

Hands were skimming her body, and Bubba looked concerned. "She's in shock, but her pulse is steady, she's not going to die."

No.

Not going to die.

But her overwhelmed brain was ready to short circuit. Her body went completely taut and then her muscles began to jerk violently as a seizure hit.

* * *

JANUARY 28TH
   11:51 P.M.

"IT WOULD BE REALLY nice if you woke up soon, sassy girl," Zander whispered as he brushed his knuckles across a sleeping Lucy's forehead.

More than fourteen hours had passed since he watched her jump out of a flying helicopter.

In those seconds it had taken her to hit the ground he'd been positive his heart was going to hammer its way right out of his chest. There was every possibility that she wouldn't survive the fall, even though it wasn't a huge distance, and even if she did the injuries she could have ended up with might have been horrific.

Though he'd lived through a lot in his life, those seconds topped the scale of the worst of the worst.

Because Lucy was his future.

His entire future was wrapped up in a five-foot-three, blonde-haired, blue-eyed package, full to the brim of smarts, sass, and strength. Without her, his life would be empty and useless. There would be no point in going on.

A whirlwind of activity had filled the first half of the last fourteen hours. Another helo had been brought in to pick them up, Lucy and the pilot had both been loaded onto backboards and transported to Landstuhl, the military hospital in Germany. It was the closest facility, and five hours after she jumped out of the helo, she was being examined by a doctor.

Two of her cracked ribs had been damaged further, her broken arm had ended up needing surgery, there was a hairline fracture in her right foot that would require her to wear a moon boot for a few weeks, and she had been diagnosed with a concussion. Some of the wounds from where she'd been skinned would need to be watched carefully for infection, and thankfully none were bad enough to need skin grafts.

Three hours after arriving at the hospital, she was wheeled out of recovery and into a private room.

While the doctors had told him—on many more than one occasion—that she was not receiving any sedation drugs, and that her brain scan was clear, he was yet to believe it.

Why wasn't she waking up?

Six hours was more than enough time for her body to have regained enough strength just to open those big blue

JANE BLYTHE

eyes for a single second. That was all he needed. One second to know that she was going to be okay.

"How's our girl doing?" Phantom asked as he strolled into Lucy's room.

All six of the SEAL team guys had decided to stay at the hospital until Lucy was released as had all the Prey guys. Nobody wanted to leave without her.

In their world, you didn't leave anyone behind, even if you would only be leaving the person safe in a hospital bed.

"She's the same," he replied. The guys kept coming in and out. Nobody wanted to overwhelm her when she woke up, otherwise, he was pretty sure that all twelve of them would be camping out in there. Well, maybe eleven as he was sure somebody would hang with the pilot who had been lucky to walk away with nothing more than bumps and bruises.

"Lucy is strong, she'll be okay," Phantom said as he pulled up the room's other chair to the opposite side of Lucy's bed.

The man's confidence should help, but it didn't.

Lucy was strong but had lived through hell these last couple of weeks. Was she strong enough to survive the aftermath?

More than that, was she strong enough to forgive him for what she'd suffered because of him and still want a future with him?

That seemed like more than he should hope for.

More than he deserved.

Because of him, the woman he was falling in love with had been abducted, flown halfway around the world, strapped to a table and had her skin peeled off with a knife, and been forced to jump out of a helicopter.

Expecting her forgiveness was like expecting her to grow wings and fly herself home.

"How are you doing?" Phantom asked, assessing him with

brown eyes that seemed to see too much. See more than Zander wanted.

Much more than he was comfortable with.

Giving what he hoped came off as an easy, dismissive shrug, he replied, "I'm fine. Zimraan's men didn't break anything." While Lucy had been in surgery and there was no possibility of him remaining at her side, he'd finally agreed to be checked out himself. He had some hellish bruises littering his body, horrible black and blue marks that he was sure would hurt when his fear for Lucy dissipated enough for him to feel anything else.

"Still with everything that happened with your team, then having to relive it all with Lucy ..."

When Phantom trailed off, giving him the opportunity to fill in the blanks, Zander remained steadfastly silent.

What did the man expect him to say?

That it was like being transported to hell?

That watching Lucy be tortured, hearing her screams, was the worst thing he'd ever had to do?

That if he was a braver, less selfish man he'd do the right thing and walk away from her now so she didn't have to see his face when she finally woke up?

All of that was true, but he couldn't make himself say it aloud.

Almost as though by speaking it he might make it become a reality.

"She needs you, you get that, right?" Phantom asked.

There was no way he couldn't scoff at that.

What Lucy needed to heal was for him to get out of her life. How could she possibly deal with everything that had happened when she had to look at his face every day and know he was to blame for most of it?

The problem was, he didn't know how to live without her.

While she might be better off if he returned to being a ghost man as she liked to call him, he most certainly would not be better off without her.

It terrified him how much he needed her.

"Zander, if you don't know it then let me say it. She needs you. She doesn't need you to be perfect, she doesn't need you to always say and do the right thing, and she doesn't need you to hide your own pain and trauma from her. But she does need you to be there. She needs to hold onto you when she feels like the bottom of the world has opened up beneath her, wanting to swallow her whole. She needs you to hold onto her, too, when you feel the same way."

"I want to believe that, but ..." Zander trailed off, the ending not needing to be said aloud. He wanted to believe it but how could he?

How could he think his presence could in any way help Lucy heal?

"Can you please trust me on that?" Phantom asked. "I learned a lot from being there for Kalee as she healed from what happened to her in Timor-Leste. And please trust me and believe me when I say this, being alone is the worst thing for her right now. Your presence is going to make all the difference in how she heals."

"She has other people. Parents, siblings, her whole Prey family," he reminded Phantom. Whether he was in the picture or not, it wasn't like Lucy was going to be alone.

"But they weren't there. They won't get it. Not really. They'll try and do their best, and yes, Lucy needs them, too. But that doesn't change the fact that she needs you. You lived through it with her, and I'm pretty sure she's falling in love with you. Don't let your demons talk you into doing something that's going to wind up hurting you and the woman you love."

With that, Phantom got up, leaned down to touch a kiss

to Lucy's forehead, then rounded the bed to squeeze Zander's shoulder before heading out of the room, leaving him and Lucy alone again.

As badly as he wanted to believe everything Phantom had said, his demons were screaming at him that the man was lying.

There was no way on earth that Lucy could need him now.

Her Prey family were no strangers to the horrors of the world. Fox and the guys had all been SEALs, and they'd all gone through ordeals with their now wives. The women of Artemis Team had all gone through more than most people could ever comprehend, and then there was what Scarlett had been through a couple of weeks ago. Lucy would be surrounded by people who would understand what she was going through and know how to help her.

People who wouldn't make her have to relive it all every time she looked at their faces.

She'd be fine without him.

Better without him.

Because all he'd done since he came back from the dead was hurt her. Crashing the plane, scaring her in the jungle, not saving her soon enough from Raul Castillo, letting her get kidnapped by people with a grudge against him, getting her tortured and almost killed. Never once had be brought anything good into her life.

Only pain.

Only suffering.

Only trauma that would haunt her for the rest of her life, just as his own was haunting him now. Reminding him of his sins, reminding him of his failures, reminding him of all the reasons he should leave, and why Lucy would be better off without him.

Dropping his forehead to rest against hers, Zander tried

to draw in enough of her scent, the feel of her on his skin, her bravery and strength, to imprint it on his soul. He needed enough of her to last him a lifetime.

All he needed was one second to see his girl's eyes open, to know that she was going to be okay, and then he should disappear for good.

CHAPTER TWENTY-ONE

January 29th
   12:29 A.M.

Fear was the first thing that registered as consciousness returned.

Lucy's eyes snapped open, needing to see only one thing.

Only one person.

Thankfully, that person was sitting right beside her bed, his face millimeters from hers.

Relief washed away the coming wave of pain, and instead she smiled, reveling in the knowledge that he was alive and safe now.

The smile fell from her face when Zander didn't smile back, and the knot of fear in her stomach returned.

She might not have lost him yet, but he was teetering on the edge.

Watching what Zimraan had done to her couldn't have been easy for him, it was reliving his worst nightmare, and

JANE BLYTHE

Lucy doubted there was anything she could do or say to reassure him. Today his demons were roaring in his mind, urging him to give her up. She knew he was worried about her getting hurt because of him, and already blamed himself at least in part for what happened in Mexico.

But she needed him.

More than he could understand.

Even more than she could understand.

"Don't leave me," she whispered the words, her body weak but her mind strong.

Surprise flared in Zander's dark eyes, and then he gave her a half smile. "You're a little mind reader, aren't you, sassy girl?"

"Know you, know you're hurting, but I'm hurting, too, Zander, and I don't want to hurt alone." If there was one thing she had learned in these last few days with Zander, it was that being open and honest was more important than she'd ever realized. For so many years she'd seen asking for help and admitting weakness as something to be avoided at all costs. But the lies and secrets between her and Zander had only wound up hurting them both.

It wasn't weak to admit you needed someone.

Asking for help was a strength. While it might not always be easy to do, it was important and something she wanted to learn to do and do comfortably. Human beings needed other humans, they couldn't do everything alone, and she no longer felt compelled to prove herself over and over again.

"Lucy, I ... this is my fault." With featherlight touches, his fingertips brushed across the lump on her head, and then over her neck where she was sure there were at least half a dozen nicks from the knife.

"How do you figure that?"

A frown furrowed his brow, and she couldn't resist reaching

244

up and smoothing it away. Anything to touch him just in case she couldn't convince him to stay. Zander might think leaving was the right thing to do for her, but he couldn't be more wrong. She needed him in a way she'd never needed another person.

"Zimraan only took you because of me," Zander said like it was obvious.

"Right, sure, but how does that make it *your* fault. Did you ask him to take me? Did you want him to take me? Did you enjoy watching what he did to me?"

"Hell no," he roared, then straightened, his hands clenching into fists as he stormed around her hospital room like his emotions were too big for him to contain.

Well, he could join the club.

Because her emotions were bubbling inside her like a kettle put on to boil. Sooner or later, they were going to come screeching out and she had no idea how she was going to deal with that when it happened.

But what she did know was that when those emotions came out, it would be so much easier to cope if she wasn't alone. If she had Zander by her side. He was what she needed, he was the one who understood what she'd been through, he had lived it with her. If there was a way to let him see inside her head and understand how much she needed him, she'd be all over it, but the facts were she couldn't force him to stay.

Nor did she want to.

She wanted him to be with her because he couldn't not, because walking away was impossible, because he needed her as much as she needed him.

"Do you see me differently now? Am I no longer beautiful to you because I'm going to have scars?" Saying the words hurt because she knew she was going to have a hard time dealing with the scars that would litter her body, but she needed to make Zander realize the truth no matter what she had to say to do it.

"Why would you say that?" he raged as he stormed back over to the bed.

Instead of answering, she continued to ask him questions. "Do you think I'm weak now? I screamed and cried when Zimraan was peeling off my skin, and I couldn't fight off his men when they were dragging me to the table."

"What the hell is wrong with you?" Zander demanded, fire dancing in his eyes.

"Just trying to figure out why you'd want to walk away from me when we should be clinging to one another."

"You are without a doubt the strongest woman I have ever known. You have survived so much, dealt with so much, and its only because of you that Zimraan is dead and no longer a threat."

"Maybe you've decided my epilepsy is too much to handle. It will always affect me and there are things I can't do because of it."

"What you deal with every single day only makes you stronger," he said fiercely.

"Do you think I'm a liar then? That I didn't mean it when I said I was always going to be there for you?"

"You're not a liar."

"Then maybe I'm stupid and don't even know what I want or what I need."

"You're smart, smarter than me."

"So, if I'm not stupid, I'm not weak, I'm not a liar, and you still think I'm beautiful, then why would you walk away from me?" This time she allowed a hint of the vulnerability she felt seep into her voice.

"Hell, baby girl, it's not you it's all me," he said, raking his fingers through his hair. "It's always me, never you, you're perfect. I didn't think it was possible, but I love you even more now. Seeing how brave you were, how you fought for yourself and your life. Then seeing you lying here, fighting for us while I feel like I'm floundering. I don't want to walk away. Damn, nothing scares me more than walking away from you, losing you. But I don't know if I'm as strong as you are, baby. You fight for what you want, but the problem is I don't think I'm worth fighting for."

Lucy just stared at him in shock.

Had he really said what she thought he had?

Everything else had faded away as she had fixated on the most important part.

"You said you love me," she whispered, totally in awe.

His brow furrowed like he hadn't even realized he'd said the words. "Is that ... okay? Is it too soon? Damn, I didn't scare you off, did I?"

A laugh bubbled up inside her and she let it burst out. "Scare me off? Zander, what exactly did you think I meant when I said I would always be there for you?"

"That you wanted to support me?"

"And why do you think that was?"

"Scarlett?"

"No, not because of your sister. Because of you. Because from the first time I met you I felt something. Because even when I wasn't sure if you could be trusted, I saw your pain and knew that whatever was going on deep down you were a good guy. Because the more time we spent together the more I fell. Because I could already see us having an amazing future with everything we both want, all our dreams coming true, everything we deserve," she added.

When he winced at her final words, Lucy held out a hand to him, praying he would take it. They didn't have to sort everything out this very second, she just had to convince him not to give up on them.

Relief flooded her system when he reached out a shaking hand to grasp hers.

He wasn't giving up.

That was all she could ask of him.

"I know you blame yourself for what happened to your team and for what happened to me. I don't have a magic answer to take away your guilt, and I can't promise you that everything is going to be easy. We've both suffered major traumas, and dealing with them is going to be a bumpy road. All I'm saying is, I want to travel that road with you. Because I love you, too."

For a second he just stared at her in shock, and then the sweetest, happiest smile broke out on his face and the fingers around hers squeezed. "You love me, too?" he asked hopefully, like he wasn't sure he should let himself believe it.

"I'm practical, straightforward, and always say what I mean, but in case you still have doubts, I'm falling in love with you, Zander Madden. It's been a crazy ride, and I'm terrified to face the aftermath of what happened to us, but knowing I can have you by my side makes it a little less scary. Stay with me? Always?"

"Always," he echoed.

And as he reached out to carefully gather her into an embrace, Lucy felt her heart settle and her anxiety recede. The next few days, and weeks, and months were going to be tough. But she had Zander and that meant everything would work out in the end.

* * *

JANUARY 28TH
4:12 P.M.

.   .   .

"How are you feeling?" Zander asked Lucy as he carried her into his house. Since she'd insisted on not remaining in the hospital in Germany and there was no medical reason why her doctors could compel her to stay, Eagle Oswald had organized a flight back home for all of them.

Of course, the flight had come with a doctor and a nurse to monitor Lucy for the almost thirteen hours it took to fly back Stateside. But now the doctor was gone as was the nurse, and everyone else had gone to their respective homes —Scarlett and Tate once again caring for Lucy's dog—so it was up to him to look after his woman.

Not that he wanted someone here per se, but he was terrified he was going to do something wrong and somehow make Lucy's condition worse. Broken bones were just that. Broken bones that would take time to heal, and she didn't have any serious internal injuries. She'd been lucky, but he didn't want to push that luck. Especially not when he was still feeling raw and uncertain.

Uncertain about himself not about the gorgeous woman cradled in his arms.

"Like I fell out of a helicopter," Lucy replied, an amused spark in her blue eyes. Since he had already asked her that at least a hundred times since she had insisted on coming home and signed herself out of the hospital, he could see why she might be amused and willing to make light of the situation.

But from where he was standing, it was the least amusing thing in the world.

While Lucy might have been the one to actually jump, she'd known what she was doing, weighed the pros and cons, come to the decision it was her best move, and taken the opportunity that presented itself.

He, on the other hand, had been forced to watch his woman just suddenly plummeting toward the earth without the aid of a parachute or anything else that might cushion her fall.

Those seconds were etched into his mind forever.

Even with everything he'd been through, everything he'd witnessed, that moment was the worst. Maybe because he'd never expected to survive being captured with his team, or known about the tracker that had been implanted in Lucy, so he hadn't been expecting to survive that either. But once help came and he realized how close they were to going home, to think he was going to lose Lucy anyway was too much. Too painful. Too horrifying.

"How can you joke about that?" he asked in a strangled voice. Too many emotions were pulsing inside him, growing quicker than he knew how to cope with.

Eyes sobering, Lucy touched a kiss to his stubbled jaw. "I'm sorry, Zander. I didn't mean to make you upset. I'm okay. I'm sore, and it's going to suck waiting for my injuries to heal, but I *am* okay. I'm not dead, and I'm not going to die. My injuries are painful, and they don't look good, I know I'm going to have scars, but they're not life-threatening and, honestly, right now that's all I care about. We both survived, and I'm happy and excited about that. For a while I didn't think we were going to, but we did, and I want to take this moment to rejoice in that fact because I can feel a storm building inside me."

Sometimes it was hard to remember that Lucy had been through a lot in such a short amount of time. She seemed like she was handling it all just fine. He was the one who felt like he was seconds away from falling apart. But he was going to have to remember that she had spent a lifetime perfecting the art of putting on a strong and put-together front. Not that she wasn't either of those things, but beneath the façade she was struggling, too, and he couldn't let her distract him from that fact.

"I feel that same storm, baby," he whispered. Being vulnerable like that was hard for him. It wasn't the way he was raised. As a child, he wasn't encouraged to express emotions, let alone anything that would make him appear weak. That wasn't fitting of a future military serviceman in his parents' opinion, nor was it appropriate "boy" behavior. His parents believed that men shouldn't express emotion ever, that they should never admit to being scared, and that crying was the equivalent of emasculating yourself and all but becoming a woman.

"That's why we need to be together," Lucy whispered back, but he could hear the thread of fear in her voice. She was still scared that he was going to bail on her.

But since his inner demons had been unable to come up with logical ways to counter all the reasons Lucy had given why he should stay, he had been able to silence them enough to remain by her side. The urge to leave, to get as far away from her as he could was still strong. He didn't want to hurt her ever again.

So, to counter the urge to put a safe distance between them, he was going to do the opposite. Take care of his girl the best way he knew how.

"I'm not going anywhere, baby girl," he assured her, and he felt her relax at his words. "Now what do you need? Something to eat? You've only been picking at food since you woke up, so you must be hungry, and you need to keep your strength up. Or I can take you up to bed if you're tired and need to sleep? The doctor said you were going to be a lot more tired than usual for the next few days, at least as your body starts to recover."

"Actually, what I really want is a long, hot bath. I feel like I've been dirty for weeks now. All I had at the hospital was a sponge bath and it wasn't enough to get the feel of dirt and blood off my skin. And don't even get me started on my hair.

But there's no way I can take a bath with this on." She shot an irritated look at the cast on her arm.

Just because he'd never washed long hair before didn't mean he couldn't, it was the same as washing short hair only there was more of it. "I'll give you a bath, baby. We can put a plastic bag over your cast to keep it dry and keep it out of the water. And I'm sure I've got waterproof bandages in my first aid kit so we can cover up your other wounds."

No baths hadn't been in the doctor's list of instructions, Lucy was just to keep her wounds as dry as possible and change the bandages if they got wet. That he could do as soon as he got her all cleaned up. Rest was important and there was no way his girl would be able to relax properly if she felt dirty.

"You're going to give me a bath?" Lucy asked, there was a tiny hint of incredulity in her tone but also a huge amount of tenderness.

"Yep, and it's going to be the best bath you've ever had," he said, making her giggle. She was right when she said they needed to enjoy this moment of relishing being alive because the storm was coming, and when it did, they would both be clinging to one another.

Carrying her up the stairs, he headed for the master bath and the huge soaking tub in it. The enormous walk-in shower had caught his attention when he'd been looking at places, but now he was glad there was the bath as well since his girl seemed to prefer them.

In the bathroom, he set her on the counter while he turned on the faucet and adjusted the heat. Then while the bath was filling, he stripped her out of her clothes, then pulled out a garbage bag and tied it around her arm. After that, he put waterproof bandages over all the cuts that had needed stitches, and the spots where Zimraan had peeled off her skin.

Looking at them, it was hard not to lose his control, but since he could sense Lucy's mounting anxiety, Zander forced himself to remain calm, and touched soft kisses to the bandages once he'd applied them.

Then he turned off the water, removed his clothes, and picked Lucy up. Lowering them both into the bath, Lucy sighed in contentment as the warm water encased their bodies.

With his girl settled between his bent knees, Zander cupped his hands together and scooped up some water to wet her hair, then grabbed a bottle of shampoo, poured a generous amount into the palm of his hand, and began to massage it into Lucy's scalp. She moaned in delight as he worked the soapy suds through every inch of her long blonde locks, and the more she did so the more he wanted to make this feel good for her.

After another round of shampooing, he shifted so Lucy's neck was balanced on his forearm, then scooped up handfuls of water to wash the bubbles out. Their eyes met as he did so, being careful to make sure he didn't get any soapy suds in her eyes. Never again was he going to cause this woman pain, not even the sting of soap in her eyes. And he would do whatever it took to protect her from pain caused by others. Lucy had been through enough, she should never have to suffer again.

When he leaned down to brush his lips across hers, those big blue eyes of hers began to shimmer with unshed tears. His heart constricted and he was filled with a powerful urge to do whatever it took to make her smile.

He wasn't ready for the storm to hit yet.

Tears began to leak from the corners of her eyes, and Zander quickly gathered her to him, holding her tight against his chest as a sob escaped Lucy's lips.

Cradling her in his arms as she wept should have made

him want to run because he knew that he was a major source of the pain she had suffered, pain that had to be let out through tears. But it didn't. Instead, holding her felt right. More than right, it felt like this was where he belonged.

Lucy needed him and he was there.

It was as simple as that.

And maybe he could let her be there for him, too.

CHAPTER TWENTY-TWO

January 29th
4:27 P.M.

LUCY WASN'T EVEN sure why she was crying.

Zander was being so sweet and tender with her, washing her hair with so much love and care. Each touch reminded her both of how lucky she was to have him, not just alive, but there in the bath with her taking such good care of her when he had to be hurting from his own injuries, but also of how close she'd come to losing him. Not just losing him to Zimraan and his need for revenge, but to Zander's own fears and insecurities.

Knowing that he was there, with her, and he'd promised to stay, filled her with too many feelings. They built inside her heart, her gratefulness warring with her fear that Zander could still change his mind until they had to come out.

Somehow, at the same time as holding her close like she was the most precious thing in his world, Zander had also managed to be clear-headed enough to ensure her broken arm was kept out of the water, draped over his shoulder as her other arm wrapped around his chest, clinging to him in a silent plea for him not to leave her.

She needed him.

More than she'd ever needed anyone else.

It was a different kind of need, it felt soul-deep, like if he went, he'd take a part of her with him that she would never be able to get back.

"Shh, baby girl, I'm here, I'm here," Zander whispered into her hair as he tucked her face close against his neck. One of his large hands cradled the back of her head, his fingers massaging her scalp just as they had been doing moments before as he worked the shampoo through her long, dirty locks. His other arm was around her waist, keeping her anchored against him the same way she was doing with him.

The thought made her smile.

They might be adrift in the middle of a vast ocean, with no clues how to navigate the emotional landscape before them, but they weren't alone. They had each other. That was a thought she kept hanging onto. The more she thought it the more she could make it a reality.

"I'm not going to leave you, baby, that's a promise."

His words set off another wave of tears, but this time joyful ones. Earlier in the hospital, he'd told her he would stay with her always, but since she continued to sense his doubts and insecurity, she continued to have doubts, too.

Maybe she was going to need to hear a few more times that Zander wasn't going anywhere.

"You swear?" she asked through her tears, nuzzling at his neck.

"Baby, I might never think I'm worthy of you, but as long as you want me here by your side that's where I'm going to be."

"I'm always going to want you by my side."

"Then I'm always going to be here."

Smiling as she lifted her head, she feathered a line of kisses along his stubbled jaw. Tears continued to roll down her cheeks, but she ignored them because warmth was spreading inside her.

This man was hers.

Forever.

He'd told her that he was going to be by her side for as long as she wanted him, and she was going to hold him to it.

She wasn't letting him go and he had better get himself used to that idea.

"I need you, Zander," she whimpered, shifting until her center lined up with his hardening erection.

"Baby girl, we can't," he groaned, although by the heated look in his eyes he clearly wanted to. "You have broken ribs, a broken foot, a broken arm, cuts and bruises everywhere, bigger wounds with stitches, and you've had two seizures in the last week. The doctors said no strenuous activity for at least a month."

"Can't wait a month," she told him. And really it was as simple as that. In the last week she had survived a plane crash, being kidnapped and tortured in Mexico, being kidnapped and tortured in Syria, and a fall out of a helicopter. It wasn't wrong for her to want to celebrate being alive. Being with the man she loved.

"Don't want to hurt you," Zander murmured, sweeping his fingertips across her wet cheeks to catch the last of her tears.

"You won't. We'll be careful. Not hot and steamy this time, just you and me making sweet, gentle love. Unless you're in pain," she added. Just because he had no broken bones didn't mean he wasn't injured and hurting, too. There were bruises over most of his body, horrible black and blue marks that made her want to cry every time she looked at them.

"No, baby, I'm not in pain. I just can't hurt you again."

"It won't hurt, I swear, and even if it did, I don't care. I need to feel you inside me, Zander. I need to feel that you're alive, that I'm alive, that we survived and we're here together. Please, Zander. I just need … you."

"Baby, I don't think I can say no to you about anything."

"Thank you." She dropped a kiss to his lips as his large hands framed her face and his serious eyes met hers. There was so much tenderness and affection in those deep brown depths that more tears filled her eyes.

"You let me do all the work though, okay?"

"Okay," she quickly agreed, anything so that he would hurry up and get inside her, filling the void in her heart.

When his lips met hers, the kiss was so soft and sweet, he was making love to her with his lips and she loved it. The fingers of her good hand tangled in his hair as he lifted her and gently lowered her onto his hard length. Already she was wet and aching with need, and he slid in smoothly in one thrust, filling her as perfectly as she had known he would.

Like the protective alpha male that he was, he kept a grip on her hips so that he was the one doing all the work, and somehow, he managed to position his hands so not only could he hold onto her hips but with every gentle thrust his thumbs grazed her throbbing bundle of nerves.

Sensations built inside her.

Wonderful, beautiful, sweet, tender sensations.

Lucy knew what it was to be loved. She came from a wonderful if overprotective family. But she had never known what it was to be cherished in this way.

It was such an amazing feeling that she was pretty sure she could have come from it alone.

Combined with the feel of Zander inside her, the friction he created with each thrust, and the brush of his thumb over her sensitive bud, there was no way an orgasm couldn't be shimmering to life inside her.

It hit her with the intensity of a bomb.

Only instead of fire, it felt like shimmery glitter exploded all around her.

It sparkled with an intensity that couldn't help but remind her that she and Zander had both survived, and that even if it was a bumpy road getting there, they could have a happy ever after that neither of them had even realized they craved.

When Zander came seconds later it seemed to increase the intensity of her pleasure, making it go on and on until she wasn't sure she could take a second more of it. But Zander was there, kissing her, holding her, his scent and his body surrounding her, cocooning her in a bubble that she would be perfectly happy to live in for the rest of her life.

"Thank you," she murmured as she touched another kiss to Zander's lips like she couldn't get enough of the taste of him, which honestly, she couldn't.

"You never need to thank me for giving you what you need," Zander told her. "Are you okay? In pain?"

"Zander, I am not lying one little bit when I say the only thing I'm feeling right now is the peace and contentment from being thoroughly satisfied by the man I love."

A pleased chuckle rumbled through his chest, and he pressed a tender kiss to her forehead. "Don't think I'm ever going to get tired of hearing you tell me you love me."

"Hmm, good thing we have the rest of our lives to say it then, isn't it?" With a sleepy sigh she snuggled closer.

"Tired, babe?"

"Mmhmm."

"Then let me get some conditioner in your hair and I'll wash this perfect body of yours, then dry you off and get you all tucked into bed."

"Sounds perfect so long as you're going to lie down with me." Although she was trying her best to be strong for Zander, knowing how much he needed her, she was exhausted. But the only way she would get any sleep was with his arms wrapped around her.

"Wouldn't dream of being anywhere but by your side."

That was perfect because it was the only place she wanted him.

* * *

JANUARY 29TH
6:51 P.M.

"WHY IS someone knocking on my door this late at night?" Zander growled, making his girl giggle.

"It's not even seven," Lucy reminded him.

"But after the hell you've been through this last week, you need your rest."

"Only I couldn't sleep. I tried. Dozed for like twenty minutes and then that was it." There were shadows in Lucy's eyes as she said that, and he knew why she hadn't been able to sleep properly and why she'd wanted to get up and come downstairs to watch TV.

Nightmares.

The silent killer.

They ate away at you a little at a time while you were at your most vulnerable. He'd suffered them plenty of times since he joined the military, and they'd become an almost nightly occurrence after his team was killed. While he wanted to protect his girl from suffering them, too, he couldn't, all he could do was hold her through them and soothe and reassure her the best he could once he woke her up.

"Go see who's at the door, Zander," she said, a hint of worry in her voice. "It could be something important. The mole is still out there, and I know I'm safe with you, Scarlett is safe with Tate, and people are watching Ella and Cassie, but I still worry."

"All right, babe." Kissing her forehead, he shifted her so he could slide off the couch, then paused to tuck the blanket snugly around her, making her shoot him an amused smile. "Don't want you to get cold," he said gruffly, surprised by how deep the urge to protect this woman from every little thing ran.

"Love you, Zander."

"Love you back, baby girl."

The words were so easy to exchange considering he'd only ever told one person in his life that he loved them, and that was his sister, and he didn't mean it the same way he did when he said it to Lucy.

He was smiling despite his irritation at someone disturbing Lucy this time of night, even if she was right and it wasn't all that late. But when he opened the door and saw who was standing on his doorstep the irritation bled away.

"Scarlett," he exclaimed, reaching out to pick his sister up off her feet so he could hug her. "Did you come to check on Lucy?"

There was a reproachful expression on her face as he set her back down. "No, Zander. Well, I mean, yes, of course. But I ... I mean we," she corrected, glancing over her shoulder where Tate was standing with a towel wrapped around what

Zander guessed was a casserole dish or something, "are here for you, too. You're my brother, I love you, I'm worried about both of you."

For a moment he didn't know what to say to that.

Over time, with the distance that had grown between them, he'd forgotten what it felt like to have his sister care about him.

Maybe over the last decade and a half, he'd forced himself to accept the fact that Scarlett didn't love him anymore. It was the only way to deal with that distance, first foster care, and then his decision to go after his parents' love by following in their footsteps had created.

But not anymore.

He wanted a close relationship with his sister. Wanted back what they'd had when they were kids, that closeness of knowing that there was always somebody who had your back no matter what.

Now he had two people to have his back. The two most important people in his life, his sister, and the woman he was falling in love with. A few days ago, he'd felt completely and utterly alone, without his team he'd had no one, and when he'd agreed to fake his death it meant cutting off ties with everyone on the peripheries of his life. All that had surrounded him was empty darkness, there was no way he'd been able to stop that darkness from seeping inside him.

Lucy had shined that first little speck of light into his world again.

The more time he spent with her the more that light grew, sending the darkness fleeing. With Scarlett's light as well, maybe there was hope for the darkness to eventually be completely banished.

"Zander? Who is it?" Lucy called out from the living room, and he could hear the growing worry in her voice.

"Can we come in?" Scarlett asked. "Is it okay that we came?"

Dragging his sister back into his arms he hugged her hard. "Of course it is."

"You can say if it's not. Tate thought maybe we would be intruding, and you'd want time alone."

Shooting a glare at the other man for saying anything that upset his twin sister, he then softened that frown into a smile as he kissed the top of his sister's head. "Scar, I know it'll take time for you to believe it, but there is never a time I don't want to hang-out with you. You're my twin sister, we're two halves of the same whole. I love you, always and forever, nothing is going to change that. I made mistakes, a ton of them. I let my need for Mom and Dad's love come between us, but in the end, I was good at what I did and I enjoyed it, well for the most part. I take full responsibility for us growing apart, and I'll do whatever it takes to mend our relationship."

Noticing Tate's approving nod, it was overshadowed when Scarlett grabbed him in a fierce hug, standing on tiptoe to kiss his cheek. "We both allowed us to drift apart, but no more. I want my brother back. I thought I'd lost you forever but now you're here, standing before me, and you're in love with one of my best friends, and I'm not going to let you go again."

"How did I get so lucky to have the best sister in the world?" he asked, affectionately tugging on her hair like he used to do when they were kids.

"I'm the lucky one," Tate said, stepping up and dropping a kiss to the top of Scarlett's head.

"With Zander for a brother, and Tate for a boyfriend, I'm the one who's lucky," Scarlett said, sharing her smile with both of them.

"Zander, if you don't answer me, I'm going to get up and walk down to the door myself," Lucy called out.

"Oh no you don't, you're not supposed to be walking on that foot," he warned, ushering Scarlett and Tate into the house and locking up behind them. "It's only Scar and Tate." Since he didn't know Scarlett's boyfriend, he was going to have to sit the man down and find out what his intentions were because nobody was hurting his twin. Scarlett had been through more than anyone should ever have to, and he wouldn't allow her to be hurt again.

"We brought dinner," Scarlett announced as they all entered the living room. "Tate has been learning to cook and he helped me make macaroni and cheese for the first time. It has to go in the oven, and I thought while it cooks, we'll make potato spirals."

"I love your potato spirals," Lucy said, beaming at her friend.

"They're great comfort food and I think we all need a little comfort right now," Scarlett said, her gaze roaming between them.

That was absolutely the truth. Scarlett had been physically and sexually tortured by Raul Castillo, and before she even had a chance to begin the healing process he popped back up in her life and then one of her best friends was hurt, too. And Lucy had been kidnapped twice, once by the weapons dealer and once by a terrorist. All of that within the last few weeks. Both women had physical and psychological wounds they had barely had a chance to acknowledge.

And worse, so long as the mole was still out there neither of them were safe.

How could any of them hope to begin the healing process when there was the constant threat of someone coming after them again?

They all needed a night off. A night to just chill out and

have fun. Eat good food and talk and laugh. And a little family bonding would be nice. He and Tate didn't know each other, and since the man had only recently entered his sister's life, Tate didn't know Lucy or really Scarlett well either.

Comfort food and hang-out time were exactly what they all needed.

"Zander and I will help cook," Lucy said, looking hungry for the first time since she'd woken up in the hospital. This might be a distraction from their problems, but nobody said you had to face your problems right away. Sometimes a distraction was exactly what the doctor ordered.

"Only if you don't overdo things," he warned Lucy as he moved to scoop her up before she could do something stupid like try to walk on her broken foot.

"Good luck with that, man." Tate smirked as he slapped him on the back.

"They're a handful, aren't they?" he said to the other man.

"Hey!" Lucy punched him in the arm, her aim off and there was no strength behind it, but he loved her cute little outraged expression.

"Adorable, too," he added, laughing when his girl's eyes shot daggers at him.

This was pure heaven. His girl in his arms, his sister by his side, a man who would likely soon become his brother there as well. Laughter and joy in the air, and a strong sense of love. As a child, this kind of family had seemed so remote from the life he'd lived, but now it was within his grasp.

There would always be a hole in his heart left behind by the seven men who had died horrific deaths in front of him, and there would always be guilt for not saving them. But Zander knew without a shadow of a doubt that every one of those seven men would be smiling down on him right now, glad he'd chosen happiness and light over vengeance and darkness.

For the rest of his life, he'd never have to worry about the darkness consuming him because in his arms he held the brightest of lights.

His light.

His Lucy.

CHAPTER TWENTY-THREE

January 29th
8:18 P.M.

"I'M STUFFED," Lucy said, leaning back in her chair and pressing a hand to her stomach. "That was amazing. I've had your mac and cheese before, and those potato spirals are my favorite, but somehow, they tasted better tonight."

"That's because I helped make them," Tate teased with a wink.

"It's so cute that you want to learn to cook because Scarlett loves cooking," she told him,

While Tate rolled his eyes at being called cute, the smile he shot Scarlett was pure warmth and joy. When Lucy cast a glance at Zander sitting beside her at the table, she saw he was smiling at her the same way.

When he smiled at her like that, it was like a lifetime of feeling she had to constantly be fighting to prove herself all melted away, and she felt a peace inside that was so soft and beautiful she wanted to curl her fingers around it and hold onto it so it never melted away. Thankfully, as long as she had Zander at her side, she didn't have to worry about holding onto that feeling because every time he smiled at her it bloomed in her chest.

"What about you, Zander? Did you inherit that same cooking gene?" she asked, and he immediately made a face and shook his head.

"Cooking and I are not friends," he told her.

"Massive understatement," Scarlett added. "In our family, girls cooked, and men ate. Although, my brother, being the sweet guy that he is and the bestest brother a girl could ever ask for, did try to help me out one time when I was sick. I think we were about nine, and I had a stomach virus. In both our parents' and grandparents' minds, that was nothing that required staying home in bed so I was sent to school. The school sent me home anyway, though, and when I couldn't get out of bed to make dinner, Zander did it for me. Well, he tried, but it was a massive fail. He set the oven on fire and we both got into trouble."

"Aww, it's so sweet that you were looking out for your sister," Lucy said, leaning over to kiss Zander's cheek even as her heart broke for the two neglected children they had been.

"Hate that you got punished for being sick, sweetheart," Tate said, pulling Scarlett's chair closer so he could scoop her up and put her on his lap.

"Me, too, but I'm so glad you had each other," Lucy added.

"It was the scars he got that day that made me recognize him on the plane," Scarlett explained. "We had to do an entire deep clean of the house with our wrists tied together as our punishment. A weird sort of three-legged race kind of thing. I was still sick, but we were set a time limit, and Zander just dragged me around with him. The rope tore off all his skin, and I felt so bad I cried. He told me it didn't matter, we were twins which meant we were joined together for all infinity."

"We always looked out for each other," Zander said, smiling at his twin like he couldn't quite believe she was sitting in his living room. A room he had sat in just a couple of days ago contemplating taking his own life because he didn't think anyone would care if he was gone.

Lucy would forever be grateful he had come to her that night rather than doing something he could never take back. Something that would have impacted people more than he realized.

Because she couldn't not touch him, she reached out and threaded the fingers of her good hand with his. Zander immediately tugged her closer and did the same thing Tate did, picking her up and putting her on his lap.

"Zander might not have gotten the cooking gene, but he has a ton of other skills. He can make the most amazing things with wood. When we were kids, he used to make me little animals in between the projects approved by our grandparents. I still have all of them." Scarlett shot a smile at her brother. "Oh, and he also knows how to sew, apparently that was something that was important in our parents' self-sufficiency, military serving lifestyle."

"You can sew?" she asked Zander.

"I'm pretty rusty, I haven't done it in a long time, but yeah, I know how to sew," Zander said, looking a little sheepish.

"That is so sweet, we'll have to get my sewing machine out at some point and make something together. I haven't sewn in a while either, but I used to enjoy it." It had been one of the things she'd done with her mom when she was a little girl and didn't have any friends.

"I'd love to do that with you, baby girl."

"See, the way to a man's heart might be through his stomach, but the way to a woman's heart is through sharing the things she enjoys with her," Scarlett said, her smile including all of them.

"Lucky for you I'm not too bad a cook," she teased Zander.

"Babe, I don't care if you're the worst cook in the whole entire world, you already have my heart."

"Aww," Lucy sighed in delight and melted against Zander, snuggling into his embrace. "You say the sweetest things."

"Hey, dude, you're making me look bad over here," Tate joked.

"You say the sweetest things, too," Scarlett quickly added, making them all laugh.

Could this night be any better?

Nightmares had quickly made sleep unappealing, even with how exhausted she was. While Lucy knew she couldn't avoid it forever, she could certainly put it off a while longer, so she'd asked Zander if he wanted to hang-out downstairs and watch some TV. That had been fine, lying curled up in his arms was her favorite place to be, and she would have been content to snuggle there for hours.

But this was so much better.

This was family.

It was everything she needed right now.

The future was a scary thing, filled with uncertainty, and oppressive anxiety over the fact that Raul Castillo and the mole at Prey were both still out there, it was all too easy to get sucked down that rabbit hole and get lost amongst the fear and pain.

Amidst all that fear and pain there were still things to be grateful for. A tracker she hadn't even known Prey had planted on her. It was Eagle's decision and one only he and Fox had known about at the time, the only way to make sure the information didn't leak to the mole. It had saved her and Zander's lives, and she wasn't the tiniest bit mad about him for sticking it on her without her permission. Without it, she and the man she was falling in love with would be dead.

She was grateful too for her Prey family who had come after her, rescued her, then stayed with her in the hospital. Rocco and his team, too, who had stuck around when they hadn't had to, and Phantom in particular who had talked some sense into Zander when his fear and guilt urged him to run.

And this right here.

People she loved, good food, laughter, the perfect medicine and everything she needed.

The only thing that would make this better was if Ella and Cassie were here with them.

"How come the others didn't come?" she asked Scarlett.

"A little bit of the guys don't want us all in one place because they think that makes us a bigger target. A little bit of we didn't want to overwhelm you with too many people all at once when you've just been through so much. A little bit of Ella felt like she needed the outlet of going to practice tonight. And a little bit of Cassie couldn't keep herself away from the lab because the plane you two crashed was found, and the wreckage was brought back to Prey. You know what Cassie is like when there's a puzzle she needs to solve, she's worse than you. She's becoming obsessed with identifying the mole, it's practically all she can talk about," Scarlett said with an eye roll because they both did know how their genius friend was when she got obsessed with something.

"Then we definitely need to do this again, only with all of us," Lucy said. "Anything to get Cassie out of the lab or she'll move in there until she gets the answers she needs." As much as they all needed to know who the mole at Prey was, Cassie took obsession to a new level. If they didn't make her leave, she would stay at Prey forever, trying to solve all of the world's problems like she didn't deserve to have a life of her own.

When Scarlett's phone began to ring, she reached over for

her bag, which was hanging off the side of the chair she'd been sitting in and pulled out her cell.

At first, Lucy didn't realize anything was wrong. It wasn't until Scarlett gasped and the color drained from her face.

Immediately, Lucy was on edge.

Of course Zander noticed, and his hand began to rub circles on her back while keeping her tucked close.

Lowering the phone from her ear, Scarlett's scared eyes met hers. "There was an explosion at Prey. In the lab," she whispered.

Lucy straightened as fear flooded her system. "Cassie was in the lab."

Scarlett nodded.

"Was it …? Is she …?" Lucy was afraid to voice the rest of her questions aloud as though speaking them might be enough to make them become a reality.

"The explosion was bad, so far they don't know if anyone was killed, but … it doesn't look good," Scarlett informed them.

Which meant there was every chance that Cassie had been killed in the explosion.

Does Cassidy have what it takes to find and dismantle the mole's bombs? Find out in the third book in the action packed and emotionally charged Prey Security: Athena Team series!

Fighting for Cassidy (Prey Security: Athena Team #3)

ALSO BY JANE BLYTHE

Prey Security: Athena Team Series
FIGHTING FOR SCARLETT
FIGHTING FOR LUCY
FIGHTING FOR CASSIDY

Prey Security Series: Artemis Team
IVORY'S FIGHT
PEARL'S FIGHT
LACEY'S FIGHT
OPAL'S FIGHT

Prey Security Series
PROTECTING EAGLE
PROTECTING RAVEN
PROTECTING FALCON
PROTECTING SPARROW
PROTECTING HAWK
PROTECTING DOVE

Prey Security Series: Alpha Team
DEADLY RISK
LETHAL RISK
EXTREME RISK
FATAL RISK
COVERT RISK
SAVAGE RISK

Prey Security: Bravo Team Series

<u>VICIOUS SCARS</u>

<u>RUTHLESS SCARS</u>

<u>BRUTAL SCARS</u>

<u>CRUEL SCARS</u>

<u>BURIED SCARS</u>

Saving SEALs Series

SAVING RYDER

SAVING ERIC

SAVING OWEN

SAVING LOGAN

SAVING GRAYSON

SAVING CHARLIE

Candella Sisters' Heroes Series

LITTLE DOLLS

LITTLE HEARTS

LITTLE BALLERINA

<u>Broken Gems Series</u>

CRACKED SAPPHIRE

CRUSHED RUBY

FRACTURED DIAMOND

SHATTERED AMETHYST

SPLINTERED EMERALD

SALVAGING MARIGOLD

<u>River's End Rescues Series</u>

<u>COCKY SAVIOR</u>

SOME REGRETS ARE FOREVER

PROTECT

SOME LIES WILL HAUNT YOU

SOME QUESTIONS HAVE NO ANSWERS

SOME TRUTH CAN BE DISTORTED

SOME TRUST CAN BE REBUILT

SOME MISTAKES ARE UNFORGIVABLE

Detective Parker Bell Series

A SECRET TO THE GRAVE

WINTER WONDERLAND

DEAD OR ALIVE

LITTLE GIRL LOST

FORGOTTEN

Count to Ten Series

ONE

TWO

THREE

FOUR

FIVE

SIX

BURNING SECRETS

SEVEN

EIGHT

NINE

TEN

Storybook Murders Series

NURSERY RHYME KILLER

ABOUT THE AUTHOR

USA Today bestselling author Jane Blythe writes action-packed romantic suspense and military romance featuring protective heroes and heroines who are survivors. One of Jane's most popular series includes Prey Security, part of Susan Stoker's OPERATION ALPHA world! Writing in that world alongside authors such as Janie Crouch and Riley Edwards has been a blast, and she looks forward to bringing more books to this genre, both within and outside of Stoker's world. When Jane isn't binge-reading she's counting down to Christmas and adding to her 200+ teddy bear collection!

To connect and keep up to date please visit any of the following

Email – mailto:janeblytheauthor@gmail.com
Facebook – https://www.facebook.com/janeblytheauthor
Instagram –
https://www.instagram.com/jane_blythe_author
Reader Group –
https://www.facebook.com/groups/janeskillersweethearts
Twitter – https://www.twitter.com/jblytheauthor
TikTok - https://www.tiktok.com/@janeblytheauthor
Website – https://www.janeblythe.com.au

There are many more books in this fan fiction world than listed here, for an up-to-date list go to www.AcesPress.com

You can also visit our Amazon page at:
http://www.amazon.com/author/operationalpha

Kristin Lynn: Worth the Risk
JM Madden: Rescuing Olivia
A.M. Mahler: Griffin
Ellie Masters: Sybil's Protector
Trish McCallan: Hero Under Fire
Naomi McKay: Twist
Rachel McNeely: The SEAL's Surprise Baby
KD Michaels: Saving Laura
Olivia Michaels: Protecting Harper
Annie Miller: Securing Willow
MJ Nightingale: Protecting Beauty
C.K. O'Connor: Delaney's Bodyguard
Melinda Owens: Betraying Katie
Victoria Paige: Reclaiming Izabel
Danielle Pays: Defending Sarina
Lainey Reese: Protecting New York
KeKe Renée: Protecting Bria
Taryn Rivers: Savage Cove
TL Reeve and Michele Ryan: Extracting Mateo
Ariana Rose: Chasing Paige
Deanna L. Rowley: Saving Veronica
Angela Rush: Charlotte
E.M. Shue: Discovering Tyler
Rose Smith: Saving Satin
Tyler Anne Snell: Cowboy Heat
Dee Stewart: Fighting for Brielle
Lynne St. James: SEAL's Spitfire
Bella Stone: Rexar
Jen Talty: Protecting Ainsley
Reina Torres, Rescuing Hi'ilani
LJ Vickery: Circus Comes to Town
R. C. Wynne: Shadows Renewed

Delta Team Three Series

Lori Ryan: Nori's Delta
Becca Jameson: Destiny's Delta
Lynne St James, Gwen's Delta
Elle James: Ivy's Delta
Riley Edwards: Hope's Delta

Police and Fire: Operation Alpha World
Freya Barker: Burning for Autumn
B.P. Beth: Scott
Jane Blythe: Salvaging Marigold
Julia Bright: Justice for Amber
Gia Cobie: Saved from Revenge
Hadley Finn: Exton
Danielle M. Haas: Crossroads of Betrayal
Deanndra Hall: Shelter for Sharla
Jenna Harte: Dead But Not Forgotten
India Kells: Game Master
Amber Kuhlman: Protecting Paisley
Reina Torres: Justice for Sloane
Aubree Valentine, Justice for Danielle
Maddie Wade: Finding English

Tarpley VFD Series
Silver James, Fighting for Elena
Deanndra Hall, Fighting for Carly
Haven Rose, Fighting for Calliope
MJ Nightingale, Fighting for Jemma
TL Reeve, Fighting for Brittney
Nicole Flockton, Fighting for Nadia

As you know, this book included at least one character from Susan Stoker's books. To check out more, see below.

SEAL Team Hawaii Series
Finding Elodie
Finding Lexie
Finding Kenna
Finding Monica
Finding Carly
Finding Ashlyn
Finding Jodelle

Eagle Point Search & Rescue
Searching for Lilly
Searching for Elsie
Searching for Bristol
Searching for Caryn
Searching for Finley
Searching for Heather
Searching for Khloe

The Refuge Series
Deserving Alaska
Deserving Henley
Deserving Reese
Deserving Cora
Deserving Lara
Deserving Maisy (Oct 2024)
Deserving Ryleigh (Jan 2025)

SEAL of Protection: Alliance Series
Protecting Remi (July 2024)
Protecting Wren (Nov 2024)

Protecting Josie (Mar 2025)
Protecting Maggie (TBA)
Protecting Addison (TBA)
Protecting Kelli (TBA)
Protecting Bree (TBA)

Delta Team Two Series

Shielding Gillian
Shielding Kinley
Shielding Aspen
Shielding Jayme (novella)
Shielding Riley
Shielding Devyn
Shielding Ember
Shielding Sierra

SEAL of Protection: Legacy Series

Securing Caite (FREE!)
Securing Brenae (novella)
Securing Sidney
Securing Piper
Securing Zoey
Securing Avery
Securing Kalee
Securing Jane

Delta Force Heroes Series

Rescuing Rayne (FREE!)
Rescuing Aimee (novella)
Rescuing Emily
Rescuing Harley
Marrying Emily (novella)
Rescuing Kassie
Rescuing Bryn

Rescuing Casey
Rescuing Sadie (novella)
Rescuing Wendy
Rescuing Mary
Rescuing Macie (novella)
Rescuing Annie

Badge of Honor: Texas Heroes Series
Justice for Mackenzie (FREE!)
Justice for Mickie
Justice for Corrie
Justice for Laine (novella)
Shelter for Elizabeth
Justice for Boone
Shelter for Adeline
Shelter for Sophie
Justice for Erin
Justice for Milena
Shelter for Blythe
Justice for Hope
Shelter for Quinn
Shelter for Koren
Shelter for Penelope

SEAL of Protection Series
Protecting Caroline (FREE!)
Protecting Alabama
Protecting Fiona
Marrying Caroline (novella)
Protecting Summer
Protecting Cheyenne
Protecting Jessyka
Protecting Julie (novella)
Protecting Melody

Protecting the Future
Protecting Kiera (novella)
Protecting Alabama's Kids (novella)
Protecting Dakota

New York Times, USA Today and *Wall Street Journal* Bestselling Author Susan Stoker has a heart as big as the state of Tennessee where she lives, but this all American girl has also spent the last fourteen years living in Missouri, California, Colorado, Indiana, and Texas. She's married to a retired Army man who now gets to follow *her* around the country.

www.stokeraces.com
www.AcesPress.com
susan@stokeraces.com

Made in the USA
Monee, IL
21 August 2024

64263511R10164